Yet you, LORD, you are our Father.
We are the clay, you are our potter;
we are all the work of your hand.

—Isaiah 64:8 (NIV)

MYSTERIES *of* BLACKBERRY VALLEY

Where There's Smoke
The Key Question
Seeds of Suspicion
A Likely Story
Out of the Depths
Run for the Roses
Crooks and Christmas Cookies
Smoke and Mirrors

MYSTERIES *of* BLACKBERRY VALLEY

Smoke and Mirrors

LAURA BRADFORD

Guideposts

A Gift from Guideposts

Thank you for your purchase! We want to express our gratitude for your support with a special gift just for you.

Dive into ***Spirit Lifters***, a complimentary e-book that will fortify your faith, offering solace during challenging moments. Its 31 carefully selected scripture verses will soothe and uplift your soul.

Please use the QR code or go to **guideposts.org/spiritlifters** to download.

Mysteries of Blackberry Valley is a trademark of Guideposts.

Published by Guideposts
100 Reserve Road, Suite E200
Danbury, CT 06810
Guideposts.org

Cover and interior design by Müllerhaus
Cover illustration by Bob Kayganich at Illustration Online LLC.
Typeset by Aptara, Inc.

ISBN 978-1-965859-23-0 (hardcover)
ISBN 978-1-965859-24-7 (softcover)
ISBN 978-1-965859-25-4 (epub)

Printed and bound in the United States of America

Smoke and Mirrors

Chapter One

"Am I the only one wishing Hannah could see just how big her smile is right now?"

Hannah Prentiss beamed at Lacy Minyard, who sat beside her at the head of a long table covered in a bright red cloth. Friends from all over Blackberry Valley lined the sides.

"I don't need to see it." Hannah grabbed hold of Lacy's hand and squeezed. "I feel it deep in my soul, thanks to you. You pulled off the perfect surprise birthday party."

Lacy's hazel eyes twinkled with joy.

Her hand still on her best friend's, Hannah took in each face to her left and to her right. "And thanks to all of you as well. You've made me feel very special this afternoon. Thank you for that, for your friendship, and for being exactly who you are. In fact, it's because of all of you that I had to think so long before blowing out my candles. I mean, what's left to wish for when I feel like I already have everything I could possibly want?"

"Like this restaurant," suggested Connie Sanchez, the church secretary and a fellow member of the monthly lunch group. She waved a hand at the empty tables and memorabilia-clad walls of the former firehouse-turned-eatery. "Which has become a real treasure in this town, I must say."

"I couldn't agree more," Sally Wright chimed in from her spot beside Connie. "My husband, who used to grouse at the mere suggestion of ever eating anywhere other than home, is now the one lobbying for us to come here to the Hot Spot at least once a week." She grinned. "So *I* must thank *you*, for *that*."

Hannah sank back in her chair and gazed around at the manifestation of her lifelong dream. Yes, the handful of tables beyond the one they used were empty at the moment, but she also knew that would change in a little over twenty-four hours.

"There's that smile again."

She met Lacy's gaze. "What can I say? I'm happy. The restaurant, being back in Blackberry Valley with Dad, Uncle Gordon, and my brother and his family, getting to see *you* again practically every day." She gestured to the women around the table. "And the kind of friends who would surprise me by turning what I thought was our normal ladies' luncheon for the month of January into a belated birthday party for me. I'm so blessed. Truly."

"And don't forget a certain—and rather handsome, I might add—fire chief you've reportedly been seen with around town a number of times this past week."

Her cheeks warming at the mere mention of Liam Berthold, Hannah swung her focus to the newest member of the ladies' luncheon group, Deputy Jacky Holt.

Jacky pantomimed pulling a notebook from the pocket of the police uniform she wasn't wearing and poised an imaginary pen above it. "What can you tell us about that, Ms. Prentiss?"

"Inquiring minds want to know, dear." Connie leaned forward in her spot opposite the off-duty deputy, as did Vanessa Lodge, the police department's young receptionist, and Miriam Spencer, the group's oldest member.

"There's really nothing to tell," Hannah said, only to stop at Lacy's answering snort.

Connie looked at Jacky. "Is that true?" she teased. "There's nothing to tell?"

Jacky grinned. "There have been reports."

"Oh?" Hannah drew back. "What kind of reports?"

"One citizen reported quiet laughter between you and the fire chief over lattes at Jump Start Coffee one afternoon this past week."

Hannah felt her brow lift, and she pointed at Vanessa. "Tattletale."

"Another mentioned bacon being hand-delivered to you here during a meeting with your staff one day last week," Jacky said across the top of her imaginary notebook.

Hannah shot a mock glare at Raquel Holden. Her server looked up and away, whistling innocently.

"And another reported a moonlit walk the two of you might have taken after Hot Spot hours Friday night."

Hannah's answering laugh mingled with Lacy's as she turned her attention to the town librarian, Evangeline Cooke. "I seem to remember passing you and Ted that night. In front of the market. You were walking your dog."

"The way he looked at you while you were talking." Evangeline set her fork and knife on her empty plate and met Hannah's gaze with a sheepish one of her own. "I couldn't *not* notice."

Jacky chuckled. "I'm just teasing you, Hannah. You don't have to tell us anything you don't want to."

"Yes, she does," Miriam huffed.

Laughter erupted around the table. Hannah waved her hand. "Fine. Okay. Yes. Liam and I have gone on a few—"

"They're officially dating," Lacy interrupted. "*Finally*, I might add."

Hannah watched the exchange of knowing looks and smiles taking place around her before she rose to her feet. "Liam and I are both very busy people, but, yes, we've decided to see how it goes."

"It's going to go wonderfully." Lacy started to stand and then sank back down, gripping the edge of the table as she did. "Whoa. That'll teach me not to get up so fast after two pieces of birthday cake."

Taking in her friend's suddenly pasty pallor, Hannah poured her a glass of water. "Here. Drink this. Don't get up until you're ready."

"But I want to help clean up," Lacy argued.

"And I want you to stay sitting." Hannah reached for her plate and Lacy's only to get her hand gently swatted away by Connie.

"Put that down right now, dear. You're the birthday girl, remember?"

"Technically, my birthday was two weeks ago."

"But we're celebrating it with you today."

"And I thank you for that, but the party is over," Hannah said, reaching for the plate once again.

"Hannah Prentiss!" Miriam scolded. "Respect your elders."

"I—"

The eighty-five-year-old met Hannah's wide eyes with a wink. She indicated the pile of opened presents on the chair between them. "We'll take care of the table *and* Lacy. You take these up to your apartment before I help myself to that apple-pie-scented candle Evangeline gave you and Jacky has to arrest me."

Hannah opened her mouth to protest, but Vanessa and Jacky each gathered up a few of the gifts, leaving Hannah with an armful of her own.

"Come on," Jacky said to her. "Vanessa and I will help you get these things up to your place, where you will remain until everything down here is cleaned up and back to normal."

"Are you sure?" Hannah asked. "I know *you're* off today, Jacky, but Vanessa—"

"Sheriff Steele okayed an extended lunch hour so I could be here for this." Vanessa checked the clock on the wall. "I have enough time to help get these upstairs before I need to head to the station."

With the help of her cane, Miriam rose to her feet, her attempt at another scowl hindered by the sparkle in her eyes. "Then it's settled. Hannah, shoo!"

Hannah planted a kiss on the elderly woman's cheek, returned the parade of hugs from the other women, instructed Lacy to wait to leave until she felt better, and then turned and led Vanessa and Jacky toward the steps to her apartment.

"Hannah, wait!"

She glanced over her shoulder to see Raquel hurrying in her direction with a wrapped gift in her hand.

"Raquel, you already gave me a gift," she protested.

"I know." Raquel set the box on top of the stack in Hannah's arms. "This one isn't from me."

Hannah looked down at the box and her name on the tag beside the bow and then back up at her friend. "Then who is it from?"

Raquel shrugged. "I can't say for sure, but I did catch a glimpse of that girl outside the door as we were finishing up with the cake and presents. Maybe it was from her."

"Girl? What girl?"

"The reporter who works with Marshall over at the paper."

"Pippa Nelson?" Hannah frowned at the box. "I've left messages for her at the *Chronicle* before every one of our monthly luncheons, but she never comes. So how would she know this one was a belated birthday celebration for me if even *I* didn't know?"

"I think Evangeline saw her out and about sometime last week and mentioned it to her."

"She didn't have to get me a gift," Hannah protested.

"*If* it's from her at all," Raquel said. "There isn't a card that I can see, but maybe it's inside the box."

"Maybe." She smiled. "Thanks, Raquel."

"My pleasure, boss. And don't worry about things down here. I'll make sure Lacy is okay and that everything is locked up before we leave."

"I can come back down and lock up."

"Don't. We've got it covered. I promise." Raquel motioned toward the table that was already cleared. Connie was sweeping, under the audible supervision of Miriam. "Staff meeting tomorrow at two, right?"

"Right."

"I'll be there."

Hannah grinned. "I know you will. And probably fifteen minutes early, as usual."

"What can I say?" Raquel asked. "Punctuality was a big deal in my house growing up."

"Punctuality, diligence, positive attitude, et cetera, et cetera."

Her cheeks tinged red, Raquel waved aside Hannah's assessment. "You should stop before my head gets too big to fit through the doors around here."

"I just call it like I see it, my friend." Hannah resumed her trek toward the back of the restaurant and the two young women waiting for her at the bottom of the steps. "Sorry, guys. I was waylaid by another present."

"Oh, who from?" Jacky asked. "You already got one from everyone who was here today."

"Raquel thinks it might be from Pippa Nelson over at the paper, but she's not sure, and there doesn't appear to be a card."

"Perhaps Jacky can dust it for fingerprints," Vanessa teased as she followed Hannah and her coworker to the former fire station's second floor.

"I have the day off, remember?" Jacky volleyed back. "Unlike you, Vanessa. The sheriff is probably getting antsy about you being gone so long."

Vanessa's laugh followed Hannah inside her apartment. "Do you see what I have to put up with working with this one, Hannah? Bossy, bossy, bossy."

When everyone was inside the tiny entryway, Hannah pushed the door closed with her elbow and led her two friends into her cozy living room. "You can leave everything on the coffee table. I'll have to decide where it's all going."

"Roger that." Jacky set down her stack of gifts. "This was really fun today. I'm glad you talked me into joining the group, Hannah."

"I am too." She took a few steps toward the door but stopped when she realized neither woman was following her. "Are you all coming?"

Jacky and Vanessa shook their heads.

Hannah glanced at her watch and then up at Vanessa. "Don't you have to go?"

"I do."

At a loss for what to say, Hannah slid her attention onto Jacky and waited.

"We want to see what's in the mystery box," Jacky said.

"Right. Of course." Hannah sat on the couch and made short work of the tape to reveal a plain white box. Carefully, she opened the lid—and drew in her breath at the sight of what was inside. "Oh. Wow. This is *beautiful*."

Jacky folded her arms. "I don't do suspense all that well. I'm just saying."

Hannah carefully extracted the contents, a tiny creamer.

A gasp pulled her attention from the gift to Vanessa in time to see the young woman surge toward her with wide eyes. Before Hannah could process what was happening, Vanessa plucked the creamer from her hands and turned it over. "I—I don't understand. How do you have this? Where did it come from?"

Confused, Hannah dug her hand inside the box, moved the tissue paper around, and then shrugged. "I don't know. There's no note. Why?"

"I know this piece, I know the set it was part of!" Still clearly stunned, Vanessa looked from the creamer in her hands to Hannah and back again. "Many years ago, my grandmother was the cook at the Taylor Estate. The job came with a small cottage on the property where she and my grandaddy raised my mama. Grandma Peggy made pottery when she wasn't working at the main house, and Mama loved to watch. She said her mother would get up before dawn to work at her wheel and sometimes, when she was working on a new piece, she would stay up all night. But as busy as she was with that and cooking for the Taylors, Mama said Grandma Peggy still made time for her and that she had a way of making every moment they spent together special. They'd garden together, have fancy little tea parties in the cottage, lie on the grass at night and look up at the stars. All sorts of things."

Vanessa turned the creamer over in her hands again, her voice thick with emotion. "One day, when Mama was getting ready to move out on her own, Grandma Peggy surprised her with a whole dining set she'd made—dinner plates, dessert plates, candlesticks, a butter dish, a sugar bowl, and this creamer. Mama cried when she saw it because she knew how hard it must have been for Grandma Peggy to find the time to make all those pieces, what with working at the main house, caring for her family, and making all those other pieces she sold at the market on Saturday mornings."

"Your grandmother sounds like she was a wonderful person," Hannah said.

"She was." Vanessa ran her fingers along the twilight-blue glazed creamer and around its brown rim. "A few days later, Mama packed it all up and moved to her own little place. But when she went to unpack, she noticed this piece was missing."

"Wait." Hannah said, drawing back. "She hasn't seen it since her mother gave it to her?"

Vanessa turned over the creamer and pointed at a tiny rose etched into the bottom. "Grandma Peggy put her initials—*PSW*—on the bottom of all the pieces she sold. But on the ones she made for my mama, she put a rose to represent Mama's name. That set has been on Mama's table for every holiday and special occasion since. Well, minus this creamer and the sugar bowl, of course."

"Sugar bowl?"

Again, Vanessa nodded. "It went missing the same time this piece did."

"I don't understand," Hannah said. "Where has the creamer been this whole time, and who's giving it to me now after all these years? And where is the sugar bowl?"

"I don't know. Mama always said the only thing that made any sense was that it was stolen, but—" Vanessa looked down at her pocket and then handed the creamer to Hannah so she could check a text on her phone. "It's the station. I really should get back."

Jacky held up her phone. "I just got a text too. Seems there's some sort of situation in Cave City, and they're looking for backup from our department. I'm going to head over there with Vanessa and see if I can do anything to help."

"Of course." Hannah stood, waited for Vanessa to type a response to whoever had texted her, and then held out the creamer. "Take this. Please."

"But it was given to you," Vanessa argued.

"It was, but it sounds like the person who should have it is your mother, not me."

Vanessa's dark eyes moved between the creamer and Hannah. "Are you sure?"

"I am."

"I—I don't know what to say. I can't believe we've found this. I really can't." Vanessa took the creamer and drew it to her chest as a smile spread across her face. "Thank you, Hannah. Mama is going to be so tickled."

A siren sounded on the street below. Hannah followed Vanessa and Jacky toward the door. "Thank you both for today. It was very special."

"It was." Vanessa and Jacky both hugged Hannah then hurried down the stairs.

When they were out of sight, Hannah closed the door then wandered back into the living room and over to the tissue-paper-filled box sitting on the coffee table. Sinking onto the sofa, she again searched it for any sign of a note or card, but to no avail.

"Where did you come from?" she whispered. "And why now? Why for me?"

Chapter Two

After propping her phone against the apple-pie-scented candle she'd gotten from Evangeline, Hannah pressed the video call button and sank into the sunniest corner of her sofa.

"Good morning, Hannah. Happy Tuesday."

"Hi, Lacy. How are you feeling today?"

Lacy lifted her favorite farm mug to her lips, took a sip, and slowly lowered it. "Just fine. Why do you ask?"

"You know, after whatever made you dizzy at our luncheon yesterday." Hannah broke off a piece of her bagel and lifted it to her mouth but stopped shy of eating it as her gaze narrowed in on her friend. "Wait a minute. You're wearing a bathrobe."

Lacy glanced down at herself and shrugged. "It's January, Hannah. I'm cold."

Dropping the piece of bagel back onto her plate, Hannah leaned forward, taking in the tiny goats she could make out on the pale pink fabric visible beneath the robe. "You're also still wearing your pajamas." She glanced at her watch. "At nine thirty in the morning."

"So?" Lacy took another sip of what Hannah guessed to be hot cocoa based on the tiniest sign of whipped cream she spied on the tip of her friend's nose. "Your point?"

"You live on a farm. You're up and on the move by six a.m. every single day."

"My mom actually took care of the animals this morning."

"Your mom?" Hannah ate her bite of bagel and chased it down with a sip of coffee. "That was sweet of her, but I'm still surprised you didn't do it and that you're wearing pajamas. Are you all right?"

Lacy lifted a piece of toast, nibbled the edge of it, and then dropped it out of view with another shrug. "I stayed up later than I should have."

"Oh?"

"I had to beat Neil in backgammon before we finally called it a night. I couldn't let his six-game winning streak grow to seven."

"Of course. I forgot who I was talking to for a minute." Hannah broke off another bite of her bagel. "I'm glad to hear he gave you a run for your money though. Someone needs to."

"So much for our lifelong friendship," Lacy quipped with an eye roll. "Traitor."

Hannah still wasn't satisfied. "Seriously, though, that thing with you at the end of the luncheon yesterday? You really think that was about too much cake?"

"You clearly didn't see the size of my second piece."

Laughing, Hannah lifted her face to the morning sun streaming through her living room window. "Yesterday was really special. Thank you for the part you played in it."

"You're loved, Hannah. By all of us."

Hannah smiled at her friend. "And I feel it."

"I'm glad. Because Blackberry Valley is where you belong, not California."

"My time in California was important, Lacy. You know that. I trained under some amazing chefs, it gave me the space I needed to work through my mom's death, and it was there I realized I wanted to have my own restaurant. *Here.*"

"I get that. I really do. But I don't ever want you to live anywhere else again." Lacy wrapped both hands around her mug. "Sprout would be lost without you."

"As cute as Sprout is, I'm fairly certain someone else would step into my shoes and spoil her silly if I wasn't here." Hannah set her coffee next to the phone and grabbed another piece of her bagel as her mind's eye filled in the face of the baby goat she'd been given naming rights to seven months earlier. "That said, I think it's safe to say that you, Sprout, and the rest of Blackberry Valley are stuck with me. I'm not going anywhere, unless the Hot Spot fails, I guess."

"Which it won't."

"Says my best friend."

"Says your best friend who has eaten there *and* sees the growing number of five-star ratings the place is accumulating on a near nightly basis."

There was no holding back her happy sigh. "We *are* doing really well."

"I never had any doubt," Lacy said. "Never."

Hannah savored the idea along with another sip of coffee. "Thank you for that, and for yesterday, and—hey! I haven't told you about the mystery gift yet, have I?"

"Mystery gift?"

"Didn't you see? Yesterday, as Vanessa and Jacky and I headed up to my apartment with all my presents, Raquel stopped me with another gift."

Lacy nodded. "Right. She saw it out on the sidewalk while everyone was cleaning up. Did you open it?"

"I did."

Lacy leaned closer to the screen, curiosity lifting her eyebrows. "What was it? Who was it from?"

"It was a ceramic creamer, and I don't know who it was from. There was no card, no note. It was just wrapped in birthday paper like everyone else's."

"And you really have no idea where it came from?"

"I don't. Raquel mentioned seeing Pippa Nelson standing outside when we were just about done yesterday, so maybe it was her. But why would she leave it out there? Why not just bring it in?"

Lacy's shoulders rose and fell beneath her robe. "Maybe she had to be somewhere at a certain time and was afraid she'd be late if she came in and people started talking to her?"

"I suppose. But the creamer wasn't just *any* creamer, Lacy. Vanessa recognized it as part of a set her grandmother made for Vanessa's mom when she was getting ready to move out on her own."

Lacy cocked her head. "And Vanessa's mom gave it to Pippa or someone else to give to you?"

"She didn't *give* it to anyone. It was stolen."

"Stolen?" Lacy echoed, drawing back. "When?"

"Not long after Vanessa's grandmother gave it to her daughter—Vanessa's mother."

"But you said Vanessa's mom was getting ready to move out on her own, so that was, what, when she was a young adult?"

"Right."

"So, we're talking *decades* ago?"

"We are. Vanessa mentioned they celebrated her mom's sixtieth birthday last year, so it would be at least forty years ago."

"Show it to me."

Hannah shook her head. "In light of what Vanessa said, I didn't feel like it was mine to keep."

"Meaning?"

"I gave it to Vanessa to give to her mom."

Lacy nodded. "Makes sense. But still. Wow."

"Crazy stuff, right?" Pursing her lips, Hannah blew out a long, slow breath. "At first I thought she had to be mistaken when she said it was her mother's, but evidently the pottery her grandmother sold at some sort of local market had her initials—*PSW*—on it, while each piece in the set she made specifically for Vanessa's mother had a rose on the bottom instead."

"*PSW*?" Lacy repeated, her eyes wide. "That was Vanessa's grandmother? I didn't know that!"

"You know her work?"

"We both do. Wait a second." Lacy got up, disappeared from Hannah's screen for a minute, and returned with a pie plate in her hand. "I bought this at the same time I bought that one I gave you for your birthday last year. Go get yours, and take me with you."

Hannah set her mug on the coffee table, picked up her phone, and made her way over to the kitchen cabinet in which she kept her most prized cooking and baking pieces. Sure enough, the moment she opened the door, her gaze fell on the fluted pie plate she'd baked many a pie in over the past twelve months.

"Take it out and look at the underside," Lacy instructed.

After propping the phone against the side of her toaster, Hannah reached into the cabinet, carefully extracted the pie plate, turned it over, and drew in a quick breath.

"*PSW*," she said. "Vanessa's grandmother. And you found this at a flea market of all places? How? It's gorgeous."

"Sometimes people are so intent on scaling down their possessions—either because they're cleaning out a deceased loved one's home or they're moving to something smaller—that they don't really stop and look at what they're letting go. I'd have paid four times what I did for these two pieces, and that was *before* I realized how sought-after her work has become over time."

"What makes it so valuable?" Hannah turned the pie plate over in her hands. "I mean, I know it's pretty. I treasure mine. But aren't there lots of nice pottery pieces to be had?"

"I'm sure there are. But Peggy's were made here during the seventies and eighties. In Blackberry Valley. From the limited bit I know, Antoinette Taylor, the daughter of Richard Taylor—the man who built that sprawling estate on the edge of town—hired Peggy Shipman Williams as her cook and provided Peggy and her family a cottage on the property. Peggy cooked and baked, raised her daughter, and eventually got her husband hired on as the estate's lead handyman. She taught herself how to make pottery using a kiln her husband built for her. I think her story resonates with people because it's about someone rising from obscurity to make a name for herself."

Hannah took one last look at the pie plate and then carried the phone back to her living room and the last few sips of coffee waiting in her mug. "Interesting stuff, for sure."

"Not as interesting as something she made for her daughter—that's been missing for more than four decades—suddenly showing up in a gift-wrapped box," Lacy mused. "For you and apparently from no one."

"Tell me about it."

"Uh-oh."

Hannah stilled her mug inches from her lips and peered at her friend across its rim. "What?"

"I know that look."

"What are you talking about?"

"The one that says even though the creamer is back where it belongs, you're going to try to figure out how it made its way to you."

Hannah took the last sip of her drink and slowly lowered the mug until it rested on her thigh. "I'm certainly curious."

"And?" Lacy prodded, grinning.

"Vanessa is my friend, after all."

Lacy's eyes sparkled. "She is."

"And there's another piece that's still missing." Hannah watched her breakfast companion's face reflect intrigue along with amusement. "A matching sugar bowl."

"And that would complete the set Vanessa's grandmother made for her mother?"

Hannah nodded.

"Then it's a no-brainer. You *have* to do a little sleuthing."

Aware of her own grin forming, Hannah leaned closer to the screen and Lacy. "*And*?"

"And what?"

"I've known you as long as you've known me, my friend. Which means I can read your look as well as you can read mine."

Lacy pulled her hands to her chest theatrically. "How can you possibly accuse me of having a look? I'm hurt."

"Are you saying if I try to figure this out, I have to do it all by myself?"

Lacy threw up her hands. "I would never say that. You know I want to be involved."

Hannah laughed. "Yes, if I need a sidekick, I know where to find you."

Chapter Three

"Every time I think we have the last of our customers for the night, some more walk in."

Hannah followed Raquel's gaze to the Hot Spot's front door in time to see a couple step inside, pause in front of the wooden case containing the various Blackberry Valley Fire Department patches, and then make their way toward her hostess, Elaine Wilby. "It has been unusually busy for a Tuesday night. I'll give you that."

"Don't get me wrong," Raquel said. "I know it's a good thing—a *very* good thing—but I don't think any of us have stopped moving since we opened."

Hannah turned in time to see her curly-haired server shrug at the clearly disappointed young man sitting alone at table three. Resting her hand on Raquel's arm, she stole the waitress's attention back with a gentle squeeze. "Take a little dessert break with Marshall, and I'll wait on these new folks."

"I can't ask you to do that," Raquel protested.

"You didn't. I offered."

"But—"

"You started your shift with a table of eight construction workers who kept you on your toes the entire time they were here. And that was on top of the near-constant turnover of your other tables both during and after them. You've earned a little time with your clearly smitten beau."

Raquel's brown eyes sparkled. "I'm pretty smitten too."

Hannah laughed. "Oh, trust me, I know. And I couldn't be happier for you. Marshall Fredericks is a good man, judging from everything I've seen the past eight months."

"*Eight* months?" Raquel echoed. "But that would mean you're including when we first opened, when he didn't give the Hot Spot the five-star review we wanted."

"He gave us the review we *needed*. The one that inspired me to make the place look like this." Hannah spread her hands wide to indicate the dozens of photos and items of memorabilia that hung on the walls in honor of the building's history as a firehouse. "And that drove us to get the menu and the service just right."

"That's true," Raquel hedged.

Hannah gently pushed Raquel toward Marshall's table. "My opinion of him has steadily climbed with how sweet he is to you and how happy he makes you. So get him some of our ice cream—on the house—and some for yourself and take a break." Hannah spotted Elaine leading the newly arrived couple across the dining room to a quiet table in the back. "I've got table eight and any of your other tables that need looking after."

"Thanks, Hannah."

"Thank *you*, Raquel." Hannah watched Raquel push her way through the double doors into the kitchen and then headed in the direction of the sixtysomething couple now seated with menus in their hands. "Good evening. Welcome to the Hot Spot. I'm Hannah. What can I get you to drink while you look over our dinner options?"

"An iced tea, please," the man requested across the top of his menu.

The woman seated across from him set her menu down and smiled. "I'd like a glass of water. No lemon, please."

"Perfect. I'll be back with those drinks in just a moment."

For the next fifteen minutes, Hannah moved between tables, delivering meals, taking and delivering dessert orders, and making change while Dylan Bowman, the other member of her waitstaff, did some variation of the same tasks at the tables in his section.

When things slowed, Hannah wandered over to Raquel and Marshall, who were laughing quietly together. "How was the ice cream, you two?"

"Almost as good as the company." Marshall peered at Hannah from behind his stylish eyeglasses. "Thank you for both of those things, by the way."

She shifted her answering smile between the food critic and Raquel. "It's my pleasure."

"I really should get back to work," Raquel said, gathering both her bowl and Marshall's before Hannah stopped her.

"The only people in your section still eating are the two at table eight. Everyone else has either paid and left or will be doing so in the next few minutes."

Raquel scooted to the end of her booth seat. "Then I should get their bills ready."

"I'm keeping an eye on them. As soon as they give me the sign, I'll take care of them." Hannah smiled at Marshall. "I'd hoped to get over to the *Chronicle* before we opened today, but the breakfast meetup I had with a friend this morning went on longer than expected, and then my dad called needing my help with something out at his place."

Marshall straightened in his seat. "Is there something I can help you with?"

"No, I was hoping to catch Pippa about a gift I think she may have left on my doorstep yesterday."

Raquel paused her hands around the empty ice cream bowls and looked up at Hannah. "So I was right? It was from her?"

Hannah shrugged. "There wasn't a card, but Vanessa and Jacky seem to think so too, since she was the only one invited to the lunch that didn't actually come."

"I wish she'd brought it in herself rather than leaving it outside," Raquel said. "I know you've wanted to meet her for a while now."

"True. But maybe she was running between stories and didn't want to get caught up in a conversation that might prove difficult to extricate herself from," Hannah said.

"With *our* group?" Raquel joked. "Perish the thought!"

Grinning, Hannah took the empty bowls and waved off Raquel's attempt to stand. "You said it, not me."

"If I hit up Jump Start for my morning coffee before work like Pippa usually does or I'm actually in the office at the same time she is tomorrow, I can let her know you're looking for her," Marshall said. "But as much as that girl is on the move, you'd probably be better off giving her a call."

"Is there that much going on in Blackberry Valley at the moment?" Hannah asked.

"No, but the deadline for the state's journalism awards is right around the corner, and Pippa is determined to find the story that will put her in contention."

Raquel frowned. "She can't *make* a story happen, though, right?"

"Depends." Marshall pushed his glasses up the bridge of his nose. "Sometimes you can if you're in the right place at the right time and you're good at seeing things from different angles. As Pippa is."

Hannah let the food critic's words meander through her thoughts for a moment, only to have to table them as a customer met her eye, smiled, and signaled for the check. "Leave the bowls here. I'll get them after I finish up."

Hannah walked over to the serving station just outside the kitchen and double-checked the man's order, printed it, and delivered it to him. He handed her a credit card, and she processed his payment.

Five minutes later, when the last customers were on their way out, she turned to find Raquel at her elbow. Hannah glanced over Raquel's shoulder and saw that not only were the ice cream bowls gone, but there was no sign of Marshall and the table had been wiped clean. "Raquel, I told you I'd take care of the bowls so you and Marshall could keep talking."

"I know you did, but he needed to get going and I needed to get back to work. Although"—Raquel glanced around—"it seems I'm a little late."

Hannah nodded to the front door. The final couple had just stepped out onto Main Street, and Elaine shut off the illuminated Open sign. "And we survived."

"I'm not sure a statement like that bodes too well for how needed I am here."

Hannah gave her a side hug. "Trust me, my friend, you are *very* much needed here at the Hot Spot. Always."

"Thank you, Hannah. For that, and for the time with Marshall tonight."

Something about the young woman's tone made Hannah pause. "Did something happen? You seem happier than usual—if such a thing is even possible."

"Marshall has a surprise date planned for us." Raquel released a happy squeal. "He told me further instructions will be coming. Isn't that so sweet?"

"It absolutely is."

"He's planning it for Saturday, but don't worry. He's aware that I have to be back here no later than three."

Hannah gave her a wink. "Three thirty will be fine."

"I'll make sure everything on the floor is ready to go when we open, so quarter to four works for me." Dylan moved on to the next table, cloth in hand. "That is, if it's okay with you, Hannah?"

"If you can do that, Dylan, then yes," Hannah said.

"Thank you, Hannah." Raquel smiled at her coworker. "Thanks, Dylan. I owe you."

Dylan looked from the cloth in his hand to Raquel as the corner of his mouth lifted in a mischievous grin. "You could let me play some of my tunes while we clean up tonight."

"Can I sing along?" Raquel countered.

Dylan shrugged and pulled out his phone. "If you promise not to make fun of whatever dance moves I do."

"Do I have to promise that too?" Elaine piped up from the hostess stand as she wiped down menus. "Because I'm not sure I can."

Dylan chuckled and tapped his phone screen. Soon the dining area was filled with the kind of music that set everyone's feet tapping.

For a moment, Hannah simply watched, the sheer joy she felt at the bond among her staff bringing mist to her eyes. Moving back to Blackberry Valley, finally acting on her dream of opening her own restaurant, being close to her family and Lacy—they were all such blessings. Every single one of them.

Feeling a vibration in her pocket, she took out her phone to find a text from Vanessa.

Mama was as surprised as I was to see her missing creamer. But she's so very grateful. Hannah was about to respond when another text arrived. I am too, of course. But I also want to know who's had it all this time and why. And most importantly, where is Mama's sugar bowl??

"I want to know the same things, Vanessa," Hannah whispered. "One way or the other, I intend to find out."

Chapter Four

It was just past eight thirty in the morning when Hannah stepped through the front door of Jump Start Coffee and surveyed the various faces dotting the tables scattered around the café. In the corner, she spotted the mayor and Sheriff Colin Steele sharing a chuckle. Another table hosted three women about her age, all seemingly talking at the same exact time while either bouncing a baby in their arms or nudging a stroller back and forth with a sneakered toe.

"Are you in line, ma'am?"

Startled, she glanced over her shoulder at a man she vaguely recognized though she couldn't put a name to the face. "Oh, right. Sorry." She stepped behind the lone woman waiting in line and began to scan the room once more, noting each face in search of—

"Good morning, Hannah."

She turned back to the counter and quickly closed the gap left by the woman in front of her, who'd ordered and stepped away. "Good morning, Zane."

The coffee shop owner, Zane Forrest, smiled warmly as he motioned to the menu hanging on the wall behind him. "So what'll it be this morning?"

"I'd like a straight-up black coffee, please. The darker the roast, the better. Large."

Her chef's brother grabbed a cup from the stack beside the coffee machine and held it in place with one hand while he filled it with the other. "Long night?"

"It shouldn't have been. *Wouldn't* have been if I'd been able to shut my brain off."

"Find a boring book and keep it beside your bed. That's what I do. Whenever I'm having a hard time sleeping, a few paragraphs of that'll put me out like a light." Zane pointed at the glass case to Hannah's left. "The blueberry muffins are pretty good, if I do say so myself."

She took in the streusel on top, the specks of blue peeking out from around them, and dug her hand inside her purse for her wallet. "I'll take one on a plate for me now, and one in a to-go bag for my dad for later. He loves a good blueberry muffin."

"Smart man." Zane made change for the twenty-dollar bill Hannah gave him. After she had it secured in her purse, he handed her a lidded coffee and both a plated and a bagged muffin. "I hope the coffee helps you wake up."

"Thanks, Zane. I'm sure it will."

Turning away from the counter, she made her way toward the tables as her gaze continued its journey across the room. Her search paid off. Tucked behind a faux tree in the back right corner, she caught a glimpse of the reason she'd resisted hitting snooze on her alarm that morning.

She threaded her way around and between tables topped with coffee cups and laptop computers, savoring the aroma seeping through her own cup's lid. She reached her destination and the young twentysomething sitting at a high-top table and poring over a notebook with equal parts interest and…frustration?

"Pippa Nelson?"

The woman raised her head and tossed a swath of her long blond hair behind her shoulder. "Yes, I'm Pippa. Can I help you?"

"I'm Hannah Prentiss. I own the Hot Spot down the street, and I've left a couple of messages for you at the *Chronicle* the last few months inviting you to the ladies' luncheon we have here in town."

"Right. Sorry." The reporter made a spot for Hannah at the table by shifting the various piles of paper around her into a single stack. "Please, have a seat."

"Thank you." Hannah perched on the empty stool across from Pippa's and set down her plate, bag, and cup. "I was hoping you could come the other day."

Pippa stilled her drink inches from her lips. "The other day?"

"Monday. Our lunch for the month."

"Ah yes, your birthday lunch." Pippa took a sip before setting her cup beside her papers. "How was it? Were you as surprised as Evangeline wanted you to be?"

"Considering my birthday was two weeks ago, yes." Hannah took a sip of her coffee, relishing the rich flavor, and followed it up with a bite of her muffin. After a moment she said, "It was very sweet of them to plan that for me. Especially after the busyness of the holidays."

Pippa's gaze crept to her papers. "That's why Evangeline said they wanted to do it. She said your birthday probably gets overshadowed, being so close to Christmas."

"My birthday was lovely, actually, but I still appreciate the surprise of it being worked into this month's luncheon."

Pippa ran her finger down the top page on the stack, set the paper aside, and repeated the same action with each of the next two sheets before rejoining a conversation she'd clearly checked out from for a few moments. "I'm glad."

Hannah moved to gather her things. "You seem busy. Maybe we can talk another time."

"I'm sorry." Pippa held her hands up with a shake of her head. "I don't mean to be rude. I'm just trying to find a story I've done in the past year that might be a good submission for the Journalist of the Year award for weekly papers, and nothing is quite cutting it."

Hannah took a bite of her muffin, followed it with another sip of coffee, and settled against the back of her seat. "Marshall mentioned something about that last night."

"Marshall?" Pippa echoed before waving off her own question. "Oh, right. His girlfriend, Raquel, works at your restaurant."

Hannah broke off another piece of muffin. "That's right. And he said the deadline to enter for the journalism award is coming up, yes?"

Pippa nodded. "Two weeks from this coming Friday. Which means I need something ready to go pretty soon or I need to write something dazzling in the next two weeks."

"I've read your articles," Hannah said. "They've all been really good."

"Thanks. But I want my submission to be a story that really grabs the judges' attention. And when it does, I want them to be mesmerized by the way I tell it."

Hannah smiled. "I'm betting on you, Pippa Nelson."

"Thank you."

"You're welcome." She took another bite or two of her muffin as Pippa's focus shifted back to the stack of pages. "Are those all the stories you wrote last year?"

Pippa paused and looked up at Hannah. "They're the ones I've written since the end of last January. That's the time period they look at, from January thirty-first of last year to January thirty-first of this year. It used to be based on a calendar year, but they pushed it out to keep the deadline from getting lost in everyone's end-of-year scramble."

"Makes sense."

Pippa returned her attention to the stack of papers. "All I know is that it gives me two more editions of the *Chronicle* to submit a really captivating story so that I don't need one of these."

Hannah finished her coffee and muffin, deciding it was time to broach the topic she'd wanted to ask about in the first place. "So. The gift."

Again, Pippa looked up. "Gift?"

"Yes, the one left outside the Hot Spot's front door during the luncheon on Monday. Was that from you?"

Pippa gave a wry grin. "I forgot a card, didn't I?"

"You did, but no worries." Hannah got up to deposit her dirty dish in the appropriate bin and returned to her spot opposite Pippa. "I do need to ask you about what you gave me."

"Didn't you like it?" Pippa asked. "I thought it would be something special to have for your restaurant guests with a cup of coffee or tea after dinner."

"No, the creamer was beautiful. Truly. It's just—"

"Uh-oh." Pippa eyed Hannah. "You said *was*."

"Yes, but that's because—"

Palming her forehead, Pippa released a loud sigh. "I must not have been careful enough with it when I dropped it off. I probably should've packaged it better."

"I didn't say *was* because it was broken, Pippa. I said *was* because I couldn't keep it."

Pippa slowly lowered her hand back to the table and met Hannah's gaze. "Why not?"

"It belongs to Rose Lodge, not me."

"Did you say *Lodge*?" Pippa asked.

"Yes, as in Vanessa Lodge's mother. Her grandmother—Rose's mom—was a potter. And that creamer was part of a dining set she made for Rose more than forty years ago."

"And what? Vanessa's mother wishes she'd kept the set together now?"

Hannah leaned forward. "No, Rose didn't willingly part with the creamer. It went missing shortly after her mother gave it to her."

"Her mother made beautiful pottery," Pippa said.

"Apparently many people agree with you," Hannah said. "Have you heard of Peggy Shipman Williams?"

Pippa's shoulders snapped back. "Peggy Shipman Williams was Vanessa Lodge's grandmother?"

"So you've heard of her?"

"I've come across things about her during research. But I had no idea she was related to—" Pippa stopped and shook her head then sharpened her focus back on Hannah. "And you gave the creamer to Vanessa?"

"I gave it to Vanessa to give to Rose."

"And she did?"

"I would imagine so." Hannah pushed an errant strand of hair behind her ear as she leaned forward. "I just don't understand how it suddenly reappeared after so many years. In a gift-wrapped box, no less."

"From me." At Hannah's nod, Pippa straightened the pile of papers she'd already looked at and set them at the bottom of the pile she hadn't. "I bought the creamer on Saturday, at a little pottery shop in downtown Cave City."

"Oh, right. The Clay something."

Pippa paused her paper shuffling. "The Clay House. You know the place?"

"I haven't been there. But when you mentioned Cave City, I remembered seeing something about a pottery place there on a flyer I got in the mail."

"Well, that's the place." Pippa swiveled, plucked her bag off the back of her chair, and quickly stuffed the papers inside it. "I'll try to get you something else sometime in the next few days, okay?"

Hannah held up her hands. "No, please. I didn't tell you about this to get another present out of you. I just wanted to ask how and where you got it—which you've now answered."

Pippa slipped her arm through the handle of the bag but stopped short of taking it all the way to her shoulder. "And you're *certain* Peggy Shipman Williams made it?"

"That's what Vanessa said."

"And it went missing forty years ago," Pippa said.

"Vanessa used the word *stolen*."

Pippa's green eyes narrowed in thought. "Do you know where it was stolen from, exactly?"

"I'm guessing the cottage Rose was raised in by her parents."

"On the Taylor Estate," Pippa said.

"From what Vanessa said, yes."

Taking one last gulp of what was surely a lukewarm drink at that point, Pippa slid off her stool and onto her feet. "Goodbye, backup articles."

Hannah stood too, her to-go bag in her hand. "Backup articles?"

"For the contest." Pippa patted her tote bag, her smile nearly blinding. "Anyway, it was nice to finally meet you in person, Hannah, but now I really must head into work. I've got deadlines to meet."

Chapter Five

Hannah grabbed the muffin bag from the passenger seat then closed her car's door and took a moment to savor the voices coming from the workshop. They were the same voices she'd heard all her life, yet in many ways there were differences in them now too.

Her brother's voice was no longer that of a young, inquisitive boy, but rather a grown man with children of his own. And her father's voice, while still strong and confident, held more of a pensive quality than ever before.

Tilting her chin toward the morning sky, she closed her eyes. "We miss you, Mom," she whispered. "But we're doing okay. Still close, still feeling your loving embrace in our hearts at some point every single day."

A gentle nudge against her calf made her look down to find Zeus, her father's border terrier. "Oh, hey, Zeus. How are you, sweet boy?" Crouching, she rubbed the dog's ears and smiled at the immediate increase in the tempo of his wagging tail. "Making sure to take good care of Dad for Andrew and me?"

Zeus flopped onto the driveway, and Hannah obediently moved her hand to his belly. "You're such a good boy. You really are."

She followed his tummy with her fingers as he rolled around on his back. Finally, he got to his feet and shook himself.

"Okay, Zeus, take me to Dad and Drew."

His tail wagging, Zeus led her down the front walk, glancing back over his shoulder at her every few steps. Halfway to the house he veered left and ran the rest of the way to the wooden shed that served as her father's workshop.

Even before she reached the open door, she could picture what she knew she'd see. The wooden worktable on which shelves had been made and various objects had been fixed over the years. The pegboard wall beside it, which neatly held the tools needed to do the building and the fixing. The homemade stool tucked beneath it that Hannah and Drew had stood on as children for better viewing of their father's projects—a stool still used on a regular basis by Drew's ever-curious youngest child, Axel.

And the picture on the wall above it of Hannah and Drew's mother, her loving smile encouraging her beloved Gabriel to keep doing the same.

"Zeus?" came her father's voice from inside. "Where are you, fella?"

Hannah winked at the border terrier as she modulated her voice. "I'm right here, Dad."

Her brother's laugh emerged through the open door a split second before her father appeared, his joy at seeing her warming her all the way down to her toes. "Hannah! I didn't hear you pull up."

She stepped around Zeus into the workshop and kissed her father's cheek. "I was driving by and thought I'd stop and say hi."

"I'm glad you did. Your brother is here too."

"I thought I heard his voice." Hannah peeked around her dad for a clear view of the workshop and the tall sandy-blond man smiling at her. "Hey, Drew. Aren't you supposed to be programming computers?"

Her brother's brown eyes danced as he leaned back against the workbench. "Not today. I took the day off."

Dad gestured toward Drew. "He and Allison are spending the day together while the kids are in school."

"Sounds great." Hannah made a show of looking around the workshop. "But doesn't that mean Allison should be here?"

Drew snapped his fingers. "I knew I forgot something when I got in the car."

Dad waved an impatient hand at Drew. "Allison is inside saying hello to your uncle before he heads over to the Taylor Estate."

"The Taylor Estate?" Hannah echoed. "Why is Uncle Gordon going there?"

"He got a call from Mrs. Adler's daughter. A pipe under the sink is apparently leaking. Her mother showed her a book with names and numbers of people who've done work on the estate in the past. Gordon was listed under a heading for plumbers."

"But Uncle Gordon is retired," Hannah protested.

Drew crossed his arms. "That's what I said."

"Come on, you two. You know your uncle. When his help is needed, he's happy to give it. Besides, he's the one who was hired to replace many of the original pipes in the main house twenty or so years ago."

Hannah crossed to the table, picked up a hammer, and hung it on the appropriate hook beside the workbench, a move that made Drew's lips twitch with amusement. "What?" she asked. "Dad's not using it, so I put it back where it goes."

"Ever the organizer," Drew quipped.

Dad sighed. "Just like Mom was."

Hannah smiled at the image of her mother moving around whatever space she was in, neatening, arranging, organizing. "I'll take that as a compliment."

Drew blew out a long breath. "I miss Mom. A lot."

Hannah reached out and squeezed her brother's elbow. "I do too. Every day."

"Ditto," Dad agreed, his voice husky with emotion as he gazed at the blond, hazel-eyed woman smiling back at them from the framed photograph behind the workbench.

Drew unlatched his arms from his chest to cover Hannah's hand with his own. "And you're looking more and more like her every day, Sis."

"I'll *definitely* take that," she said.

Silence fell as the three of them gazed at the photo.

Hannah relived a memory of being snuggled up on the porch swing as her mother read aloud from one of the hundreds of books they'd enjoyed together. She recalled the subtle yet steady creak of the swing. She could smell the scent of freshly cut grass. She could taste the warm chocolate chips in the cookies they'd shared on a napkin laid across their laps. She could hear the change in pitch in her mother's voice depending on the character who was talking in the story.

"The kids asked about her before bed last night. They wanted to know what Grandma was like and if I miss having a mom," Drew said, breaking the silence.

His children had never gotten the chance to know their grandmother, which broke Hannah's heart. Mom had been so full of love that her grandchildren would have been blessed beyond words to experience it. *We'll just have to make sure they still feel her love from us*, she reminded herself.

Dad slid his attention off the photograph of his wife and onto his son. "And what did you tell them?"

"I told them I couldn't tell them everything there was to know about her before one bedtime, but I told them about her smile and her laugh and how everyone who knew her loved her. And then I told them that, even though she's with God now, she'll always be my mom."

Dad cleared his throat with a quick cough. "Sounds like maybe we should plan a family night to watch some of the home movies your mom and I recorded back in the day. Let them see her with their own eyes."

"I'll make some popcorn," Hannah said. "That alone will guarantee Axel's attention for a little while."

"I like this idea," Drew said. "A lot. Let me talk to Allison about it today, and we'll toss out some possible dates in the next few weeks, if that works for both of you."

Dad gave Hannah a hopeful yet tentative smile. "You could bring Liam."

"We'll see, Dad. It might be a little early in our relationship for him to see me in some of my dorkier phases."

"You say that like they ended at some point," Drew teased. He dodged Hannah's playful swat. "I'm kidding, I'm kidding. But seriously, let's do this. It sounds fun. And I think you should bring Liam too."

"You name the time, and I'll take it from there." Dad shooed his son toward the door, and they all followed Andrew outside. "Now go enjoy your time with Allison and tell that brother of mine he should be heading out to the Taylor place if he wants to be back in time to play pickleball at the rec center with me and the guys at one."

"Got it. Thanks, Dad. I'll also tell him about the family movie night we're planning." Andrew set off in the direction of the house then paused and glanced over his shoulder at Hannah. "We should double-date with you and Liam on a Sunday afternoon sometime. If Dad and Uncle Gordon will look after the kids, that is."

"Family movies first," Dad said. "Then, yes, after that, you should."

Hannah watched her little brother make his way up the porch steps and through the front door of their childhood home and then turned back to her father, her thoughts taking her to a very different house—a much bigger, fancier, more expensive house. "Dad? You know Vanessa from church, right? Vanessa Lodge?"

"Of course. Did something happen to her?"

"No, no, she's fine." Hannah lifted her shoulders as a shield against a sudden burst of cold air through the trees. "Did you know that her mother grew up on the Taylor Estate?"

Dad watched Zeus meander about the yard. "At the time, no. Rose and I ran in different circles at school. But later, after your mom and I were married and we got to know Rose and her husband, Mac, better at various community events, I remember putting two and two together. Why?"

Hannah lifted her chin to the midmorning sun and willed its warmth to chase away the effects of the wind. "Rose's mother, Peggy Williams, worked there as a cook. I think Vanessa said something about her grandfather—Peggy's husband—also working on the estate."

"Ray Williams. Yes, he worked out there too. First as a handyman, and then he became chief of staff."

"Did you ever do any work on the estate?" she asked.

"A few times. I was brought in to help rewire the stable when you were in kindergarten. I remember that because Drew wasn't in school yet and he wanted to go with me so badly."

Hannah grinned. "The horses?"

Dad nodded. "He loved them."

"We both did growing up. But you said a few times, right? What else did you do there?"

"There was an electrical problem in one of the outbuildings some years after that." He scratched his jaw in thought. "Actually, it was the cottage where Peggy and Ray lived. Real nice, welcoming folks. He'd had some sort of knee surgery and couldn't move about too easily. He was quick with the jokes and had me in stitches the whole time I was working. And she was a potter, if I remember correctly."

"She was," Hannah confirmed. "Apparently, she taught herself how to make pottery, and her work became almost famous."

"She gave me a bowl after I finished that day," Dad said. "Your mother was over the moon about it."

"*Really?*" Hannah asked, shocked that she hadn't heard of this before. "Which bowl?"

"The one we used for popcorn on family movie nights."

Hannah gaped at her father. "The big brown one? The one that got broken during Drew's seventh-grade birthday party?"

"That's the one."

"I loved that bowl," she said. "Now I'm extra upset that it broke."

"Your mom felt the same way."

"I'll have to tell Vanessa about that the next time I see her. I think she'll be pleased to hear how her grandmother's work was and still is appreciated." Hannah looked down at her watch and noted the rapidly closing window she had to get things done before needing to be at the restaurant. "I was hoping for some more time with you, but I really need to drive out to Cave City before I have to be back at the Hot Spot."

Dad walked Hannah out to her Subaru. "What do you have to do in Cave City? Is it an errand I can run for you while you're working?"

"Not really, but thanks for offering, Dad. I appreciate it." She pulled her keys from her pocket and opened the car door. "I need to speak to the owner of the pottery shop there."

"A pottery shop?" Dad grinned. "How's that for irony? Or should I say a coincidence?"

She studied her dad with a raised eyebrow. "Meaning?"

"I bring up pottery and you're off to a pottery shop." He snapped his fingers to gain Zeus's attention and summoned the dog to stand at his side. "Maybe while you're there, you can see if they might have a popcorn bowl that'll work for our upcoming home movie night with the crew? Bonus points if it looks like the one that broke all those years ago."

She kissed her father's cheek and then settled herself behind the steering wheel. "I'll see what I can do, Dad."

Chapter Six

Taking in the array of shelves in front of her as well as to her left and right, Hannah found herself gravitating toward the display showcasing various hues of blue—pie plates, dinner plates, dessert plates, serving bowls, individual bowls, and mugs. The obvious skill with which they'd been made drew her in for a closer inspection of a platter and then a peek at its underside.

She pulled the rectangular piece of pottery closer with the supposition she'd read the numbers printed on the price tag incorrectly, but she hadn't. "All right," she murmured, placing the piece back on its shelf. "No platter for me."

"Welcome to Clay House Pottery." A woman about Hannah's height but roughly a decade older breezed into the room through an open doorway at the rear of the shop, wiping her hands down the front of her apron as she did. "I'm so sorry it took a few moments to get out to you, but I had something coming out of the kiln at the exact moment you walked in."

Hannah waved aside the woman's apology and gestured to the platter and the other wares surrounding it. "You have some truly beautiful pieces here."

"Thank you. That's music to my ears." The woman beamed from behind the register. "I'm Morgan Wyatt. Please take as long as you'd like to browse. The dinnerware is safe for the oven, microwave, and dishwasher, and we can ship anywhere in the country if you're thinking about gifting to a loved one outside the area."

With a last wistful glance at the platter, Hannah strode over to the counter and Morgan. "Actually, if it's okay, I just wanted to ask you a question or two if I may."

"A question?"

"Yes, but I won't take too much of your time."

Morgan's shoulders slumped along with her smile. "Oh. I was hoping you'd come in because you'd heard about my shop or one of my pieces." She slowly lowered herself onto a stool positioned behind the register. "Don't mind me. I just worry sometimes about whether I can keep this place going."

"I'll be honest, I saw a flyer once, but I didn't remember you were here."

"And that's half my problem." Plucking a pen from the counter, Morgan heaved a long, slow sigh. "No one seems to know I'm here. I mean, I'm on the main road, so you think that would help. But people are focused on the places they intend to visit, like the ice cream shop one block over, the taco place beyond that, and that sports store across the street everyone seems to love."

Hannah glanced back at the shop's front window and the lack of foot traffic. "How long have you been open?"

"A month this coming Saturday," Morgan said.

"Have you run any ads in either *The Blackberry Valley Chronicle* or *The Cave City Press*?"

Morgan nodded. "I have, but people tend to look right past those these days."

"Maybe you can get one of them to do a story on you and your store," Hannah suggested. "That would probably help a lot. Human interest pieces are always more fun to read than ads."

The shopkeeper let loose a laugh laced with sarcasm. "I'm trying, my dear. I really am."

"I'll keep my fingers crossed."

Morgan blew out another breath, shook her head, and dropped the pen onto the counter. "Maybe you could tell your friends about the store? Word of mouth is important too. Tell them I make every piece in here by hand. Nothing is mass produced."

"I'll be sure to do that. And I'll make an effort to get back here and really spend some time looking around when I don't have to be at my own job in"—Hannah glanced at her watch and grimaced—"a little over twenty minutes when it'll take me ten to fifteen minutes to get there."

Morgan slid off her stool and onto her feet. "Oh? What do you do for work?"

"I opened a restaurant in Blackberry Valley last year."

"The Hot Spot?"

"That's right. Have you been?"

"No. But I've heard about it." Morgan's laugh was short. "From people who've eaten there and a story or two in the paper. You know, the normal word-spreading ways."

"Give it time. It'll happen for you too."

"I hope you're right." Resting her hands on her hips, Morgan scanned the shop. "Anyway, I've bent your ear long enough, I'm afraid, and you still haven't had a chance to ask whatever question brought you here in the first place. So now I'll be quiet and let you talk."

Hannah thought about the box she'd unwrapped and opened less than forty-eight hours earlier. "I was given a piece of pottery from your shop as a birthday gift the other day and I—"

"Wonderful!" Morgan exclaimed. "The rectangular platter with the stamped pinecone in the center?"

"No."

"The coffee mug with the flower handle?"

"No. It was a creamer."

A flash of something Hannah couldn't quite identify skittered across the shopkeeper's face only to disappear in favor of a series of quick chin taps. "A creamer?"

"That's right. It was a pretty blue color with a ribbon of brown along the top?"

"That's strange. I haven't made anything like that. Are you sure it was purchased here?"

Hannah started to answer but stopped as her phone began to ring from inside her front pocket. Pulling it out, she took in the familiar face on the screen and the time on the clock above it. "Excuse me, Morgan, it's my chef. I should take this."

At the woman's nod, she crossed to the front of the shop and answered the call. "Hey, Jacob, I might run five or ten minutes late today, but I'll be there."

"You can't be late, Hannah," Jacob said. "Not today."

She glanced back at the counter and Morgan. "Is something wrong?"

"Wrong? No. Right? Yes." She heard Jacob's voice grow quieter as if he'd moved the phone away from his mouth to engage in a conversation with someone else that she couldn't quite hear. A moment later, he addressed her again. "Seriously, Hannah, you need to come. Now. Before you miss this opportunity."

"What opportunity is that? Who's there with you?"

"Marshall Fredericks."

She tightened her hold on her phone. "Is he wanting to run another review on the Hot Spot?"

"Nope. He's not here with the *Chronicle*. He's here as *The Gourmet Guy*. With a camera crew." *The Gourmet Guy* was Marshall's popular food blog.

"A camera crew?" she echoed.

"Who, I must add, will only be sticking around for another twenty minutes."

"Twenty minutes, *tops*!" Marshall hastily clarified in the background of the call.

"Can you at least tell me what's going on?" Hannah asked.

"Remember a few weeks ago when Raquel told us that Marshall reached out to that local news station about his blog?" Jacob prodded.

"I do. Are they going to do a story about it?"

"They are."

She felt her mouth spread wide with her answering smile. "That's fantastic. Did Marshall know this was happening?"

"He did, but he didn't know it was going to happen today. But apparently this crew was covering something close to Blackberry Valley anyway, so they reached out to him and asked if he could talk to them now."

"Oh, wow. That's cool."

"It gets cooler, Hannah."

"I'm listening," she said.

"Marshall said there was no way he was about to pass up the chance to get some free advertising and so he told them yes."

"Smart."

"But since he wasn't expecting this today, his apartment wasn't as clean as he would want it to be for a camera crew." Jacob stopped, drew in a breath, and released it. "So he called Raquel, who apparently tried to call you, but it went straight to voicemail."

Surprised, she quickly pulled back the phone, pressed a button, and furrowed her brow at the tiny red circle above the phone icon that indicated the presence of a voicemail. "I must've been in a dead zone when she tried," Hannah said, returning the phone to her ear. "But I'll listen to it the moment we hang up."

"You don't have to. When you didn't answer, she called me, and I took it upon myself to 'run things,' as you always tell me to do when you're otherwise occupied."

"Good. I want you to do that."

"I figured as much, so that's why I went ahead and gave permission. On your behalf."

She shifted the phone to her other ear. "Permission? Permission for what?"

"To film Marshall's segment here—at the Hot Spot."

She felt her mouth gape.

"Now, before you ask, all hands are on deck, and any sign of the camera crew's presence will be long gone before we open at four o'clock," Jacob said, his excitement evident. "This is a huge PR opportunity for us, Hannah. It really is."

"I'm on my way."

"Be safe, but hurry."

"I will." She ended the call, shoved the phone back in her pocket, and readdressed the woman clearly watching and listening from behind the counter. "I'm sorry for that interruption, but I have to get to the restaurant right away. We have an opportunity to get in front of a wider audience of potential customers, and you know what that could mean."

Morgan's shoulders slumped, sending a twang of guilt through Hannah. She hadn't thought before she'd spoken, and she hadn't meant to be unkind. But she probably shouldn't have mentioned her good fortune when she was already successful and Morgan was struggling to get her business off the ground.

But all the shopkeeper said was, "I do. You can't pass that up."

"I'll be back, for sure."

Her hand on the door's handle, Hannah waited for her words to reverse the shopkeeper's slumping, but they didn't. If anything, they made it...*worse*? Before she could even try to process the odd reaction, though, the door opened, pulling her forward.

"Pippa!" She hurried to gain her footing as the reporter's shocked eyes found hers in the suddenly open doorway.

"Oh, Hannah, I'm so sorry! I guess I wasn't paying attention when I opened the door and—"

"*Finally*!"

At the exasperated note in Morgan's voice, Hannah glanced back inside to find the shopkeeper's attention on Pippa. Unfortunately, she had no time to figure it out. A chime from her phone and a subsequent peek at the screen made her jog toward her Subaru.

Chapter Seven

Glancing from the dashboard clock to the road she turned onto, Hannah called Vanessa on her hands-free system.

The police receptionist answered right away. "Hey, Hannah, I can only talk for a minute."

"That's okay, because that's about all I've got too," she replied.

"You at your place?" Vanessa asked.

"No, I'm in the car, heading into work."

"Jacky said she saw a news van pull up outside the restaurant. Is everything all right?"

"We're getting a story. Or more accurately, we're getting the opportunity to be the background for a story."

"Is it correct to assume it's a *good* story?"

"It should be."

"That's fantastic, Hannah!" A pause on Vanessa's end was followed by something that sounded like papers being shuffled. "I'm guessing it's also safe to assume that's not why you're calling me?"

"It's not."

"I'm all ears." The shuffling sound stopped.

"Is there any chance you can take a picture of the creamer and send it to me in the next day or so?" Hannah asked.

"How about as soon as we get off the phone?"

Hannah let up on the gas pedal as Blackberry Town Hall and then the Hot Spot came into view. "Oh no, I don't want you to leave work to take a picture. Just when you get a chance."

"I already have one—several, in fact," Vanessa said. "Mama is in all of them, of course, but then you'll get to see how overjoyed she was when I gave it to her."

Hannah slowed still further as her gaze fell on the white paneled van bearing the news logo on its side, the very sight of it outside her restaurant stirring up a mixture of nervousness and anticipation. She parked and drew in a steadying breath.

"Hannah? Are you still there?"

"I am. Sorry." Hannah peeked in her rearview mirror in time to see a face she recognized from the local news affiliate.

Vanessa's laugh filled the Subaru's cabin. "I take it you're at the restaurant?"

"That's right." She cut the engine. "And I suddenly have the urge to fall asleep."

"Fall asleep?" Vanessa repeated.

"It's apparently how I dealt with stage fright when I was in kindergarten. I slept right through my role as a sheep in the church's Christmas pageant that year."

"Well, you can't do that this time," Vanessa said.

It was Hannah's turn to laugh. "That doesn't mean I don't want to."

"Be that as it may, the Hot Spot is incredible. Everyone who's been there knows that. This is just a chance to put it on even more radars. So go do exactly that."

"Thanks, Vanessa."

"My pleasure."

Hannah paused her finger in front of the red circle on the dashboard screen. "I can't wait to see your mom's face in the pictures."

"I'll send them to you right away. I have to go. There's a call coming in on Sheriff Steele's line. Good luck with the TV shoot."

"Raquel, your boyfriend is the man!"

Hannah raised her head from the cell phone she and her staff were huddled around to watch their spot on the five o'clock news. "Dylan is right, Raquel. Marshall *is* the man."

Raquel beamed. "I know, but it's nice to have others appreciate him too."

Hannah grinned and tapped the screen. "This story was just supposed to be about him and his blog. But then he included the Hot Spot to help get our name out even more. There aren't any words, other than thank you so much—to him *and* to you."

"I didn't do anything," Raquel protested.

Hannah's answering laugh mingled with Jacob's and Dylan's. "Other than capture Marshall's heart."

"He didn't do this because of me," Raquel protested. She gestured around the kitchen. "He did it because this place and Jacob's food are worth showcasing."

Jacob puffed out his aproned chest with pride. "The food *is* pretty great. But a lot of that is the spectacular local ingredients Hannah sources."

"Our top-notch chef sure doesn't hurt," Hannah said with a grin. "But that two-minute segment we just watched means we've left our customers unattended. So let's table the celebration in favor of them. At least for now anyway."

Dylan straightened the waist apron that carried his order pad and made a beeline for the door, Raquel right behind him.

When they had disappeared into the dining area, Hannah turned to her chef. "That? On the TV just now? That was real, right? I wasn't imagining it?"

"If you were, we were too. And so was everyone responsible for the notifications coming from in there." He nodded to where the staff left their phones during their shifts. "Started the moment Dylan's face popped up in the background of Marshall's last shot and hasn't stopped since."

"What do you think that means?" Hannah asked.

"Every friend of his who happened to be watching the news is texting to let him know they saw him on TV." Jacob stepped behind the grill and began plating one of the Hot Spot's most requested menu items—the Rookie Meltdown. "As I imagine my phone would be doing, if I didn't have the ringer set to silent."

Hannah wandered over to the swinging doors and studied the view of the dining room their porthole-shaped windows provided. She watched the redhead moving with ease between his assigned tables. "Is it just me, or have you noticed Dylan seeming a little subdued when he clocks in the past few days? I've wanted to ask him about it, but every time I think about pulling him aside to see if he's okay, it's time to open and he's turned back into his happy, normal self."

"I can't say I've noticed." Jacob added a side of fries to the burger plate and set it under the heat lamp. "The kid I see coming and going through the kitchen door during work hours is always smiling."

She watched Dylan top off both water glasses at table five before heading in her direction. "He's good with the customers."

"Now that he's not dropping things on them, I have to agree," Jacob quipped as he plated a Pull Box sandwich and set it beside the Rookie Meltdown.

"He never dropped anything on anyone, Jacob," Hannah said, chuckling. "Just near them. And only once or twice."

"Once or twice?" Jacob repeated. "You're being kind."

Hannah stepped back in preparation for Dylan's entry. "The customers have grown to love him almost as much as they love Raquel."

Dylan breezed into the kitchen and grabbed the plates from under the heat lamp. "Table five watched the segment on their phones too. They said it was fantastic."

"They watched from their table?" Hannah asked. "How did they know?"

Dylan grinned. "I wanted them to know they might not see me for a few minutes while we watched in here."

She smiled at the young waiter. "Smart thinking."

Setting his back against the swinging door, Dylan said, "I'm trying."

"I know. And you're succeeding—very well, in fact."

"You really think so?" he asked.

"I *know* so, Dylan."

Dylan glanced at Jacob, who gave him a nod of reassurance. From the stoic chef, that was high praise. Dylan straightened his shoulders, lifted his plates a little higher, and pushed through the double doors.

Hannah beamed at her chef. "Thanks for that, Jacob."

Jacob stopped stirring long enough to meet her gaze across the empty warming shelf. "For?"

"Giving Dylan a quiet 'attaboy' just now." She took one more look through the porthole window before turning back to her chef. "I feel like he really needed that for some reason."

"All I did was nod."

"Maybe. But I could tell it meant a lot to him."

Jacob continued stirring the sauce she knew would soon be expertly drizzled across the Five Alarm Burger. "As long as he knows he can always get better, I'll give him a nod of encouragement every now and again."

"Ever the philanthropist," she said, laughing.

Her phone vibrated in her pocket. She pulled it out, looked at the screen, and drew back at the notification box alerting her to a dozen unread text messages. Dad, Uncle Gordon, Drew, Lacy, Miriam, Jacky, Neil, Pippa, Evangeline, Allison, and—her smile grew—Liam "Best Boyfriend" Berthold. The time listed next to each name let her know that they had seen the Hot Spot's inclusion in the feature piece on Marshall's food blog. Thankfully, she also knew every single one of them would understand that a reply from her would have to wait until the restaurant closed.

Still, her finger hovered above the one from Liam, the sight of his self-appointed nickname wrapping her in a pleasant warmth she felt from the top of her head to the tip of her toes.

But before she could open his text, a new one came through from Vanessa, so Hannah opened that one instead.

Sorry for the delay in getting this to you. I got sidetracked with some tasks from the sheriff, and by the time I

FINISHED, I'D COMPLETELY FORGOTTEN ABOUT YOUR REQUEST. MY APOLOGIES.

Another vibration delivered a stack of four photos.

Opening the first one, Hannah saw Vanessa's mother, Rose, seated in an armchair in what was clearly the family's living room. Rose's eyebrows were pinched downward as she looked at Vanessa, who had her hands behind her back.

She thumbed to the next picture. In it, Rose's expression was no longer one of curiosity but one of complete shock at the creamer that rested on Vanessa's extended palm.

A third picture showed a rapid transition into joyful celebration for both Rose and Vanessa, who winked at whoever had been tasked with capturing the reveal.

The fourth and final picture was a closeup of Rose, the creamer clutched to her chest, tears on her cheeks.

"Wow," Hannah murmured. "Such a beautiful moment."

"You say something?" Jacob asked.

Shaking her head at him, she set the thumb and forefinger of her free hand on the screen with the intention to zoom in but stopped as the picture was pushed higher on the screen by another message from Vanessa.

I THINK THAT MOMENT WITH MAMA WILL BE WITH ME FOREVER. SHE SAID SHE GOT A MISSING PIECE OF HER MAMA BACK, THANKS TO YOU. I WISH I'D BEEN ABLE TO GIVE HER THE CREAMER AND THE SUGAR BOWL, BUT A SINGLE BLESSING IS BETTER THAN NONE, RIGHT? ESPECIALLY WHEN IT CLEARLY MEANT SO MUCH TO HER.

Hannah beamed at the message.

I know you just asked for a picture of the creamer, but I had to send you the ones of me giving it to Mama, since you're the reason I was able to. Mama doesn't understand how it ended up coming to you all these years later, but she says she's grateful it did.

And I am too. Thank you, Hannah!

The clunk of one, two, and then three plates onto the warming shelf stole her attention toward Jacob. Another vibration, though, brought her eyes back to her phone.

Here's a pic of the creamer by itself.

Tapping the newly received photograph, Hannah stared down at the item she'd pulled from an unmarked gift box two days earlier—a gift Pippa said she'd purchased from the pottery shop in Cave City over the weekend yet the owner claimed to have no recollection of selling.

She recalled the moment she'd asked Morgan about the creamer, seeing the odd expression she'd caught on her face in response. It had been quick, sure, but it had been there just as surely as Hannah herself had been.

The only question now was whether it was due to a poor description of the creamer on Hannah's part—or something far less innocent.

Chapter Eight

Hannah took one last look around the Hot Spot's empty dining room. "It looks great in here, guys."

"Wait." Dylan hurried over to a table, plucked a cloth from his waist apron, and carefully rubbed at a spot along its edge. "Nope, it's nothing. Just a little bit of the cleaning spray I missed during wipe-down."

"Thanks, Dylan. You did a great job on the tables, as always."

Beside Hannah, Raquel rose up on the toes of her shoes. "So we're good to go?"

"You're good to go," Hannah repeated, waving Dylan away from the table. "*All* of you."

Raquel started toward the staff room to retrieve her personal belongings but stopped at the door to look back at Hannah. "Any chance I could put a scoop of tonight's mint chocolate chip ice cream in a to-go container for Marshall? I'd like to set it outside his front door, ring the bell, and then get back in the car and drive off before he sees me."

"Are you seriously asking me that question, Raquel?"

The waitress's ever-present smile dimmed. "You can take it out of my next check. I just know he'll really like it."

"Which is why I want you to give him as many scoops as you think he'll eat, and it's on the house," Hannah said, motioning toward the kitchen door. "After what he did for the Hot Spot by insisting part of the news feature on him be shot here today, he can have all the ice cream he wants."

Dylan's laugh was echoed by Jacob's from beyond the kitchen door. "Um, Hannah?" Dylan asked. "Have you seen how much ice cream Marshall can eat? You might want to make sure you don't ever say that around him, or we'll all be out of work."

Hannah joined the laughter.

"Dylan isn't wrong, Hannah." Raquel pushed on the kitchen door to reveal Jacob removing his apron and hat. "But, since he *did* help us out, I'll take him two scoops instead of just one."

"Raquel?" Jacob balled up his apron. "What Marshall did today was huge for the restaurant. You'd better make it three scoops."

"And when he calls you while you're driving home after your ice cream ring-and-run, please make sure to thank him from me," Hannah added.

Jacob held the swinging door open while Raquel set about the task of filling a large to-go cup with ice cream.

Raquel looked up midscoop. "You thanked him when he and the news crew left, remember? Several times, in fact."

"I repeat, Raquel, what Marshall did today was huge for this place," Jacob said.

"We can't thank him enough," Hannah agreed.

"All right." Raquel finished filling the container and capped it with a lid. "I'll let him know."

"Thank you. And don't you dare clean that ice cream scoop," Hannah said. "Just leave it in the sink. I'll take care of it. You—all of you—get out of here. Have a great rest of your night."

She waved away Raquel's hesitation and then watched as her devoted staff filed out of the Hot Spot.

Turning, Hannah headed toward the kitchen and the ice cream scoop that needed cleaning. Halfway to the sink, a steady vibration from inside her pocket had her reaching for her phone instead.

"Hi, Vanessa. I got the pictures you sent, and I'm just now realizing I never texted you back to tell you that." Hannah leaned against the counter and let loose a tired exhale. "It was a busy Wednesday night around here, to put it mildly, but I loved seeing your mom's joy over being reunited with the creamer her mother made for her."

"They were the best pictures, weren't they?" Vanessa gushed.

"They were."

A noise that sounded as if Vanessa was on the move quickly faded to the return of her melodic voice in Hannah's ear. "I wouldn't normally call a person at nearly eleven o'clock at night, but I figured with the restaurant and all, you might not be in bed yet."

"Not only am I not in bed, I'm still downstairs in the restaurant."

"Am I interrupting something?"

"Hardly. You're saving me from having to clean an ice cream scoop at this exact moment," Hannah said, laughing. "And I thank you for that."

A door closed in the background before a quieter Vanessa returned in her ear. "Mama just went to bed, so I can't talk too loud, but I didn't want to wait on this until tomorrow."

"Is something wrong?"

"Pippa Nelson called me on my way home from work this evening. She asked all sorts of questions about the creamer she gave you."

"What kind of questions?" Hannah asked.

"Stuff about my grandmother and her pottery, about the set she made Mama, and when Mama first noticed it was missing."

"I guess that makes sense," Hannah said. "I mean *I'm* curious about how something that's been missing for more than forty years could show up as a birthday present for me. And Pippa is the one who bought it."

"She's a reporter. She's trained to be curious. It's a requirement for her job. I get that, Hannah. I see it all the time from her in my work at the sheriff's department. But there's more than curiosity behind this," Vanessa said.

"Meaning?"

"She's excited."

"How so?" Hannah asked.

A crunching sound was replaced by a quick sip of something in her ear. "Pippa is certain the resurfacing of Mama's creamer is the perfect story for some big journalism award she's trying to get."

"She told me about that award." Hannah reached inside the sink with her free hand and grabbed the ice cream scoop. "She's going to use a story on this as her entry?"

"That's what she kept saying," Vanessa said. "That, and a whole lot about some professor she had in college who was a big believer in throwing out as many lines as possible in the hope of getting a decent nibble or two."

Wedging the phone between her shoulder and her ear, Hannah turned on the faucet. "That makes sense."

"But there's a problem, Hannah. Mama isn't one who likes to be the center of any sort of fuss. Asking her to sit down with a reporter and answer a bunch of questions about her mama and her life and the creamer would be exactly the kind of thing she'd hate."

"Then tell Pippa that." Hannah rinsed the ice cream residue from the scoop and then pulled the door of the commercial washer open. "I'm sure she'll listen."

Vanessa's laugh held no sign of humor or lightness. "I'm not sure you'd be saying that if you'd been on the call with her."

"Do you want me to talk to her?" Hannah asked.

"Kind of, but no. I'll take care of it, if I need to. In the meantime, Mama asked me to tell you she'd like you to come to the house sometime soon. She wants to thank you herself, and she wants to use the creamer with you."

Hannah smiled as she started the washer. "Tell her I'd love to come."

"I will. And now I'll leave you to finish up whatever you need to do in order to be able to call it a night."

"I just did. But thank you." Hannah made her way back into the dining room. "And thank you again for the pictures."

"My pleasure."

"Have a great night, Vanessa."

"You too, Hannah. Good night."

Lowering the phone to her side, Hannah crossed to the front door, readied her hand on the lock, and then paused as her gaze came to rest on the tall, brown-eyed man smiling at her through the glass pane.

Chapter Nine

"Liam, hi!" She opened the door and stepped forward into his ready embrace, breathing in the comforting scent of the man responsible for the sudden smile claiming her face. "This is a nice surprise."

"I was hoping you hadn't gone up to your apartment yet," he said.

"I got sidetracked by an ice cream scoop and a phone call."

"Lucky me."

She backed against the open door. "Do you want to come in for a little while? I could make you coffee if you're on a break from work. Help you stay awake."

"I was thinking we could take a walk if you're not too tired. Not very long, but maybe around the park or down to the library and back? I need a little Hannah time."

Joy filled her at his words. Liam Berthold was a good man, someone who was becoming more and more important in her life with each passing day. What the future held for them only God knew, but she was excited to find out.

Stepping onto the sidewalk, she pulled the door shut, locked it, and fell into step beside the handsome fire chief, his hand finding hers as they headed in the direction of the park. For a full block, neither said anything, and that was okay. Just his presence at the end of a long day was a comfort, and she thanked God once again for bringing him into her life.

At the start of the next block, he tightened his hold on her hand. "I'm sorry we haven't had a chance to talk since dinner on Sunday, but the past three days have kept me even busier than normal. I had some training to put my crew through, a meeting with the mayor, and another with someone from the state fire safety board. Plus my usual shift duties. And Gramps needed my help with some stuff at his place. He says hi, by the way."

Hannah stopped, turned to face Liam, and found his eyes in the light of the moon. "Hey, no apologies. We talked about this, remember? You're the town's fire chief. Your grandfather lives nearby, and he's getting on in years. You have a lot of people counting on you all the time. I have a restaurant to run and a family I missed a lot of time with when I lived in California. We're busy."

"That's just it," Liam said, studying her closely. "I don't want to be so busy I don't even get to hear your voice."

Aware of a growing warmth in her cheeks, she pivoted back toward the park. "Be careful what you wish for," she said, laughing.

"Meaning?"

"A lot has happened since I last saw you."

"I've heard." When they reached the park, he guided her to the nearest bench. "Bits and pieces, anyway. But I want to hear about everything from you."

She sat, waited for him to do the same beside her, and then gazed up at the stars. "Bits and pieces, huh?"

"Let's start with Monday's luncheon with the ladies."

"What did you hear about that?"

"That it was really a surprise belated birthday celebration for you."

"I had no idea they had that up their sleeve." She lowered her gaze to his. "Did you?"

His smile grew into a full-blown grin. "Evangeline might've mentioned it to me after church on Sunday. But she swore me to secrecy."

Straightening her shoulders, Hannah tried her best to be indignant, but she failed. "Liam, it was so nice. Everyone was there. They took care of the food and the drinks and an absolutely perfect cake."

"I had a truck at the ready," he quipped.

"A truck?"

"Thirty-six candles means thirty-six flames."

She swatted playfully at his arm. "It's rude to remind a lady of her age. I should tell your grandfather."

"He'd probably take your side." He captured her hand with his and hung on to it gently. "Seriously, I'm glad. You're a special person who means a lot to a lot of people, Hannah Prentiss. Clearly the ladies wanted to make sure you knew that."

"Thank you, Liam."

"Just calling it like I see it, that's all." He draped his arm across the back of the bench, his fingers brushing lightly against her shoulder. "I also heard about—and then made sure to watch—you on the five o'clock news today."

"I was only in the background."

"I saw you and the restaurant quite clearly, thank you very much."

"They wanted to do a feature on Marshall's blog and had a last-minute slot to fill. He talked them into filming it with the Hot Spot as his background. Which I still can't believe. It was amazing press for us."

"I repeat, you're a special person who means a lot to a lot of people. I mean, who in your field actually *thanks* a food critic for dinging their restaurant?"

"The Hot Spot is much better now thanks to what Marshall called me out on. That's why I thanked him."

"Okay, but I stand by what I said. I imagine your reaction was not something he's used to in his job—at least from people who don't get a perfect review. That's probably why he wanted to include you in his moment. To help give the Hot Spot a little added attention."

"Maybe. But I'm thinking there was another factor that also came into play." She grinned. "Like a certain server with beautiful curly brown hair and big brown eyes that literally sparkle every time she looks at him."

Liam's laugh echoed in the night air. "Okay, so maybe he had *two* reasons to shine a spotlight on your restaurant."

"Three, if you count the container filled with tonight's homemade mint chocolate chip ice cream Raquel has probably dropped off on his doorstep by now."

"Wait!" He held up his finger, his eyes narrowing. "Does that mean the next time there's a fire that a news crew asks me to weigh in on, I can get some hand-delivered ice cream at *my* door?"

Grinning, she rolled her eyes toward the sky. "If you mention the Hot Spot, I'm sure Raquel would do the same for you under those circumstances."

"I don't want *Raquel* bringing it by," he protested. "I want the Hot Spot's boss lady to deliver it."

"Get us the kind of airtime we got today, and I'll see what I can do," she said, her answering laugh mingling with his. Then she remembered that she was filling him in on her story. “I got a strange present after the luncheon on Monday.”

His brows dipped. “Strange? How so? And who from?”

“It was from Pippa Nelson, although she forgot to include a card or her name anywhere on the wrapping paper or in the box.”

“I thought you said everyone was there,” Liam said.

“Every one of the usuals were there.” She let out a quiet sigh. “I’ve made sure to invite Pippa to the luncheons prior to this, but she never comes. She never even responds. Evangeline apparently spoke to her about this one and the fact that it was a belated birthday celebration for me, but she still didn’t come.”

“Yet she gave you a present?”

Hannah nodded. “Left it outside the door of the restaurant while we were inside eating cake.”

“Why didn’t she bring it in?”

“She didn’t want to get waylaid, I guess.”

“By the ladies in this town?” he asked, drawing back in mock surprise. “They don’t waylay people. How can you make such accusations?”

“I know. I’m not sure what I was thinking.” She rested her head on his outstretched arm. “I’m serious here. About the gift being strange.”

He met her gaze, his warm brown eyes steady and welcoming. “Tell me about it.”

And so she did.

She told him about the beautiful twilight-blue creamer. She told him how surprised Vanessa had been when she saw Hannah lift it out of the box. She explained the piece had been made as part of a complete dining set more than forty years earlier and given to

Vanessa's mother before she moved out on her own. She told him how the creamer and sugar bowl had disappeared, never to be seen again until the moment Hannah pulled the creamer out of the gift box from Pippa.

"Wow." He seemed to mull over what she'd said. "Any idea where it's been this whole time?"

"Pippa claims she bought it at a new pottery shop in Cave City over the weekend. But when I stopped by there this morning to ask the shop owner where she'd gotten the creamer, she said she didn't recall selling it." Memories of her time in the shop flooded Hannah's thoughts, a mishmash of words and expressions that left her feeling unsettled. "I know this might sound silly, but I'm not entirely sure the shopkeeper was honest with me."

"Why do you think that?"

"She had a strange look on her face when I asked about the creamer. It was quick, and I didn't get to probe further, on account of getting the call from Jacob about the TV crew and having to leave as quickly as I did, but I saw it."

"But you said she didn't remember selling it, right? So maybe what you saw was simply confusion, or her trying to remember," Liam suggested.

"Maybe." Hannah shrugged. "But maybe it was something else."

"You don't believe her?"

"I don't know."

"Nothing changed when you showed it to her?"

Hannah held up her hands. "I didn't show it to her. I gave it to Vanessa to give to her mother the moment I learned it had been taken from her all those years ago."

"So then maybe you caught a funny face from the clerk because she wasn't the one who sold it to Pippa? Maybe it was another employee?"

"The shop is a one-woman operation, and the woman I spoke with, Morgan Wyatt, *is* the one woman," Hannah said.

Liam scrubbed at his jaw. "If you turned it over to Vanessa as soon as you got it, is it possible you didn't describe it well enough for Morgan to visualize?"

"It is possible," Hannah admitted. "Since then, I've had Vanessa send me some photos of the creamer. I figured I'd stop back in at the store in the next day or so and show Morgan. But now, remembering that odd expression on her face when I first mentioned the creamer, I'm not so sure she didn't remember it." Hannah released a tired breath. "Because, really, in a store that small with next to no foot traffic—according to her—I can't help but wonder how many creamers she could've possibly sold in the past few days that would make it so she couldn't remember the one she sold to..."

Her eyes widened as something clicked.

"*Pippa*," she said.

"Which you already knew," Liam pointed out.

"I did. But Pippa walked into the shop as I was walking out, and it sounded like there was familiarity between her and Morgan. At the time, I was in a hurry to get back to the Hot Spot, so it didn't really register."

His gentle laughter filled the air around them. "The plot thickens, it seems."

"It does."

"Have you brought Lacy up to speed? I know she loves this kind of thing."

"I talked to her before I went to the pottery shop this morning," Hannah said, giving in to a shiver the cold night practically demanded. "But yes, I'll catch her up on all of this when we talk in the morning."

Liam immediately reached into the pocket of his coat, pulled out a beanie with the Blackberry Valley Fire Department logo across the front, and gently worked it onto her head. "We won't tell Gramps I didn't think about you not wearing a hat until just this moment, okay? He'd have my head."

"I wasn't cold until just this moment," she protested.

"He'd still have my head."

She tugged the beanie down over her ears with a grateful smile. "I won't tell him."

"And I promise I'll do better next time—sleep-deprived or not." He turned his back flush to the bench again, his arm sliding around her shoulders once more. "And the sugar bowl that went missing at the same time as the creamer? What's its status?"

"Still missing."

"Interesting."

"It is. But if I figure out the mystery of the creamer, maybe it'll lead me to the sugar bowl. I'm hoping so anyway."

"Maybe it will." Tilting his head back, Liam pointed out the Big and Little Dippers and a few other constellations before returning his full attention to Hannah. "Do you know where these pieces went missing from forty years ago?"

She burrowed closer to his side as, once again, her gaze traveled upward. "Probably from the cottage Vanessa's mother, Rose, grew up in. On the Taylor Estate."

"It's been a while since I've thought of that place," Liam said, resting his cheek against the top of her head.

Reveling in the warmth of his breath against her hair, Hannah nodded. "Rose's mother, Peggy, worked as a cook on the estate. Her father worked there also, first as a handyman and then as head of the staff."

His chin bobbed on her head with his nod. "Interestingly enough, I was actually out there today to check a faulty smoke detector."

"Fire chiefs make house calls for that?"

"I've been known to make a few, as have members of my department over the years," he said. "Whatever keeps the residents of Blackberry Valley safe. Today's request came via the mayor, as opposed to a call directly to the firehouse."

"That's strange," Hannah murmured.

"Not really. His ties to the Taylor family go way back, apparently. His dad was friends with Jack Adler, who married Theresa Smith. Theresa was the daughter of Antoinette Taylor-Smith. Antoinette's father was Richard Taylor, the man who had the estate built."

She laughed. "My head hurts trying to keep track of all that."

"Yours and mine both," Liam said. "Which is why I look to my grandfather to fill in that kind of stuff when I need it. Which, fortunately, isn't all that often."

"From what I've seen, you do pretty well putting names to faces."

"Faces I see often, maybe. I'm not as good with family trees." He reached down and captured her hand with his. "Changing the subject slightly, guess who I saw while I was out at the Taylor Estate today?"

"My uncle Gordon."

"Guessing games are more fun when you don't guess right the very first try," Liam said. "But yes, I saw your uncle. He was finishing up some work on a pipe under the kitchen sink when I came out of Mrs. Adler's room. We didn't want to disturb her, so we stepped outside for a few minutes and talked a little football."

She felt an incoming yawn and hurried to stifle it with her free hand. "Sorry. I promise it's not the company."

He grimaced at his watch and stood, gently tugging her up beside him. "I'm glad to hear it, but I'm being selfish—wanting to fit in some time with you but not keeping close enough tabs on how late it's gotten, and after you've already put in a full day and then some."

"This time was wonderful, Liam. Needed, even." She fell in step beside him as they made their way back in the direction they'd come, the lantern light above her restaurant's front door glowing a welcome. "So thank you."

"Thank *you*." He released her hand in favor of placing an arm around her shoulder as they walked, his nearness bringing a smile to her lips that he matched. "Hey, any chance I might be able to land a chair at the Prentiss family home movie night Gordon told me about? I'd love to see you through the years now that I'm finally smart enough to pay attention."

"I was two grades behind you, Liam. It makes sense that I wasn't on your radar when we were kids," she said.

"Maybe. But I can't help thinking we might've had fewer years in distant towns if you had been."

"I needed the time I had working in restaurants in California to figure out what I wanted—and it ultimately brought me back here, to Blackberry Valley." She squeezed his hand. "You needed to perform the way you performed in order to become fire chief at such a young age."

"My brain knows you're right, but it still feels like wasted time to me." He stopped at the restaurant's front door and turned her to him, his gaze finding hers in the lantern light. "I'd still love an invite to family movie night whenever it happens."

"You'll get one," she said. "Under one condition."

His left eyebrow lifted. "And what might that be?"

"You promise not to hold any of the awkward phases you might see on the screen against me."

Closing the gap between them, he pressed a kiss to her forehead. "You've got yourself a deal."

Chapter Ten

Hannah watched the sign on the door of the Clay House Pottery Shop change from Closed to Open then pushed her way inside.

"Good morning, welcome to..." Morgan Wyatt's greeting trailed away, along with its accompanying smile. "You're back."

Hannah reached into her purse and took out her phone as she approached the counter. "After I left yesterday, I realized that I probably didn't do a good enough job describing the creamer I asked you about. This time, I've brought a picture of it with me to make it easier."

"Oh. That's, uh, great."

Hannah tapped the screen, scrolled to the photo, and held it out for the shopkeeper to see. "Here it is. This is what a woman named Pippa Nelson said she purchased here this past Saturday. In fact, she came into your shop yesterday afternoon when I was here."

"I really don't remember it," Morgan hedged.

"Please." Hannah stepped closer. "If you could just look and see if it jogs your memory."

"I'm not the only potter in the area, Miss—I didn't catch your name."

"Prentiss. But you can call me Hannah."

Morgan pulled out a cloth from somewhere beneath the countertop and began wiping everything in her reach—the register, a cup of pencils, and the roll of gift wrap mounted on a large spool to her left. "People sell pottery in farmer's markets and flea markets all over the area."

"No, she bought it here. It was even wrapped in that paper you just dusted. And tied with the lavender ribbon I see over there." Hannah pointed at the opposite counter and the half dozen colors of spooled ribbon. "Which looked lovely together, by the way."

"Other people could have that paper and ribbon," Morgan muttered.

"Please. Just take a look."

"Fine." Morgan plucked the phone from Hannah's hand and glanced at the screen. "Okay, yes, I have a vague recollection of that piece." She tried to hand Hannah back the phone but when Hannah didn't take it, she set it facedown on the counter between them. "Was it cracked?"

"No."

"Not a color you like?"

"No, it's not that either."

"Then I don't understand what the issue is."

Hannah flipped the phone over so the creamer was visible once again and pointed at it. "You told me you make everything that's for sale in this store."

"That's right."

"But you didn't make this creamer."

Morgan closed her eyes, and her throat moved with a hard swallow before she opened them again. "Fine. Okay. I found it, someone liked it enough to buy it, and I'm not exactly in a position where I can turn down a sale. Maybe one day that won't be the case, but it is now. Sadly."

"You *found* it?"

Morgan nodded.

"Where did you find it?"

"I'd really rather not say."

Hannah studied the woman closely. "Knowing what Pippa does for a living, I'm quite certain she asked you these same questions yesterday."

Morgan's gaze traveled to the front window and its view of the sidewalk, though Hannah was virtually certain the woman saw none of it. "I told her it was in a shipment of supplies I got."

"Is that the truth?"

"No. But your friend is a reporter. I don't want her publishing something that will scare off potential customers."

"I get that, but I'm not a reporter, Morgan. Can you please just tell me where you found it?"

"Back there." Morgan pointed Hannah's attention to the door the shopkeeper had emerged from the previous day. "In my studio."

Of all the things she might have said, Hannah would never have expected that. "Like in a box or a crate you came across when you took over the building?"

"No. It just showed up on one of my shelves, and I decided to put it out here."

"I'm afraid I don't understand," Hannah said.

"Yes, I suppose that does sound strange." Inhaling deeply, Morgan squared her shoulders. "Come with me. I'll show you exactly where I found it."

Hannah retrieved her phone and followed Morgan through the doorway to the right of the register and down a very short hallway that opened into a room about the same size as the one they'd just left. Instead of a storefront window, there was a large silver box with cords coming out of it in front of the fourth wall. In the center of the room, she counted six stools at six pottery wheels. And behind her, tacked to a bulletin board, was a QR code to scan to make a donation to the local art guild.

Morgan must have seen where her gaze had gone. "All donations are appreciated, regardless of their size."

"Is it a pretty active guild?" she asked.

"It is," Morgan said. "Cave City and the surrounding area is ripe with people active in many art forms. Pottery just happens to be my chosen medium."

Hannah pointed at the silver box in front of the far wall. "I take it that's a kiln?"

"It is."

"And these tables?" Hannah motioned to the area in front of them. "They're giving me a classroom vibe."

Morgan beamed. "I held my first class in here Friday night."

"How did that go?"

"I only had three students—two from the area, and one from somewhere in the Northeast who's in town visiting family. But considering the shop is new and I haven't had any help promoting it from any of the papers in the area yet, I'll take that as a win." Morgan strode over to the shelf unit on Hannah's right and pointed at four small bowls lined up on the center shelf. "I started them off with a bowl because it's a good piece to use for teaching technique." Morgan touched one of her students' slightly lopsided bowls. "They'll get better as the class continues."

Hannah indicated the fourth bowl, its shape perfect. "I take it you made this one?"

"Yes. To demonstrate technique."

Hannah took in a slew of unglazed dishes and bowls more in keeping with what was sold in the front room. "And you made these too?"

"I did. I'm just waiting to get them into the kiln."

"And you're saying the creamer I was given simply showed up on one of these shelves?"

Whatever lightness Morgan had managed to find disappeared with a long, slow nod. Crossing to the opposite wall, she pointed at a bottom shelf. "Right here, in fact."

"And it was the only piece you couldn't account for?"

Morgan's nod was short, curt.

"There wasn't anything else?" Hannah prodded, thinking of the sugar bowl.

"No."

Hannah scanned the surrounding area before returning her attention back to the shop's owner. "When did it appear?"

"I noticed it Saturday morning."

"Which is the same day Pippa says she bought it for me."

Morgan's face reddened. "Trust me, the irony that a piece I didn't make sold faster than any I have made was not lost on me."

"I'm sure it wasn't anything personal."

A jingle from the front room cut short Hannah's words and sent Morgan scurrying toward the hallway. "I have to go up front, Hannah. Every person who comes in is a potential customer I can't take the chance of losing. Feel free to poke around back here."

"I understand. Thank you."

And then Morgan was gone, the cheery greeting Hannah had earned the previous day reaching her ears once again. Absently, she ran her finger across the spot where Rose Lodge's missing creamer had suddenly reappeared after over four decades, her thoughts too jumbled at the moment to cull for anything useful.

From there, she maneuvered around the individual workstations and over to the kiln, vaguely aware of Morgan's voice interspersed with another woman's inquiring about different pottery pieces and their pricing. She touched the cool silver covering of the machine and then left it behind in favor of a closer look at the students' bowls.

The first of the three was good. Good proportion, roundish shape.

The second was passable.

And the third—

She was powerless against the quiet laugh that bubbled up inside her as she stared at the misshapen bowl. "This would so be mine," she murmured, grinning. "And the first one would be Lacy's. Nearly indistinguishable from the teacher's."

On a whim, she set the two bowls side by side and took a photo of them. When she was satisfied with her shot, she sent it with the caption, IF WE WERE TO TAKE A POTTERY CLASS TOGETHER.

She switched the bowls back into their original positions, deposited the phone into her bag, and crossed to the bulletin board.

"Wonderful choice," Morgan said from the front room. "Truly wonderful. And I'll get to work on the matching candlesticks you requested right away. Expect to hear from me late next week or early the next."

Hannah heard what sounded like something being set down on the counter followed by a woman's voice. "That'll be perfect, thank you."

"And will that be cash or charge for your purchase today, as well as the deposit for the candlesticks?" Morgan asked.

"Cash."

Hannah studied the local art guild's logo at the top of the flyer seeking donations, pulled out her phone to snap a picture of the bulletin board as a whole, and then slid it back into her bag.

Morgan's voice reached her once again. "If you'll leave me with your name and number, I'll call you the moment the candlesticks are ready to be picked up."

"Of course. I'm Wendy Wallace-Holliday."

Hannah heard the voice continue, knew numbers were being given, but her every thought skipped back in time at the mention of a name she hadn't heard in decades.

Chapter Eleven

"Wendy?" Hannah called as she stepped into the pottery shop's main room. "Wendy Wallace? Is that really you?"

Pausing with her fingers on the handle of the front door, the woman spun to look at Hannah across the shoulder strap of her designer bag, her expression quickly morphing from confusion to surprised recognition. "Hannah Prentiss?"

Hannah smiled and waved. "Yup, it's me."

"Wow." Wendy moved toward Hannah. "It's been a long time."

Laughing, Hannah embraced her elementary school classmate. "A very long time indeed."

"I feel like I heard you'd left the area." Stepping back, Wendy made no attempt to hide her visual head-to-toe inspection of Hannah. "Am I wrong about that?"

"No, you're not wrong. I went to California for college and stayed there for a few years after graduating. It broke my heart when your family moved to Louisville when we were in second grade, but now here you are, shopping in Cave City."

"*Living* in Cave City, actually," Wendy corrected before raising her left hand and showing the pair of rings it sported.

Hannah admired the jewelry. "Congratulations!"

"We've been married almost five years now. With a three-year-old and a one-year-old who keep us hopping."

Hannah followed Wendy's gaze down to her own ringless left hand and shrugged. "Nope, not married."

"I'm sorry. I shouldn't have assumed." Wendy cocked her head. "Anyway, tell me what *is* going on in your life. So you moved back to Blackberry Valley?"

Hannah nodded. "I did."

"I imagine your parents are thrilled."

"My dad is, very much. My mom passed away from cancer several years ago."

Wendy sucked in a breath. "Oh, Hannah, I'm so sorry. I didn't know. How are you doing?"

"Life has to go on, of course, but not a day goes by that I don't miss her."

Wendy set her hand on Hannah's shoulder and squeezed. "I can't imagine. I call my mom at least once a day whether it's about something with the kids, or the house, or the pool we're getting ready to put in, or even what outfit I should wear to one of my husband's work things."

"I'm glad you have her," Hannah said, and she meant it.

"So did you come back to help your dad?" Wendy asked.

"Being able to see him on a more regular basis is certainly a huge asset in my decision to come home, but I mainly came back so I could finally open my own restaurant."

Wendy startled. "A restaurant? That sounds like quite an endeavor."

"It is. But I love it. I have a great staff, and we're getting busier every week."

"Wait," Wendy said, holding up her hands. "You've already *opened* your restaurant?"

"I did. Last spring." Hannah felt her smile returning. "It's called the Hot Spot, and it's housed in the original firehouse on the main road through town."

"I've been meaning to get over there and try it out myself," Morgan interjected from her spot behind the counter. "I've heard nothing but good things about it."

Wendy beamed at Hannah. "I've also heard a few people at my church talking about it. I just had no idea it was yours. I'm so proud of you."

"Thank you."

"I guess that's kind of like having a husband and kids, only you get an occasional day off now and again, I imagine," Wendy said. "Anyway, I should probably get going. The nanny is watching the kids, and I want to get home before the housekeepers come. They tend to miss some spots when I'm not there to oversee their work."

"I understand." Not from personal experience, of course, but she understood the need to get back to the demands of one's life.

Wendy addressed Morgan. "I'll be waiting for your call about the pieces I ordered."

"I'll be in touch soon," Morgan assured her.

Wendy patted Hannah's arm. "It was good to see you. Good to catch up and hear about where you are in life. Tell your dad hello from me, if you think he'll remember me."

"I'm sure he will, and I'll make sure to do that. Take care, Wendy."

"You too, Hannah."

And then Wendy was gone, the door swinging shut in her wake.

"Wow, she was something, wasn't she?"

Hannah glanced over her shoulder at Morgan. "You made a sale. That's wonderful!"

Morgan grinned. "I did indeed. And if the paper actually features an article on the shop like that reporter said they're going to, maybe I'll start seeing more of that."

Slowly, Hannah wandered back to the counter, her thoughts still playing tag with bits and pieces from her chance meeting with someone she hadn't seen since second grade.

"For what it's worth, I don't believe marriage is the only way to have a happy life," Morgan said. "I love the business I've built, and I have a wonderful family and great friends. It's too bad not everyone believes that."

Before Hannah could respond, her phone dinged with an incoming text. She checked it to find a message from Lacy.

A POTTERY CLASS TOGETHER? SIGN ME UP!

She let the message soothe her with a sense of normalcy before asking Morgan, "Do you have plans for other classes moving forward? Beginner ones like the one you started last week?"

"Absolutely. Would you like to be added to my newsletter list so you know when new classes are starting?" At Hannah's answering nod, Morgan pushed a sign-up sheet and pen across the counter. "Just your name and email address will do."

Hannah picked up the pen, began to write her information, and then stopped, her gaze lifting to Morgan's as a curious thought struck. "Your first class was Friday night, right?"

"It was."

"And you said you found the creamer I showed you in the picture when you came in the next day, right?"

Morgan's throat moved with her swallow. "Yes."

Hannah considered the information as she finished filling out the form, and then she slid it across the counter as she gave voice to the thought tickling her mind. "Could I see the names of the people in your class?"

Morgan set the sign-up sheet back in its original spot beside the register before saying, "I can't give out that information. But I will tell you that friend of yours wasn't in it." She nudged her chin toward the front door. "In case that's what you were wondering."

Chapter Twelve

With a glance at her dashboard clock, Hannah passed the recently refreshed WELCOME TO BLACKBERRY VALLEY sign and turned instead of continuing straight, her thoughts already skipping ahead to the sweet-faced little goat she'd been itching to see since her last visit to Lacy's farm.

So much of her days were spent indoors. During restaurant hours, she was inside, talking to diners, pitching in on occasion in the kitchen, and making sure everything ran smoothly. Before and after restaurant hours, she often sat at her desk in her small office or on the couch in her living room, updating the books or placing orders for various needed perishables and supplies.

So when she had a window of time in which she could slow things down a little bit, a stop at Lacy's was near the very top of her list. Something about the unhurried pace of the animals in the barn and in the fields calmed her, as did the feel of the sun on her face and the sight of Lacy's always welcoming smile.

As she approached her best friend's property, she slowed enough to allow herself a peek at the pasture and the trio of horses quietly grazing. Smiling, she greeted each one silently in her head.

Soon, she pulled up the dirt driveway that took her to the heart of Bluegrass Hollow Farm. She followed the lane to the small parking area beside the barn, cut the engine, and stepped out, lifting her face toward the winter sun. It was chilly, sure, but not as cold as it had been the previous week or as cold as the seven-day forecast promised it would be again.

Still, even with the warmer-than-normal temperatures, she hastened to the open barn.

"Well, isn't this a nice surprise."

Hannah spotted her friend by the empty horse stalls and closed the gap between them with several long strides. "Hey, Lacy. I was on my way back from that pottery place where the mystery creamer came from and saw that I had enough time to squeeze in a visit with you before I have to get to the Hot Spot."

"A visit with *me*?" Lacy asked, resting her pitchfork against the closest wall. She jerked a thumb toward the pen where three of the farm's cutest residents spent their mornings. "Or do you mean a visit with your new best friend?"

Laughing, Hannah held up her hands in surrender. "No one could ever take that title from you. But I wouldn't mind squeezing in a little time with Sprout too."

"Sprout has two siblings, you know."

"I know, I know. And I bring treats for all three of them every time I come, as you know."

"Yes, but don't think I haven't noticed the extra helping Sprout gets when her siblings aren't watching."

Hannah pantomimed locking her lips and tossing away the key.

"Fine. You don't have to say anything. But Mimi and I know the truth." Lacy joined Hannah on the other side of the open stall.

"You think Mimi has noticed?" Hannah fell in step with her friend, her smile spreading as she caught her first glimpse of the trio of seven-month-old kids.

Lacy nodded. "Mamas see everything. Even mama goats."

"Noted. Though this time it's just me." Hannah stepped over the pen's low wall and made a beeline for the cinnamon-colored goat. "I didn't have time to go back to my place and pick up any sort of treat."

Sprout looked up from the hay she was eating to push her head gently against Hannah's leg.

"From where I'm standing, Hannah, it looks like you're treat enough for your girl," Lacy said from her spot outside the pen.

Grinning, Hannah cupped Sprout's face in her hands and placed a soft kiss on the goat's head. "Hello, sweet girl. I've missed you."

A nudge from her left and another nudge from behind made her turn to greet the goat's two siblings, the black one named Flower, and the white one named Niblet. "Hello to both of you too. Have you been nice to Sprout while I've been gone?"

Lacy laughed. "No favoritism in that statement."

She scratched the top of Flower's head then Niblet's, sheepishly gave Sprout an extra scratch, and then straightened. "If you didn't want me to play favorites, you shouldn't have let me name one of them. That gave us a special bond. I can't help it."

"You know I'm kidding, right?" Lacy said as Hannah reluctantly joined her outside the pen once again. "Watching you with Sprout is really sweet."

"I really do love all three of them, and Mimi too." Hannah looked back into the pen to find Sprout watching her instead of the hay her siblings were eating. "But there's just something special about Sprout."

"Then my letting you be the one to name her makes sense."

She blew a last kiss to Sprout and then turned back to Lacy. "How so?"

"You said there's something special about Sprout."

"There is. For me anyway."

"And there's always been something special about you for me," Lacy said.

Hannah coughed to clear the sudden lump in her throat. "Ditto. So how are things around here?"

"Busy as usual." Lacy led the way back to the empty horse stalls and the pitchfork.

Hannah grabbed a nearby shovel and held it at the ready as Lacy continued turning over the straw in Razzle Dazzle's stall. "Not that I haven't said this a million times already, but I really wish you'd get some help out here. It's a lot for you to be doing alone all the time."

"Neil helps when he can, and so does Mom. Though, right now, she's recovering from some sort of bug she picked up somewhere."

"I get that, and I'm glad you can lean on them a little." Hannah scooped up some manure and dropped it into a waiting wheelbarrow. "But I know you well enough to know you won't have your mother doing too much, and I also know Neil is busy with the bookstore. Owning your own brick-and-mortar business is no joke."

"I help him with his inventory," Lacy proclaimed with a grin.

Laughing, Hannah used the shovel once again. "By stealing the mysteries from his shelves?"

"Borrow, not steal. He gets them all back. In time." Straightening up, Lacy set the tongs of the pitchfork against the stable floor and wrapped her hands around its handle. "Speaking of mysteries, where are we with the decades-old reappearance of Vanessa's mother's creamer?"

Hannah arched her eyebrow. "*We*?"

"Of course."

Hannah set the tip of her shovel against the floor and mimicked Lacy's stance as she eyed her friend with amusement. "I'm just teasing. Your input is always appreciated."

"Good answer. Now tell me what you've found—" Suddenly, Lacy swayed and had to catch herself against the nearest wall. "Whoa."

"Lacy?" Hannah set the shovel against the wheelbarrow and hurried over to her friend. "You okay?"

Lacy exhaled slowly, deliberately, nodding as she did. "I—I think so. I just felt lightheaded for a moment. But it's passing." She took another deep breath. "I didn't really eat much this morning."

"Silly girl. Aren't you the one who was always spouting the merits of eating breakfast way back in high school?"

Lacy shrugged. "I know. But my stomach was a little squirrely when I woke up."

Noting the color returning to her friend's face, Hannah gently extracted the pitchfork from Lacy's hands and set it beside the shovel. "Has your mom had stomach issues from the bug she's been fighting?"

"Maybe."

"Then I think we need to get you inside for a little while."

"I can't," Lacy protested, albeit weakly. "I need to finish this last stall."

"No, you don't." Hannah slid her arm around Lacy's shoulders and guided her to the stall's open door. "Once you're settled inside with a glass of water and some crackers or something, I'll come finish this before I head out."

"I can't ask you to—" A second, bigger sway made her cling to Hannah. "Okay, yeah, maybe I do need to sit down and eat something."

Slowly, carefully, Hannah guided Lacy out of the barn and into the fresh air, toward the farmhouse. Once inside, she hung up her friend's coat, settled her on the living room sofa, and then bustled into the kitchen. She poured a glass of water, toasted two slices of bread, and carried everything back into the living room to set on the end table beside her friend.

"Hydrate, eat, and stay put for a while." Hannah took inventory of the coffee table and the empty sofa cushions beside Lacy. "Where's your phone?"

Lacy looked at Hannah across the top of her water glass. "In the kitchen maybe? Or in the coat I was wearing."

Crossing to the coat stand just inside the front door, Hannah felt around inside its pockets until she came across the phone, pulled it out, and carried it back to Lacy. "Keep this with you. If you start to feel worse, call Neil or me, okay?"

"I'm fine, Hannah."

Hannah checked the time. She had a little over thirty minutes to finish cleaning Razzle Dazzle's stall, stop at the apartment for another shower, and get to the Hot Spot for the usual preopening tasks. But she couldn't leave her best friend in such a state. "I'm not budging from this spot until you promise you'll call one of us if you need to."

"Fine. Yes. I'll call." Lacy picked up a slice of toast, took a bite, and sank deeper into the couch. "But leave the stall alone. I have a feeling I'll be fine after I eat this."

"You probably will be, but I'm still going to finish it up. Just in case." Hannah headed toward the door, only to glance back at Lacy as she reached it. "Feel better, okay?"

Lacy smiled. "Thank you, Hannah. But don't think this gets you out of telling me the latest on the mysterious creamer. And the still-missing sugar bowl."

"I know." She opened the door. "Maybe if we're lucky, I'll have more to share when we next talk."

Chapter Thirteen

Hannah had just finished writing the evening's specials on the last of the new tabletop chalkboards when the youngest member of her staff loped inside.

"Hey, Dylan," she said, setting the board back on its easel stand.

The tall, lanky redhead stopped, blinked rapidly in an attempt to adjust to the change in lighting, and waved as Hannah approached the hostess stand, a trio of colored chalk sticks in her hand. "Hi, Hannah. Sorry I'm late. I was on my way out the door when my mom grabbed me to have a conversation."

She set the chalk in its spot on the stand's second shelf and then wiped the brightly-colored dust from her hands. "Actually, we didn't have a staff meeting today, so you're not late. Let your mom have time with her great son. I'm sure she's proud of the fact you'll be starting your college classes soon."

A muted snort was quickly shaken off and followed by a shove of his hand through his hair. "Actually, she thinks..." Dropping his hand to his side with a loud exhale, Dylan glanced around the dining area. "Looks like we're all set up. Sorry again I wasn't here to help."

"No problem. We had it handled." She tilted her head until he made eye contact. "Are you okay?"

He blew out another breath, closed his eyes briefly, and then gave her a bright smile. "I'm good, Hannah. Really."

"I'm not sure I'm buying that."

Raquel burst through the front door, her arm stretched toward them with a single red rose in her hand. "Marshall was waiting outside the door just now with this. Isn't he the sweetest?"

Dylan laughed. "I can't say I'm surprised." He took off his jacket and hooked his finger beneath the collar.

Raquel set her free hand on her hip, her right eyebrow inching upward though her smile never faltered. "Meaning?"

"Marshall reminds me of my friend's puppy every time he looks at you." Dylan nudged his chin toward the kitchen's swinging door. "I'm gonna hang up my coat and see if Jacob needs any help before we open."

Hannah opened her mouth to protest in the hopes of getting her earlier conversation with the twenty-year-old back on track but stopped as Elaine made her way through the front door.

"Marshall makes puppy-dog eyes whenever he looks at me?" Raquel glanced down at the rose in her hand. "Really?"

"Really," Hannah and Elaine chorused in unison.

Raquel's smile grew still wider as she pulled the flower to her chest. "He's just the best, isn't he?"

Hannah chuckled. "Hang up your coat and put the rose in water. Then we need to get this place open, okay?"

"You got it," Raquel said dreamily. She pushed the kitchen door open to reveal Dylan standing beside Jacob, watching as the chef stirred something on the stove.

"I hope that whatever Dylan opts to pursue in college, it'll be something that has him around people. He has a real special way about him," Elaine said.

Hannah watched the hostess shift the seating chart to the side of the reservation book as she considered the woman's words. "He does, doesn't he?"

"I realize I only really see him here, but people respond to him." Elaine grabbed a pen from the shelf and set it on the book. "Maybe he should be a teacher or a social worker."

Hannah peered through the porthole-style windows on the double swinging doors to the kitchen. She couldn't hear what they were saying, but it was clear Dylan hung on Jacob's every word. "Or maybe something in the hospitality arena."

"Something that would have him staying here with us?" Elaine joked.

Hannah grinned. "Maybe. But there are lots of options for him there."

"Back when we first opened and he was as clumsy as he was, could you have envisioned yourself talking like this about him?"

"I plead the Fifth," Hannah said.

"Smart." Elaine motioned Hannah's attention toward the front door and the sixtysomething couple peering in at them. "It's four o'clock. Time to get our evening started."

"You're right." Hannah poked her head into the kitchen. "All right, gang, we're opening the doors. Let's have a great night, okay?"

Dylan vacated his spot beside Jacob in favor of Hannah and the dining room, with Raquel close on his heels. Apron ties were secured, order pads and pens slipped into pockets, and customer-centered smiles put in place.

For the next few several hours, they went about their duties like the well-oiled machine they'd become. Elaine took the occasional phone call, led customers to their tables, and handed out menus. Raquel and Dylan filled drink orders, discussed dishes, answered questions, brought food to the tables, and collected payment. Jacob stirred and cooked and plated dish after dish, occasionally pausing to peer out at the expression of a diner who'd opted to try one of his evening's specials. And Hannah moved between newly seated customers to greet, to chat, and to make sure that everyone was happy with their choice to patronize her lifelong dream.

"You must be Gabriel and Frieda's daughter."

Looking up from the table chart Elaine had temporarily abandoned to seat a family of four, Hannah took in a woman in her early sixties, who smiled at her over the hostess stand. "I am," she said, offering her hand. "I'm Hannah. And you are?"

"Linda Macon. I lived down the street from your parents until you were in kindergarten, when we moved." Linda swiped away an errant strand of graying hair and studied Hannah with wide green eyes. "You are the spitting image of your mother, God rest her soul. The hair color, the eyes, the genuine smile—all of it."

Hannah breathed in the words, let them sit in her heart for a moment, and then stepped to the side with the woman as Elaine returned to her post. "I'm sorry, but I don't remember you. I take it you and my mom were friends?"

Linda nodded. "We were. We did stroller walks together two or three mornings a week when you and my daughter, Vivian, were babies. Then I had Trevor, and she had Andrew. We still tried to meet up often, but it was a little harder, since things were more hectic."

"Where did you move to?" Hannah asked.

"Missouri. Just outside of St. Louis. My husband was transferred there for his job. I grew to love it there eventually, but I missed time with your mother. She was a bright and peaceful spot in so many of my days."

Unsure of what to say, Hannah remained silent.

"I was sorry to learn of her passing from your father when I drove through the old neighborhood today," Linda said. "Frieda was such a light. A true light."

Hannah felt the hitch in her answering smile but tried her best to hold it steady. "I miss her every day."

"I'm sure you do, dear." Linda squeezed Hannah's hand. "I met Gabriel's sweet dog, Zeus, and I was glad to hear that Gordon lives with them now. Less lonely that way, I'm sure."

Hannah looked past Linda to see Elaine greeting a party of six. "Dad is doing well. He keeps busy with church, Zeus, and a host of projects he and Uncle Gordon are always undertaking. Not to mention being a grandpa."

Linda's smile returned. "He told me about Andrew and his wife and their three children. He even showed me pictures."

Hannah laughed. "I'm sorry if you had other plans for that hour."

"No, dear, I enjoyed it. That's what grandparents do, you know."

She grinned. "I take it you have a few of your own."

"I do. Vivian has three, and so does Trevor."

"Very nice," Hannah said. "I imagine they keep you busy."

Linda smiled in response. "Gabriel mentioned that Andrew is a computer programmer now. And his wife does something with children's books, right?"

"She's a freelance proofreader."

"That's what it was. I saw a bit of Frieda in their little girl as well."

Hannah nodded. "Yes. Of Andrew's three, Ava favors my mother the most in appearance. Andrew Junior—or, AJ, as we call him—has her gentleness, and Axel, the youngest, has her curiosity. Although, being five, his is a bit more super-charged."

Linda abandoned eye contact with Hannah in favor of looking past her to the dining area for a few moments. "And you have this place."

Something about the woman's slight change in tone brought Hannah up short. "Yes, this is my restaurant."

Linda patted her hand. "Well, it got you back here, to Blackberry Valley, which is good. Just know that some people find their footing later than others. I'm sure it will come for you too, dear, as it did for your younger brother."

What?

"Anyway, I wanted to stop in real quick and see you with my own two eyes before my husband and I continue south for the cruise we're taking out of Florida. He's waiting in the car for me. But be well and know that I'm praying for you to find your way in life like your brother has."

Linda waved and headed out the door, leaving Hannah's mind in turmoil.

Chapter Fourteen

Hannah wasn't sure how long she'd been sitting there, staring into the darkness outside her living room window, when she finally glanced down at her watch.

Thirty minutes—thirty minutes since she'd let herself into her apartment above the restaurant after another successful evening.

Normally, when she got home, the first thing she'd do would be to flip on all the lights, take off her shoes, get a glass of water, and then unwind on the couch for a few minutes. Looking down at her feet and then at the empty coffee table in front of her, it was clear that the only part of the routine she'd adhered to that evening was the couch part.

"I *found* my footing," she said to the ceiling. "I found it the moment I opened the Hot Spot."

She sat with her words and the conviction behind them for a moment before blowing out a breath. Marrying two years after graduating college was the path *Andrew* had chosen. She'd taken a different one, and that was okay. Perhaps one day she would get married and have kids, but now wasn't that time.

She closed her eyes, shook her head, and then pushed herself off the couch. Linda Macon was one person. One—

"I guess that's kind of like having a husband and kids..."

Hannah stepped into her kitchen, plucked a glass from the cabinet beside the sink, and filled it with water. She took a long drink and decided to dismiss Wendy Wallace's words also.

"The Hot Spot makes me happy," she said aloud. "I love my staff, I love my customers, and I love how I feel every time I step inside it, knowing that with God's help, I made it happen. *I* did."

She finished her water and set the glass down on the counter with a thud. "Far too many restaurants fail in the first year. And the Hot Spot isn't failing. In fact, I'd venture to say it's thriving!"

She knew her mother's friend hadn't meant any harm with her words. Wendy Wallace probably hadn't either.

Hannah's experience, her choices in life thus far, had simply been different than theirs. That was all. Slowly, she wandered back to her front door and the spot where she'd dropped her bag upon entry. Balancing carefully, she nudged off her left shoe with the toes of her right before switching to the other.

"I'm fine with where I'm at in life," she said. "More than fine, in fact."

When her shoes were in place beside the door, she reached inside her tote bag for her phone. She read the GOOD NIGHT text from Liam that was now too late to respond to, listened to a voicemail from Lacy saying Hannah had missed her calling as a professional horse-stall cleaner, and made a mental note of an email she needed to attend to in the morning.

Then, reaching into her bag again, she pulled out the packet of saltwater taffy one of her favorite customers had given her toward the end of the night, helped herself to a piece, and thumbed through the three or four pictures she'd taken on her phone that evening.

Raquel carrying the rose Marshall had given her out of the kitchen after her shift.

Hannah's former middle school gym teacher and some of his friends celebrating a successfully eaten plate of Inferno Wings.

The list of their evening's specials on one of the tabletop easels.

She swiped one more time and saw the two pottery bowls she'd captured for Lacy.

And—

"What is that?" she murmured, confused.

Expanding the picture, Hannah stared down at a piece of wrinkled paper barely visible on a narrow table beneath the makeshift classroom's bulletin board. On the paper, below the handwritten heading FRIDAY NIGHT POTTERY CLASS, three names were listed.

She recalled Morgan's voice. *"I only had three students—two from the area, and one from somewhere in the Northeast who's in town visiting family. But considering the shop is new and I haven't had any help promoting it from any of the papers in the area yet, I'll take that as a win."*

"Three students," Hannah repeated aloud as she zoomed in even closer on the names now visible on her phone's screen.

Doug Bell.

She squinted at the next line and the next name, the faintness of the pencil used to write it making it difficult to read in its entirety. *S...Winfield.* The handwriting seemed feminine, but she couldn't make out the first name.

Giving up, she moved on to the next line and—

"Pippa Nelson?" Hannah yelped aloud. "*Pippa Nelson* is in Morgan Wyatt's pottery class?"

She stared at the young reporter's name. "She said she bought the creamer there. She *didn't* say she was taking a class there too."

Why hadn't Pippa mentioned that? Wouldn't it have been a natural thing to bring up when they'd seen each other at Jump Start and Hannah inquired about the creamer and the pottery shop?

Her gaze returned to the names above Pippa's, the first one tickling at something she couldn't quite identify.

"Doug Bell," she read aloud. The name was familiar, but try as she might, she couldn't place a face with the name or really anything beyond a sense of having heard it somewhere before.

"Lacy will know," she finally said as, once again, her attention narrowed in on Pippa's name.

Pippa, who'd given her the creamer.

Pippa, who'd purchased the creamer from Morgan.

Pippa, who'd been in the very space Morgan said the creamer appeared in the wake of her first pottery class—a class Hannah now knew Pippa had taken.

Coincidence? Maybe. But she doubted it.

As Hannah stared at the image, she recalled Vanessa's words. *"Pippa is certain the resurfacing of Mama's creamer is the perfect story for some big journalism award she's trying to get."*

Chapter Fifteen

Lifting her face to the Friday morning sun, Hannah silently counted each trilling ring.

After the fourth one, she heard Lacy's voice. "Hi! You've reached Lacy. I'm sorry I missed your call, but I'm probably out in the barn looking after the animals, sitting against a tree reading a book, or doing a myriad of other things on the farm. I'll get back to you as soon as I'm able, but until then, have a blessed day."

Hannah checked for traffic and crossed Main Street. "Hey, Lacy, it's me. I didn't see your voicemail last night until it was way too late to respond, but I am honored to know that if the Hot Spot doesn't work out, I could have a career mucking stalls. Thank you for that."

She tilted the phone away from her mouth momentarily as she greeted an elderly man walking the opposite direction with a newspaper in his hand and a tweed flat cap on his head.

"Anyway, I wanted to check in and see if you're feeling any better or if you succumbed to whatever your mom had. I hope the former, but know that I'm here if it's the latter. Love you tons. Bye."

Slipping her phone into her shoulder bag, Hannah peeked through the windows of Blackberry Market, spotted its proprietor, Joe Wilson, bagging groceries, and waved. She thought about her own sparse pantry and made a mental note to write out a shopping list and make a stop at the market before work sometime soon.

She drew in a breath of chilly air and let it out, the need for answers proving to be far stronger than her dislike of the cold. Try as she might while getting ready for bed the previous night, and again while waiting for sleep to quiet her thoughts, she couldn't come up with a good reason why Pippa hadn't mentioned taking a class at the Clay House Pottery Shop.

She hurried across the street and to the *Chronicle* office. Maybe Pippa's failure to mention taking a class at the same shop where she'd bought the long-lost creamer was a simple oversight. But from everything she'd heard and read regarding Pippa, the woman was sharp. The whole thing just didn't add up.

Hannah stepped through the door and into the *Chronicle*'s front room, a small, tiled space that played host to a pair of metal-framed chairs and a table stacked high with newspapers. She peered beyond the room into an equally small space and spied her reason for being there looking back and forth between a notebook and monitor screen, fingers flying over the computer's keyboard.

"Excuse me, Pippa?" she called out, earning herself a quick glance up and a momentary pause in typing. "Good morning. Can we talk?"

Pippa held up a finger, continued typing for a bit, and then dropped back against her swivel chair. "Do you think you could stop by for a chat every Friday morning at this same time?"

Hannah laughed. "Not a fan of Fridays, I take it?"

"Friday *mornings*," Pippa corrected, motioning Hannah to come closer.

"Oh? Why is that?"

"That's when I try to knock out the not-so-interesting parts of my job."

Hannah leaned toward Pippa's computer screen. "The *Chronicle* prints the minutes from the garden club's monthly meeting?"

"More or less." Pippa sighed. "Though I have to find a way to write them that turns them into a story that someone might want to read. You know, for the one or two souls who might actually find them buried on page ten."

Hannah raised an eyebrow at the surprising amount of text. "It's January. Outdoor plants are pretty much either dead or dormant. Yet that much happened at their last meeting?"

Pippa shrugged. "What can I say? I can make a story out of even the most mundane event."

"I can see that." Hannah took in the reporter's desk topped with half a dozen notebooks, pens, and the newest issue of the paper. "I haven't had a chance to read this week's paper, but are you pleased with it?"

"I'd have been more pleased if our conversation at Jump Start the other morning had happened a bit sooner," Pippa said.

"Why?"

"Then I could've gotten the creamer story in before deadline." Pippa picked up the paper, scanned the front page, and set it back down. "Then again, there's always next week."

"Assuming we have answers by next week."

"Watch me." Pippa's green eyes lit behind her glasses as she swiveled her chair to fully face Hannah. "So, what brings you by this morning?"

"I saw your name on a list yesterday."

"Oh?" Pippa straightened in her seat. "A good list, I hope."

"It was a class roster, actually."

"A class roster?"

"Yes. At the Clay House Pottery Shop in Cave City."

"Oh. Right. That class." Pippa swiveled back to her desk, her face and any expression it held now shielded by a curtain of hair. "It slipped my mind."

Hannah stepped to one side for a better view of Pippa. "I'm surprised you didn't mention that the other morning when we talked."

Pippa shrugged. "Probably because I wanted to forget it."

"Forget you were in the class?" Hannah prodded.

"No. Forget how horrible I was at it." Pippa yanked open her desk's top drawer, sifted through a slew of pens and paper clips, and then pushed it closed again. "We made bowls. Or, rather, my fellow classmates made bowls. I'd be lucky if mine could hold even a single drop of soup."

Hannah recalled the photo she'd texted to Lacy as a funny example of what Hannah herself would've likely created as a student in the same class. Resisting the urge to chuckle at the memory, she asked, "What made you take the class?"

Pippa again opened the top drawer and closed it without getting anything out. "I took it as a way to work a different creative muscle. I write all day long. I'm a firm believer that the deeper I make my creative well, the more I'll have to draw from."

"Makes sense." Hannah leaned against the desk. "What else have you tried?"

Pippa paused her hand shy of what Hannah suspected was to be a third opening and closing of the drawer. "Tried?"

"In terms of creative endeavors like this pottery class."

The young woman coughed. "Um, that was the first."

"You have to start somewhere, right?" Hannah suggested.

Pippa's shoulders relaxed a bit. "Right."

"So, out of curiosity, what made you choose pottery as the first thing to help deepen your creative well?"

Pippa picked up one of her notebooks, thumbed through it, and set it back down. "I don't know. I just picked it."

"Was it something you've always had an interest in?"

"I don't know. I guess—"

"Pippa?" Jack Delaney, the *Chronicle*'s editor-in-chief, poked his head around the partition that separated his desk from the editorial pool and nodded a silent greeting to Hannah before turning his full attention on the paper's lone news reporter. "I just got a call from someone out on Millhouse Road about a cat that's stuck in a tree. A fire truck left a minute ago to make the rescue, and I need you to get out there and grab a picture for the Around the Town page."

Rocketing to her feet, Pippa grabbed a notebook and pen, shoved them into a bag at her feet, and then retrieved a camera from the top of a nearby file cabinet. "Sorry to cut this short, Hannah, but I have to go."

"Right, of course," Hannah replied, though she doubted that Pippa was actually sorry. "Duty calls. Maybe we could pick this up later? Say, over coffee? My treat."

"Maybe? I mean, it's likely I'll be busy, but we'll see."

Hannah smiled when the paper's food critic came in through the back door. "Good morning, Marshall."

"Good morning, Hannah," he replied. "Morning, Pippa. Looks like you're on the run already."

Nodding, Pippa shoved the camera in her bag. "Cat trapped in a tree."

"Photographic gold, right there," he teased. "It'll probably be the big story of the day."

With a wry smile, Pippa hoisted the bag onto her shoulder, shoved her chair into place beneath her desk, and turned her attention to Hannah. "I've got a full schedule today, I'm sorry."

"No problem. I could do tomorrow." Hannah stepped back to afford Pippa a clear path to the front door. "Say, eight o'clock at Jump Start?"

"I, um, have other plans," Pippa said, making a beeline toward the reception area and the door beyond. "I'm sorry."

"Eight works for me," Marshall called, grinning.

Hannah made a face at him. "No, you have a date with Raquel tomorrow morning, remember?"

Marshall's smile widened still further. "Oh, I remember. Trust me. I just thought that if you were buying, I could fit a cup of joe in beforehand."

"You can't." Hannah hurried after the young reporter. "One more question about that creamer, Pippa. Do you remember seeing it on a shelf in the back room of the Clay House either during or after your class? And if so, do you remember if anything was sitting on the shelf beside it?"

She heard Marshall call another jest from the editorial room behind them.

Pippa pushed the door open, stepped onto the sidewalk, and shot a firm "No" across her shoulder.

"Is that no for Marshall, or for—"

But it was too late. Pippa was already halfway down the block, making haste toward her car. Or rather, away from Hannah.

Chapter Sixteen

Sidestepping the puddle of soapy water outside the Blackberry Valley Fire Department's two open bays, Hannah took note of the missing ladder truck as well as which three hooks were currently void of turnout gear—C. Walker, A. Lestrade, and D. Roarke. By now, she imagined the three firefighters had arrived at the scene on Millhouse Road and set up the right ladder for their rescue mission.

A nudge on her leg stole her attention to a pair of hopeful brown eyes. It was the department's one true volunteer, a dog who'd simply reported for duty one day and never left, according to the firefighters.

"Hi, Smoky!" Hannah squatted and offered the firehouse dog a scratch behind his ears. "Did you know everyone is out on a call to save a cat? It climbed to the top of a tree all by itself, but now it can't get down without some help."

Smoky's tongue lolled out of his mouth as Hannah's continued to pet him.

"I thought I heard your voice out here." Liam strode into the empty bay and greeted Hannah with a warm hug and a kiss. "And I was right. As interesting and wonderful as this morning has already been, finding you out here has made it even better."

She smiled at Smoky's tilted head and perked left ear. "I'm as curious as you are, Smoky." Hannah faced Liam again. "You had me at 'as interesting and wonderful as this morning has already been.'"

"Not the part after that?" he teased.

"Well, that was nice to hear, of course, but still." She swept her hand at the empty space around them. "You passed on playing superhero for a trapped kitty?"

He laughed. "I figured I'd give Archer a chance to earn his keep around here."

"Of course."

"How'd you know that's where the guys went?" Liam motioned for Hannah to follow him down the side hallway and into his private office.

She waved goodbye to Smoky as he settled in to wait for the rest of the department to return. "I stopped by the paper to talk to Pippa, so I was there when Jack asked her to go take pictures of the rescue."

"Then I'm extra glad I put Archer on the call with Declan and Colt. With any luck, Pippa will get a shot of him I can tape to his locker and tease him about for the foreseeable future."

"Men and their need to constantly rib each other," she groused.

"It's what we do." He directed her to the chair across from his desk and claimed his own. "Everything go okay at the restaurant last night?"

Hannah set her bag down and settled into her seat. Her thoughts returned to the conversation with her mother's friend and the doubt it had stirred inside her. "It was a…great night."

His left eyebrow pushing upward, Liam leaned forward on his desk. "Was that hesitation intended?"

"No, not really." She pushed a few stray wisps of hair off her cheek. "Jacob's evening specials were a hit with all who tried them,

Raquel's feet were ten feet off the ground the whole night thanks to Marshall, and—"

"What did he do?" Liam asked.

"He was waiting outside the Hot Spot with a rose when she arrived for work."

Liam gave an exaggerated eye roll. "Of course he was."

She laughed. "That doesn't mean you or any other guy has to do the same."

"Go on with what you were saying about your evening before I interrupted."

"Several customers commented on how personable and efficient Dylan was. He was thrilled when I shared that with him at closing, and we had no hiccups to speak of all night long."

Liam plucked a pen from the top of his desk and spun it in his fingers. "But you hesitated to describe it as a great night."

She blew out a slow, measured breath. "If I did, it was a little residual woolgathering, I guess."

"About?"

Hannah willed herself to shake away her concerns once and for all. "Work was great. No hesitation. What's been so nice about your morning?"

He studied her for a moment, clearly debating whether to challenge the subject change. Finally, he swapped the pen for a piece of paper on his desk, which had been mailed to him if the creases in it were any indication. "I don't know if I've ever mentioned to you my dream of starting an explorer program at the high school."

Hannah shook her head.

Liam went on. “Not everyone feels compelled to go the traditional college route. It’s great for those who want to, of course, but it’s not for everyone. Some prefer to go into a trade.”

“Like my dad and Uncle Gordon,” Hannah said.

“Exactly. And *others* are drawn to a career of public service such as the military, police work, or what we do here,” Liam said. “But it seems those routes aren’t discussed in schools as much as the other career options.”

Hannah certainly remembered feeling that way when she’d been in school. She couldn’t recall her chosen profession being lauded as a great career option.

“It’s something I’ve wanted to see changed for a while now. At least here in Blackberry Valley.” He placed the letter on his desk and leaned back in his chair, tenting his fingers beneath his chin. “But if it’s going to happen, I want it to be done right. Like with instructional videos, merchandise, and job-shadowing days for those kids who are interested in what we do here or in the sheriff’s department. But doing it right requires funding we don’t have.”

“Understandably.”

A smile grew across Liam’s face. “Until this morning, that is. When I opened this letter.”

“I’m intrigued,” she said, his excitement contagious.

“Remember when I told you I stopped out at the Taylor Estate the other day to check that faulty smoke detector in the main house?”

She nodded. “I do.”

“I told you, I saw your uncle out there, and he and I discussed my idea. I knew he’d be interested and supportive of such a program.” He rubbed his hand along his jawline. “Apparently, even though I tried to keep my voice down so as not to disturb Mrs. Adler, she must have heard me talking about it, because I got this letter from her. Along with a check for a truly impressive amount of money." He showed her the check.

She read the memo line aloud. "'BVFD Explorer program.' Wow, Liam, this is incredible. Congratulations!"

"Thank you." He set the check back down in front of him. "And a *huge* thank-you to Mrs. Adler for apparently being awake enough to hear me talking about this and deciding she wanted to get involved."

"Now that you have the funds, how long do you think it will realistically take to get it off the ground?" Hannah asked.

"I could probably do it in a month, maybe two. But that would put us in February or March, and I think we're too far into the school year to have the kind of impact I want for this." He set his elbows on the arms of his chair and leaned back. "I think I'll wait till fall and the new school year to actually start it up. That way I'm not rushed and can make sure it's done well."

"I think that makes a ton of sense," Hannah said. "But you don't have to wait to advertise it. You could build anticipation for it with flyers or something that lets interested kids know it's coming."

He nodded. "I like that."

She sat with his idea and the vision he'd shared and found her thoughts sifting through possible projects and experiences the participants could have until a chuckle from Liam drew her attention back to him. "Did I miss something?"

"Nope," he said, grinning. "I'm just enjoying watching your wheels turn on this."

"It's exciting."

"It is."

She pointed to one of the framed photographs on the shelf behind him. "Something tells me that man right there would love to help you with this. In whatever way you think he could."

Liam followed her finger, and his eyes widened. "You really think Gramps would want to be a part of this?"

"Have you met your grandfather?" she teased. "I think he'd enjoy every minute of it. And I think it would be interesting for the kids to learn how and why the call to firefighting ran through so many generations of your family."

Liam beamed at her. "That's a great idea, and I think you're right. He'd love being a part of the planning and the implementation. I'll talk to him about it the next time I see him. Thank you, Hannah."

"My pleasure."

He gaze met and held hers. "So did you just come over to brighten my morning?"

"You mean brighten your already very bright morning?" she asked. "Maybe. Although I'm not sure I was necessarily conscious of it."

"Nothing cryptic in that answer," he joked, his laugh rich and deep.

Her thoughts traveled back to her previous stop at the *Chronicle*, and she let her next words form. She stood and made her way to the window with its view of the station's bays and Smoky. "What's your read on Pippa Nelson?"

"My read?"

She glanced back at him. "You know, your thoughts. Impressions. That sort of thing."

Liam tilted his head from side to side, clearly hesitant to answer. "Pippa is a sweet girl."

"What about her work as a reporter? Do you find her to be thorough? Intrusive? Considerate? Ethical?"

A heavy silence fell between them and lingered long enough that Hannah couldn't help but feel her internal antennae rising. When he finally spoke, his words came slowly, almost reluctantly. "Pippa is thorough. I'll give her that."

"But?" she prodded, sensing more.

"The last month or so she's been a little *too* inquisitive. Like she's trying to find some big scandal she can expose."

Hannah crossed back to her chair but remained standing. "I'm listening."

"Sometime last month, I found her poking around the ladder truck. When I confronted her, she got all flustered and said something about the hydraulics that had failed on a similar truck out in California. She said she was worried for our safety."

"But she didn't come to you and express that?" Hannah asked.

"She did not." He stopped and raked a hand through his thick black hair. "I got the sense that maybe she *wanted* to find an issue. So she could have a big story."

"Why would you think that?"

"Because when I told her I'd already had the truck inspected because we'd been informed about that incident, she seemed really disappointed." Liam glanced at the open door before continuing. "And between you and me? Colin said something in passing the other day that makes me think he's been picking up something similar about her where the police department is concerned."

Hannah made a mental note of that.

"Though why she'd be doing any of this, I don't know. This is Blackberry Valley. Not some big city where crime and intrigue are so rampant that the paper has to pick and choose what to publish."

A series of loud, staccato beeps announced the return of the other firefighters. Hannah faced the window in time to see the ladder truck slowly reversing into its assigned bay. Liam pushed off his desk and stood. "Now I can get some bacon."

She laughed. "You mean because Colt is back?"

"That's precisely what I mean." He gestured to his open office door and the narrow hallway beyond. "And if you have time to stick around, you can have some too."

"I must admit, the thought of Colt's bacon is tempting—to say nothing of more time with you—but I'll have to pass this time." She grabbed her bag off the floor in front of her chair and hoisted it into place on her shoulder. "I've got one more stop I need to make this morning before I need to be back at the restaurant to do some pre-opening work."

He slid his arm over her shoulders and pulled her in for a side hug. "I guess I'll just have to indulge in an extra piece. For you."

"The trials and tribulations," she said, laughing.

"Exactly." Lowering his hand to the small of her back, he guided her into the hallway. "I'm glad you stopped by. It really did make my morning even more special."

Hannah smiled up at him as they turned toward the trio of voices coming from the garage. "I'm glad, because it made mine special too."

"Even without Colt's bacon?" he teased.

"Even without Colt's bacon."

"Wow. You must really like me."

"I do." A few steps shy of the garage, she paused. "Hey, quick question."

"I have an answer. Let's see if they match," he said.

"Do you know anyone by the name of Doug Bell? It sounds vaguely familiar to me, but I can't place it."

"Sure. Doug's a history teacher at the high school. You want to know anything about this town—past or present—you talk to him."

Hannah certainly intended to.

Chapter Seventeen

Hannah stepped through the doorway of Legend & Key Bookstore and drew in the familiar scent of books, lazy afternoons, and new people and places to experience with every turn of a page. It was, without a doubt, one of those places where she could find something for just about any mood she found herself in.

Motivational books when she needed a push to reach a little bit harder with the restaurant.

A sweet romance when she craved a happily-ever-after story.

A local history book when she wanted to learn more about Blackberry Valley or its corner of Kentucky.

Or a mystery she'd been compelled to try based on Lacy's recommendation.

Each genre took her to a different place or jogged a different part of her mind, but all expanded her horizons in some way. And for that, she was grateful.

"Good morning, Hannah!" called a familiar voice.

She lowered her gaze to the unmanned counter and a stack of books sitting beside an open cardboard box. "I *hear* you," Hannah said, peering around. "But I don't *see* you."

"That's okay. I'm coming to you." Neil stepped out of the aisle devoted to local, regional, and state history.

"There you are," she said, stepping aside to allow him passage to the counter. "How did you know it was me when you were back there?"

"I'm psychic."

She laughed. "Try again."

Neil pointed her attention to a mirror mounted in a back corner. Sure enough, she saw the front door reflected in its surface. "One of my two new additions to the store," he said.

"Okay, that's a good one. What's the other?"

He sifted through the stack of books beside the box and plucked out one she recognized as a self-help title, and another a beautifully covered Bible. "I'll let you find it yourself."

She looked over at the counter and saw the same register and pencil jar he'd always had. She pointed at the two books in his hand and then the stack that remained. "New books?"

"Yes, but this is a non-book addition."

Turning, she surveyed the room as a whole. The shelves, the layout, the—

"The sign!" Without waiting for confirmation, she hurried over to the far wall and the new sign that hung below the clock.

"THAT'S THE THING ABOUT BOOKS. THEY LET YOU TRAVEL WITHOUT MOVING YOUR FEET."
—JHUMPA LAHIRI, AUTHOR OF THE NAMESAKE

Pointing at the sign, she glanced back at Neil. "It's perfect. And so true."

"Lacy saw it in a catalog and said I had to get it for that wall."

"And so you did." Hannah followed Neil to the self-help section and then the religion section as he shelved both new books. "Like the fabulous husband my best friend always credits you to be."

He paused his hand on a Bible's spine and shook his head, his smile dimming. "I'm not so sure about that. Not today, anyway."

"Why?" she asked. "Is something wrong?"

"Lacy is battling some sort of bug, and it's hard seeing her feeling so awful."

"I knew she was a little off the last time I saw her, but then she sounded better in a voicemail she left later in the evening." Hannah sighed. "I hoped she'd turned the corner on whatever it was she picked up from her mom."

Neil led the way back to the counter and the last of the new books he still needed to shelve. "So did I. But I made sure she had what she needed before I left, and I gave her strict orders to call me if she wants me to come home."

"Which she won't do." Hannah knew her best friend well.

"That's why I spoke with my mother-in-law before work this morning to give her a heads-up on how Lacy is feeling. She's going to come up with some reason to visit and call me if Lacy starts feeling worse," Neil said.

She watched him as she processed his words. "Is her mom feeling better?"

"She is."

"Well, that probably means Lacy will feel better soon too."

"I hope so." Neil pulled three mysteries off the stack, set them on the counter to his left, and then picked up a book on the Revolutionary War.

Grinning, she tapped her finger on the stack of books he'd set aside. "You're taking these home to Lacy, aren't you?"

He looked at Hannah across the upper rim of his glasses. "How do you think I maintain 'fabulous husband' status after all these years?"

Their laughter mingled as he set off, books in hand, to the appropriate shelves. "So what brings you by this morning?" he asked as he returned to the now-bookless counter and Hannah.

"Has Lacy told you about the piece of pottery I got from Pippa at my surprise birthday luncheon on Monday?"

"Piece of pottery?" he echoed. "I don't think—wait." He broke down the box and tucked it just inside the door of the shop's small stockroom. "She did mention something about pottery when she first started feeling under the weather. We tabled it and never got back to it, I'm afraid. Did you like it?"

She pulled her phone from her bag, found the photo, and turned the screen for Neil to see. "This is it."

Taking it in with a passing glance, he nodded. "It's nice."

"It went missing from the cook's quarters on the Taylor Estate more than forty years ago." She held the phone steady as his gaze ricocheted back to the picture. "Fast forward to this past Friday evening, when it mysteriously showed up on a shelf in the back room of a pottery shop in Cave City, where Pippa purchased it for me the next day."

He took the phone and examined the photo more closely as Hannah continued. "I wouldn't have known it had been missing all these years if I hadn't opened it in front of—"

"You say it went missing from the Taylor Estate?" he interrupted.

Startled she replied, "Yes."

Repositioning his glasses, he again studied the picture. "Does it have the initials *PSW* on the bottom?"

"No."

His shoulders slumped.

"But it's hers. On this particular piece, along with the others from this set, she put a tiny rose where she'd normally have put her initials."

Neil's gaze jerked up to Hannah's. "She?"

"Vanessa Lodge's grandmother—Peggy Shipman Williams," Hannah said. "Peggy made the creamer and all the other pieces in that set for her daughter, Rose."

"Hence the rose instead of the initials," Neil said. "How fascinating."

"So you're familiar with Peggy's work?"

Neil handed back her phone. "Familiar with how she fits into Blackberry Valley's and, more specifically, the Taylor Estate's history. Peggy Williams was hired to work at the estate by Antoinette Taylor as a cook, which should've been the end of the story. But Peggy's food was reportedly so good and so revered by guests that this woman who was hired simply to be a cook ended up having way more influence than one might expect. So much so, in fact, that she not only got her husband hired onto the estate, but she was also allowed to keep a potter's wheel he found in an unused outbuilding. She went on to teach herself pottery and became a self-made businesswoman because of it."

"Wow," Hannah mused. Vanessa had told her a lot of that, but she hadn't realized how influential Peggy had been at the Taylor Estate.

"It's even more impressive when you take into account Peggy's full-time job as the Taylor family's cook, her role as a wife and mother, and the fact that she never had anyone teach her the first thing about pottery."

"Did Antoinette know Peggy sold pottery on the side?"

"I can't say for sure. But Peggy had a booth at every flea market around the area from what I've been able to gather, so I'm not really sure how Antoinette could *not* have known," Neil said. "Blackberry Valley is a small town now, and it was an even smaller town then. And Peggy would've had to fit her selling around her work for the Taylor family."

"I hear her pieces can go for some big money these days," Hannah said.

"It's a feel-good story with some real history behind it." He motioned to the photo on Hannah's phone. "How much did Pippa pay for that creamer, do you know?"

"I don't." Hannah slipped her phone back into her bag. "I'd like to think she wouldn't have spent a crazy amount on a birthday present for me, no matter how nice it was. Though, with everything I've heard so far about Peggy's work and the value of it these past few days, it's hard not to think she might've spent a lot."

Neil rubbed at his clean-shaven jawline. "You say she bought it at a pottery shop in Cave City, right?"

"Yes. The Clay House Pottery Shop."

"Interesting."

She eyed him closely. "What's interesting?"

"Is the shop owner a pottery enthusiast?"

"She's a potter herself," Hannah said.

"And she didn't know to hang on to a Peggy Shipman Williams' piece?" Neil pondered aloud.

"It had a rose on it rather than her initials, remember?"

He held up his index finger. "Right. You said that. So it's likely she didn't realize what she had."

Especially since it simply showed up in her shop, Hannah thought but didn't say.

"I must say, though, Hannah—not only am I intrigued by the question of where it's been this whole time, but I'm also quite curious about why it's reappeared now."

"And why not the sugar bowl too?" she added.

Neil's brow furrowed. "Sugar bowl?"

"The set's sugar bowl went missing at the same time as the creamer."

"Wow," he said, shaking his head. "Lacy must really be feeling awful if she hasn't filled me in on all of this."

The bell over the front door jingled, alerting Hannah to the fact that the conversation needed to end if she wanted it to remain private. Besides, she needed to get going.

Hannah tapped the stack of mysteries Neil had set aside for his wife. "These can keep her busy until she's back to her old self. Once she is, though, her inquiring mind is all mine."

Chapter Eighteen

Hannah peered over at Dylan at least a half dozen times, clocking how efficiently he performed his preopening while her head and her heart zoned in on something very different—an underlying stiffness.

She'd sensed it the moment he'd walked in, his waist apron balled up in his hands. Yes, he'd returned her greeting with his usual cheer. Yes, he'd plunked himself down at a table and started rolling utensils inside napkins without being reminded. And, yes, he'd even cracked a smile or two over some of the grumblings from Jacob coming through the kitchen doors.

But even with all of those things, she felt tension emanating from the young man. It was as if a cloud had parked itself over his head and showed no signs of budging.

Glancing at Elaine, who was behind the hostess podium reviewing sections and reservations, and then through the kitchen door at Jacob as he moved between the sink and the counters, Hannah made her way to Dylan and the growing pile of wrapped utensils beside his right elbow.

"I think we've got enough for today," she said, lowering herself onto the bench across from her youngest employee. "Maybe even for tomorrow too."

Dylan paused his hand on the handles of the napkin-topped fork and knife, took in the pile he'd completed, and slumped in his seat. "You're right. I guess I was on a roll."

"I appreciate your hard work." She watched him finish the final set and then reached across the table to put her hand on his forearm. "You're starting your college classes soon, right?"

"Week after next."

"Are you excited?"

"I want to be."

"You should be," she said, drawing back her hand. "It's exciting stuff—something you set in motion all by yourself."

"I did."

Something about the tone of his answer made her lower her voice so that only he would hear. "What's going on, Dylan? I've been sensing something off with you for a few weeks now."

Dylan sat up straighter. "Has a customer complained?"

"No, nothing like that," Hannah assured him. "In fact, you've been mentioned by name in a few glowing reviews this week alone."

His mouth spread wide with his first full smile of the day. "They mentioned me?"

"Absolutely." She grabbed her phone and pulled up two reviews that had come in over the past twenty-four hours. "See for yourself." She handed the phone to him.

Dylan stared at the screen. "Wait. I'm 'a delight'? And 'knowledgeable'?" He met Hannah's gaze, his eyes wide. "Seriously?"

"Seriously."

He took in the review on the screen again before scrolling down to the next one. His eyes moved back and forth from left to right, his lips closing around a long, low whistle. "'A pleasure to have as a waiter'? And they'll ask to be seated in my section next time they come?"

"That's right."

He looked from Hannah to the phone and back again. "They obviously haven't had Raquel yet."

She shook her finger at him. "Don't say that. Raquel is a fantastic server, no doubt, but you are as well. The growth you've shown since the Hot Spot opened has been phenomenal, Dylan. Truly. I'm so proud of you."

"I'm still not Raquel."

"You're right, you're not. You're Dylan. And Dylan is pretty great, if you ask me." She gestured to the phone. "And if you ask the folks who wrote those reviews."

Silence fell between them for a moment as he silently read both reviews again. When he finished, he handed the phone back to Hannah. "It's nice to know I'm doing *something* right."

She leaned across the table. "You're doing a lot of things right, Dylan."

Setting his elbows on the table, he pressed his hands to his cheeks and sighed. "My mom thinks I made a mistake starting classes this semester. She says I need 'direction.'"

"Direction?" Hannah echoed.

Dylan's nod was slow. "She thinks I should decide on a major before I start school. But I'm not sure I want to take the path she wants me to."

"Which is what?"

"Something to do with math."

"Do you like math?" Hannah asked.

Dylan's shoulders rose and fell in a half-hearted shrug. "Well enough. But I don't necessarily want to spend my life doing it, you know?"

"I totally understand. I was the same way, but with the language side of my brain. My high school counselor thought I should be an English teacher."

His brow lifted. "Why didn't you want to do that?"

"Because as much as I enjoyed those classes, none of them made me feel the way I did when I was in the kitchen with my mom."

The light returned to his eyes as they bore into Hannah's. "That's how I feel here, at the Hot Spot. I like interacting with the customers, I like talking about the menu, I like knowing I did a particularly good job when I get an extra-big tip, I like our staff meetings and hearing about the behind-the-scenes stuff that needs to happen to make this place run, and I like watching Jacob's brain work when he's coming up with a new seasonal item—the flavor combinations, the importance of texture, the way he decides to plate it. Stuff like that."

"Then maybe some aspect of restaurant work should be your career path."

And just like that, the light in his eyes drained away. "Maybe. I don't know. That's why I want to take different classes and see how I feel about them."

"Sounds like a good idea to me," she said.

"I know Mom's looking out for me and doesn't want me wasting my money taking classes I might not end up needing." He spread his arms toward their surroundings. "I didn't know how this place would make me feel. I just needed a job. But now that I'm here, I really like it—something I wouldn't have known if I hadn't applied and you hadn't hired me. So now I want to see if I like anything else as much as I like this. I want to check out my options until I find the one that feels right to me. I don't want to declare a major, take a bunch of classes, and end up stuck in a program that it makes me miserable."

"That makes sense to me," Hannah told him. "The good news is that you're just starting your college classes, Dylan. You need to be thinking about what you want to do, but it's okay if you're not ready to commit to a specific field of study yet."

He laughed, the sound void of anything genuine. "From your mouth to my mom's ear."

"She'll come around, Dylan. It's entirely possible she said those things to you because she had a stressful day at her job and was wishing she'd chosen a different career path for herself. I know it hasn't been easy for her since your dad passed, and I'm guessing she had to take a job without necessarily wanting it to be a career. I imagine she simply wants you to be able to plan ahead for the career you want and build it now, rather than getting dumped into it. In the meantime, like you said, pay attention to how the classes you take make you feel. God gives all of us gifts. The key is learning to recognize yours."

"It's definitely not science. For a little while during my junior year, I thought it might've been history, but when I got a different teacher my senior year, I realized it wasn't that either. And then there's math, which may or may not be it. I mean, I'm decent at it, and people in math-centered jobs tend to have more stable careers.

But it just doesn't excite me." He gathered the pile of wrapped utensils and put them into the large basket Elaine kept beside the menus at the hostess stand. "But if one of these days I had my own restaurant like you do, I'd have to do math sometimes, right?"

"You would."

"But not geometry or algebra?"

Hannah laughed. "Nope, no geometry or algebra."

"I did like fractions when I was younger."

"Which is an important skill for a chef," she pointed out.

He sat back on his seat for a moment, his eyes fixed on a point somewhere far beyond the confines of the Hot Spot's dining area. "I think coming up with dishes—the combination of flavors—the way Jacob does is so cool."

"Then make room for that on your list of possible careers."

"I will. But I like interacting with the customers out on the floor too," he said. "Which is why I'm not ready to declare a major yet. There are a lot of things that interest me. I'm just not sure which one interests me the most."

She sat with his honesty for a moment, mulling over the best way to respond. "You'll know in time."

Dylan's nod was slow and pensive. "I've seen your dad here a bunch of times. He was good with you going the restaurant route, yes?"

"I don't think he was wild about all the years I spent in California after I graduated from college, but that was about me being so far away, not about my chosen career." She started to rise to her feet but stopped and sank back. "Just this past week, though, I've had two people make me question where I am in life."

Dylan pointed across the table at Hannah. "You?"

She nodded. "I'm thirty-six. I'm not married. I don't have children. The bulk of my world is this restaurant. That's odd to some people."

"Did it bother you when they talked about it?" he asked.

"For a little while," she said. "Longer than I wanted it to. But God made us all different, all unique. I believe I'm where I'm supposed to be right now." As she said it, the truth of it sank in.

"'Where I'm supposed to be,'" he repeated before meeting her eyes again. "I want to be able to say that too someday. With the same kind of conviction you have, Hannah."

"You will. You have plenty of time."

He gazed around the room, apparently taking in the empty tables, the rolled cutlery, Raquel hustling through the front door, and, through the porthole windows, glimpses of Jacob clattering around in the kitchen. "I might be leaning toward hospitality."

Smiling, she stood. "You'd be great at it. But, again, there's no rush to figure it out today. You haven't even started your classes yet."

He stood too, grabbing hold of the now-full basket. "Thanks for listening, Hannah. It really helped."

"I'm glad. One more thing," she added as an idea occurred to her, "Do you know a Doug Bell? He's a history teacher at the high school."

Dylan deposited the basket next to the stack of menus and turned back to Hannah. "Yeah, I know Mr. Bell. He was my favorite teacher and the reason I enjoyed history my junior year. He made everything sound interesting, no matter what it was. A battle, a treaty, you name it. Sounds boring, I know, but like I said, he made it interesting. Anyway, one of the best parts about Mr. Bell was how he was available every single day after school if his students needed a little extra help—which I did. A lot."

"Every day?" she asked, glancing down at her watch. "Think he'd still be there now on a Friday?"

Dylan craned his neck to see the time on Hannah's wrist. "Definitely. Why? You want to talk to him about something?"

"I do, but we'll be opening soon."

Dylan held up his hand. "Mr. Bell is cool. If you need to talk to him, I can cover here until you get back."

"I can't do that."

"Yes, you can. I know what I'm doing." He opened his arms wide to encompass his coworkers in the gesture. "We *all* do, thanks to you."

Chapter Nineteen

Hannah headed straight down the main hallway of Blackberry Valley High School, the security officer's verbal directions looping through her thoughts. Eighteen years ago, she'd walked this same hallway five days a week during the school year, yet now it felt like it was all new.

Yes, the walls were still made of cinder block, and the drop ceiling and fluorescent lighting felt the same, but beyond that, she recognized little. Even the students she passed dressed and carried themselves so differently than she and her friends had.

At the end of the hallway, she turned left, her feet slowing as she spotted the lockers lining both sides. She smiled at the memory of how she and Lacy had decorated each other's lockers for graduation. Ribbons and confetti and balloons had rained out of hers the last time she'd opened it. She made a mental note to check in with Lacy on her way back to the restaurant.

Every twenty lockers or so, she came to another classroom, its number listed on a placard to the left of the door. When she reached Room 115, she looked through the open doorway and saw a man sitting at a desk at the front of the room, hunched over a stack of papers. Along the top of the wall behind him was a series of pictures spread out across a timeline that circled the walls she could see. Facing the man's desk were twenty-five smaller desks lined up in five rows of five. On the wall above the man, a clock ticked away the seconds and minutes until he could call it a day and the Hot Spot started its own.

She lifted her hand beside the doorframe and knocked softly. "Mr. Bell?"

The man smiled a greeting and pushed back his chair. "Yes, can I help you?"

Motioning for him to remain sitting, she crossed into the room and offered him her hand. "I'm Hannah Prentiss. I own the Hot Spot here in town. Nice to meet you, Mr. Bell."

"Doug, please. I thought you looked familiar." He motioned her to the student desk in front of his own and set his red pen on the stack of papers he'd been grading. "I've eaten there a time or two. In fact, one of my former students is on your payroll."

She smiled. "Yes, Dylan Bowman. He's an amazing young man with a bright future wherever he lands."

"I couldn't agree more." His smile grew pensive as he leaned forward. "Since I'm assuming you're not here for remedial work, what brings you to my classroom?"

Pausing to compose her thoughts, Hannah glanced at the photographic timeline. She pointed up at a picture almost directly above his head. "That's the old firehouse where my restaurant is."

He glanced back at the picture and nodded. "It is."

She squinted at the number listed above it. "That's the year it was built."

"It is," he said again.

She took in more years written in black marker on cards affixed to the wall, recognizing different buildings and key places in

Blackberry Valley. "You teach a class on Blackberry Valley's history?"

"I teach a *section* on Blackberry Valley's history, and that's the unit we're doing now. Just started, actually."

Pivoting in her seat, she scanned the pictures on the timeline and the years listed along with each one. She saw the library, the very school building they sat in at that moment, and—

"That's the Taylor Estate," she said, pointing again.

"You are correct." He retrieved his pen and slowly turned it between his thumb and index finger. "Antoinette Taylor had great wealth—what is commonly known as 'old money'—inherited from her father upon his passing. When she and her husband took over the estate, they had it outfitted to be their primary residence, but they also had a house on the coast in Rhode Island. Both homes were equipped with paid staff, strictly for the comfort of Antoinette and her family."

"Like Peggy Shipman Williams, right?"

His green eyes lit at her knowledge. "Yes, like Peggy, who was hired as the family's full-time cook. And, for a time, like my grandfather."

"Oh?" she asked, her curiosity rising. "What did your grandfather do at the estate?"

"Everything and anything that had to do with upkeep of the buildings and the land."

"Did he live on the property like Peggy's family did?"

"No. My grandfather had a modest place out on McCauley Road. He and my grandmother raised my father in what was little more than a one-bedroom cabin." The chair creaked as Doug leaned back, his arms crossed in front of his chest. "Oh, he had *dreams* of being able to provide his family a bigger home, of being able to see a little bit of our country, and of putting my father through college so he could have a better and more fulfilling life. But none of that came to pass, on account of Antoinette being strong-armed into replacing him."

Something about his words niggled at her thoughts, but she pushed it aside as he continued.

"Now, Antoinette's daughter, Theresa Adler, owns the estate, but the Taylor name remains as a nod to her grandfather and to her mother, who kept the Taylor name even after marriage. Time will tell if that continues though. Theresa's daughter will likely inherit the house and the land, and she might just turn around and sell it."

"Do you teach your students specifically about Peggy?" Hannah asked. "The fact that she was a self-taught potter and actually made a small business for herself?"

He appraised her through narrowed eyes. "You've done your homework."

"Not a lot. Just bits and pieces I've come across." She shrugged. "As a female business owner myself, I guess I'm impressed by her story. It couldn't have been easy for her to teach herself a craft, perfect it enough to create something worthy of selling, and then amass an audience for it, all while working for Antoinette and raising her daughter."

"Her own, and, in many ways, Antoinette's as well," he said. "Antoinette didn't necessarily have a reputation for warmth."

"She allowed her cook to not only use the potter's wheel Peggy's husband found, but also to make a business for herself outside the kitchen," Hannah countered. "That has to point to *some* warmth, don't you think?"

He nodded again. "One could certainly make a case for that, I suppose. Though, from what I was told growing up, any warmth she may have had only seemed to go in Peggy's direction."

Hannah considered his description of the estate owner and then moved on. "Is that why you're taking the pottery class in Cave City? Because of its tie to the unit you're in with your students right now?"

His brow rose. "How do you know that?"

"Right." She weighed what she wanted to divulge against what she didn't—yet—and squared her shoulders. "I was in Morgan's store the other day, and she mentioned that she'd just started teaching a pottery class. She showed me the room where she teaches, and I was intrigued enough to take a picture of the space. Then, when I looked at it later on my phone, I realized I'd accidentally gotten the student roster in the shot. Your name was familiar to me, but I couldn't place why at first. Liam put your name in context for me."

"You mean Liam Berthold? The fire chief?"

It was on the tip of her tongue to add that he was also her boyfriend, but she held back. "Yes."

"I see," he said, busying himself with his pen, the stack of papers, and, finally, the smooth edge of his desk.

"So?" she prodded. "Is that why?"

He looked up at her. "Why what?"

"Why you're taking the class?"

He stood and began wiping all evidence of his day's teachings from the whiteboard. "This is the first time I've ever spent so much time on Blackberry Valley's history. I've touched on it in the past, but as a blip inside our state's history. This year, based on feedback from last year's students, I decided to spend more time in our own backyard. The Taylor Estate and the cook play a big part in that, as did the cook's pottery. I enrolled in the class so I could talk more knowledgeably about it to my students."

"Are you enjoying it?" she asked.

He set the eraser on the sill along the bottom edge of the board and slowly turned back to Hannah. "There's only been one class so far, but it was…interesting. In fact, I'm happy to say my first effort didn't yield the worst in the class. It didn't yield the best either, but it wasn't the worst."

She thought about the bowls, assigning each one to a name on the roster as he made his way back to his desk.

"Are you thinking about taking the class yourself?" he asked, resuming his seat.

"I'm giving it some thought," Hannah said, recalling her text from Lacy. It really would be fun to try a new hobby with her best friend. "With one of my girlfriends, if I do. But I'm not sure. I'm not super crafty."

"It's not the cleanest thing I've ever done, but it's satisfying." He glanced behind her at the clock, reached under his desk for a leather satchel, and began stuffing it with the papers, clearly signaling an end to her visit. "Though, as a teacher myself, I'd recommend waiting for another class to start so you aren't trying to play catch-up on the basics."

"That makes sense. Thank you for the advice." She'd come there planning to show the photo of the creamer to the history teacher in the hopes he'd remember having seen it during or after his class, but something inside her told her to wait.

She stood and offered her hand with a smile. "Thank you, Doug, for your thoughts on the class. And the brief history lesson about Blackberry Valley. Makes me want to learn more."

"If you have any questions I can answer, you can find me here."

"Thank you. You can count on it." Hannah meant every word. She wanted to talk again with Doug because something about his attitude regarding the Taylor Estate troubled her. She definitely needed to figure out a way to examine that.

Chapter Twenty

By the time Hannah made it back to the restaurant, the slow build-up between four and five o'clock was starting to give way to the dinner rush. Since it was a Friday, she and her staff soon found themselves in nonstop motion for the next two hours.

When Elaine wasn't fielding calls from people looking to make a reservation, she was seating those who had one and doing her best to fit in people without one in as timely a fashion as possible.

Raquel and Dylan moved between their assigned tables, explained the specials, answered questions about the menu, and gave their thoughts on various dishes when prompted. They struck the perfect balance between attentive and unobtrusive, making their current guests feel welcome and at leisure and quickly preparing tables for their next guests.

Jacob stirred, grilled, fried, and plated over and over again. Hannah kept an eye on him to make sure he drank plenty of water, because he was on the move in such close proximity to the hot grill and the warming lamps.

She also bustled between the hostess stand, the various tables, the kitchen, and the front door as she pitched in whenever and wherever she was needed. She added names to the waiting list while Elaine seated other parties. She took phone reservations for the following evening and delivered drinks to tables while her waitstaff tabulated bills. Sometimes she washed her hands, threw on an apron, and helped Jacob with large and complicated orders.

It was crazy, but it was also everything she'd dared hope for as a first-time restaurant owner. Still, as the time ticked toward eight o'clock, she was a little relieved to see the waiting area thinning. Raquel and Dylan had more time with their guests, and Jacob was occasionally able to pause for longer drinks of water.

"Hannah?"

She found a smile for the curly-haired server who always looked unfazed, no matter how busy things got. "You and Dylan have been absolute machines tonight, Raquel. Thank you."

"I didn't see any moss growing under your feet either." Raquel lifted a pitcher of ice water in a gesture. "So go make your dad's night and sit with him for a little while. Elaine, Dylan, and I can take it from here."

Hannah scanned the tables and was surprised to spot her father and her uncle. "I didn't see them come in." She took in the full drinks and lack of menus on the table between Dad and Uncle Gordon. "And you've already taken their order?"

"I have. You were ringing up a credit card when they arrived. Their appetizer should be about ready." Raquel gestured to the delivery window. "And there it is. Go sit with them, and I'll bring it over."

"Miss?"

Hannah and Raquel turned toward table one, where a woman sat with her husband and two small children. The woman asked for their check, and Hannah squeezed Raquel's forearm. "You take care of that table, and I'll take my dad and Uncle Gordon their appetizer."

"And sit with them for a little while too?" Raquel prodded.

Hannah laughed. "Yes."

"Good."

She and Raquel went their separate ways—Raquel toward the young family, and Hannah first to the kitchen and then toward the growing smiles on the faces at table six. She set the plate of hot wings between the brothers, added an extra set of napkins for the messy fingers that were sure to come, and planted a kiss on her father's cheek. "Hi, Dad. Hi, Uncle Gordon."

Her father patted the vacant spot beside him. "Can you sit with us for a little while?"

"Actually, I've been ordered to do exactly that." Hannah lowered herself onto the seat with a groan. "Oh, wow. It feels so good to sit down."

"Not that you haven't had proof for quite some time now, but in case you've somehow missed it, the Hot Spot is the place to be on a Friday night in Blackberry Valley." Uncle Gordon helped himself to a wing smothered in hot sauce, his brown eyes flashing with excitement. "I think it would have taken us twice as long as it did to get a table if we weren't your family."

"Elaine doesn't play favorites. We're slowing down for the evening." Hannah waved away her father's offer of a wing and sank back against her seat with a long sigh. "But if you want less wait, come on a Tuesday, Wednesday, or Thursday night next time."

"And miss seeing you living your dream?" her father asked. "Waiting is a small price to pay to see that, my dear."

"Thanks, Dad." She looked from the plate of wings to her uncle's mad dash for a sip of water and chuckled. "I keep telling you it might be wise to go with the Glowing Embers instead of the Flamethrowers. They're still good, just not as hot."

Uncle Gordon's sip turned into several gulps before he set the glass down with a shake of his head. "We may not be able to handle the Inferno level the way those youngsters Liam works with can, but we're not ready for the old people ones yet either."

"The Glowing Embers level is not for old people, Uncle Gordon," Hannah protested, laughing. "But do you want me to get you some milk? Water doesn't do much to help with spice."

"Why not?" Dad asked.

"It has to do with the compound that makes things spicy," Hannah explained. "It's called capsaicin, and water just washes over it rather than washing it away. Milk, on the other hand, contains a protein that binds to the capsaicin and actually moves it out of your mouth."

Returning to his half-eaten wing, her uncle shrugged. "We've got this, don't we, Gabriel?"

Hannah's dad laughed as his brother again sought solace for his mouth with another, bigger swig of water. "Whatever you say, Gordon."

Raquel swung by to top off the men's water glasses and set a fresh one in front of Hannah.

They thanked Raquel, and then Hannah settled her attention on the man seated opposite her. "Uncle Gordon? Dad mentioned something the other day about you doing some work out at the Taylor Estate this week."

Uncle Gordon polished off a wing, another two gulps of water, and nodded. "That's right. I fixed a leaky pipe under a bathroom sink."

"And?" Hannah's dad prodded.

"And I replaced a worn washer inside one of the faucet handles." Uncle Gordon started to reach for another wing then gulped water instead.

"And?" his brother urged.

Uncle Gordon raised an eyebrow at Dad. "And I took care of a drip in the kitchen sink as well. Which is nothing different than you would've done if you'd spotted things you could easily take care of while fixing a GFI or a broken light switch."

"Uncle Gordon has a point, Dad," she said.

Her father waved her off. "Whose side are you on?"

She chuckled as the Prentiss brothers ribbed each other for a few moments. When they took a break in favor of eating another wing or two, she steered the conversation back in her intended direction. "Did you often work out at the estate before you retired?"

Uncle Gordon nodded. "Your dad and I both did."

"But with few exceptions, we weren't out there all that often until much later in our careers." Her father reached for one last wing but set it on his plate as if trying to convince himself he could eat another. "Before that, they had staff to do it all."

"Like Ray Williams, Vanessa Lodge's grandfather," she said.

"Yes."

"The other day, you told me about a time you were out at the estate to fix something in the cottage where Ray and Peggy lived."

Uncle Gordon slanted a look at his brother. "Why did Ray Williams need you to fix something he was more than able to fix himself?"

"He was laid up after knee surgery. Peggy wouldn't let him off the couch." Dad grinned. "I think you and I both know something about overprotective wives."

"Did your paths cross much before that?" Hannah asked. "Specifically with Ray?"

"Yes."

"Other than the stable rewiring job when you were little, not really. Before that, Gordon and I just knew of him through our work in the trades." He turned to his brother. "I do remember hearing you talking about the fires Ray had to put out when he first took over out there. Remember those?"

"I do indeed," Uncle Gordon said. "Crazy stuff."

"Ray was a firefighter too?" Hannah asked.

"Not *literal* fires," her uncle said.

"Actually, one of them *was* a literal fire," her father corrected. "Remember?"

"That's right. There was one actual fire—a barn fire," her uncle said. "I was in my early twenties, and just starting out. I remember hearing about it over lunch with the guys. Seems Ray, who'd just gotten the job at the estate, had built an addition to the barn for Antoinette's newest horses shortly after he started. Built it, outfitted it, painted it, the whole nine yards. Less than a week after it was finished, it caught fire."

"Were any horses killed?" Hannah asked.

"Thankfully, no," Dad said.

Uncle Gordon's right eyebrow lifted, and he snapped his fingers. "And that canopy of trees along the front entrance to the estate you see now? They weren't the first ones there."

"Or the second," Dad added.

"What do you mean?"

"The first attempt at lining the drive with trees was unsuccessful. They were chopped down. Right?"

Uncle Gordon nodded. "Same happened to the second round as well. All within months of Ray starting his job. Being new at my own job, I remember thinking how awful that must've been for him."

"Wait. So the trees were literally chopped down?" Hannah asked. "Who would do that?"

Uncle Gordon shrugged. "Probably the same person who later slashed the tires on every vehicle on the estate—not once, not twice, but three times, if I remember correctly."

She gasped. "But why?"

"They never found the culprit, so I can't answer that question. But there was a lot of talk going around."

"What kind of talk?"

"There were rumors that maybe it wasn't the estate that was being targeted, maybe it was Ray Williams," Uncle Gordon said. "He didn't get hired on because of someone's retirement. He was brought in to replace someone who was still of working age."

Something poked at her memory, but before she could home in on it, Uncle Gordon continued. "The police even checked out Ray's predecessor for the barn fire, the tire slashing, and the vandalism with the trees, but the guy apparently had alibis."

"Did anything else happen?" she asked.

"Not that I recall," Uncle Gordon said. "But word on the street was that the police kept a close eye on the estate after all that."

A tap on Hannah's shoulder drew her attention to Dylan, who stood beside the table with a look of apology on his freckled face. "I'm sorry to interrupt, but the credit card machine appears to have a glitch of some sort, and I'm not sure how to fix it."

"You're doing exactly what you should—telling me." She slid out of the booth and onto her feet. "Dad, Uncle Gordon, thanks for giving me a reason to sit for a few minutes, but duty calls."

"We understand, sweetheart. But come back if you get another chance," her father said. "We promise not to bore you again if you do."

She put her hand on his shoulder and squeezed. "Oh, trust me, Dad, this conversation was anything but boring."

Chapter Twenty-One

With a bowl of freshly popped popcorn in one hand and the remote control in the other, Hannah sank onto the couch in her living room. It had been a long day. While she felt every bit of it in her neck, shoulders, and back, she couldn't deny the sense of pride running through her as she settled on the cushions and set the bowl in her lap.

A small part of her knew she should probably use the next thirty minutes or so before bed to fold some laundry or go over her Saturday to-do list for what would likely be another busy night at the Hot Spot. But a larger and more insistent part knew she needed this downtime.

She popped a few kernels into her mouth and aimed the remote at the wall-mounted TV opposite the couch. Slowly, she flipped through the channels, passing sitcom reruns, a home and garden show, and the weather report on eleven o'clock news broadcasts, finding nothing of interest. After a second pass through the same monotony, she moved her finger from the channel button to the power button and watched the screen go blank. Sighing, she leaned past what remained of her salty treat and grabbed the pen and small spiral-bound notebook she'd left on the coffee table that morning.

"To-do list it is, unfortunately." Sighing, she shifted the bowl to the empty space beside her and opened the notebook. "Maybe instead of a pottery class, I need to take one on how to relax."

She clicked the pen, paged past previous days' lists, and stopped when she came to a clean page. Lowering the pen to the paper she started to form the *S* in *Saturday* but instead found herself writing *Questions to Ask.*

Studying the new heading, she thought back over the past few days and the snippets of history she'd learned, the people she'd met, and the information she'd been mulling over. Again, she began to write.

> *Morgan:*
>
> *Who has access to the back room?*
>
> *Were any students left alone in the back room either before or after class?*
>
> *How would a rose—as opposed to* PSW*—on the bottom of a piece made by Peggy impact the piece's value?*

She paused, her thoughts moving away from the pottery shop owner.

> *Pippa:*
>
> *Did she know Morgan prior to taking the class?*
>
> *Was anyone else in the back room when she arrived?*

She paused, tapping her pen against the page as her mind wandered. Suddenly, she sat up straight, the memory of her father's words from the restaurant that evening bringing to mind a very different conversation.

"Oh, he had dreams *of being able to provide his family a bigger home, of being able to see a little bit of our country, and of putting my*

father through college so he could have a better and more fulfilling life. But none of that came to pass, on account of Antoinette being strong-armed into replacing him."

Leaving the notebook and pen on the cushion beside the popcorn bowl, Hannah went in search of her phone, finding it on the counter beside the microwave. She opened her text conversation with Vanessa.

Hey, I'm sorry for the late hour, but are you awake?

She hit send, hoping that if Vanessa wasn't awake, the notification wouldn't interrupt her sleep.

Seconds later, a response came in. I am. What can I do for you?

She began typing again. Did you tell me your grandmother had something to do with your grandfather being hired at the Taylor Estate?

Vanessa's reply appeared. You could say that. As Mama tells the story, Grandma Peggy told Antoinette that my grandfather needed good steady work, and if he couldn't find it, they'd have to move on from BV. If you'd ever eaten Grandma Peggy's food, you'd understand why Antoinette hired my grandfather.

Hannah gave a low whistle as her thoughts shuttled back to her conversation with Doug Bell. Before she could fully process it, her phone yielded yet another message from Vanessa.

I'll have to make you some of her biscuits one day soon. Once you taste them, it'll all make sense.

Slowly, Hannah made her way back to the couch, her thumbs moving across the screen. I'd love that. How old is your mom?

She's 61.

Hannah considered the answer against her father's and uncle's current ages and the age her uncle would've been as an apprentice and did some quick mental math.

So that would have made her about 18 when she got the dining set from your grandmother, right?

That's right.

She took in Vanessa's answer. Considered it. Stowed it away.

Before she could formulate another question, Vanessa texted again. I should probably go. We're moving some filing cabinets and desks around at work tomorrow, and I told the sheriff I'd be there to oversee it all. Good night, Hannah!

She wished her friend a good night and hurried back to the couch to scribble in her notebook.

Doug Bell's grandfather lost his job to Peggy's husband—a loss that affected his family. Did he retaliate by setting fire to the barn? Chopping the trees? Slashing tires? What more might he have done?

She paused the pen after the last question mark, remembering that her uncle said the senior Bell had been questioned and cleared. And yet Doug Bell had been at the pottery class, and he had historical family ties to this case. She drew an arrow pointing down to the next line, her next question.

Where does Doug Bell fit into all this?

Chapter Twenty-Two

With a plated cinnamon roll in one hand and a large to-go coffee in the other, Hannah slowly scanned the handful of tables that peppered Blackberry Valley's favorite morning meeting spot, Jump Start Coffee. She smiled and nodded at the mayor's wife and daughter, EMT Gary Perkins and his grandmother, and Pastor Bob Dawson and his wife, Lorelai, before finally catching sight of Lacy's raised hand off to her right.

Pulling her plate and cup closer, Hannah expertly wove her way to her friend's table. "Hey, Lacy, sorry I'm late. It took me a while to fall asleep last night." She pointed her cup-holding hand at the empty tabletop. "Where's your food?"

Lacy lifted a small plastic cup of water above the table's edge for Hannah to see and then lowered it back down to her lap. "Nothing looked good to me."

"Then clearly you didn't see those gigantic blueberry muffins in the case. They had your name written all over them." Hannah set her cinnamon roll and coffee cup on the table and then hiked her thumb in the direction she'd just come. "I'll go get you one and be right back."

"No, I'm good. Sit."

She jerked her thumb over her shoulder again. "Seriously, you should eat."

"I will. When I'm ready." Lacy pulled one hand from around her cup and tapped the tabletop. "I think I've kicked whatever I had, but my appetite hasn't fully returned yet. I can get a muffin once it does."

Reluctantly, Hannah sat, looking across at her friend. "You still seem a little pale."

"It's January. Not exactly prime tanning weather."

Hannah examined the skin on her own hands and arms, shrugged, and reached for her cup, savoring her first sip of coffee. "How was our sweet Sprout this morning?"

Lacy leaned back against the chair. "I wouldn't know. Neil took care of all the morning chores before he had to head over to the bookstore."

"Good man." Hannah set her cup down and reached for her fork. "He's a keeper, that one."

"Without a doubt." Lacy gave her a soft smile.

Hannah took a bite, relished the explosion of cinnamon in her mouth, and pointed at the remaining roll with her fork. "Would you like some?"

Lacy's gaze pinged off the plate. "No, thank you."

"Still queasy?" Hannah asked.

"No. Just not hungry." Shifting in her seat, Lacy looked back at Hannah, her hazel eyes tired. "Tell me something."

Hannah rested her fork on the edge of the plate and reached for her coffee again. "What kind of something?"

"Something happy."

"Hmm." She took a sip, her gaze traveling over the tables she'd passed on her way to theirs before landing back on Lacy. "I won't know any specifics until later this afternoon, but it seems Marshall is taking Raquel on some sort of surprise date this morning."

Lacy's answering smile stopped short of her eyes. "Those two are really cute together."

Hannah nodded across the top of her cup. "I couldn't agree more. In fact, they remind me a lot of you and Neil."

"And I think you and Liam are pretty cute together too."

Aware of heat rising in her cheeks, Hannah set the cup back on the table. "Not that we have a whole lot of time to spend together."

"I have faith that the two of you will find the right balance."

"You do, huh?" Hannah busied herself with another bite or two of her cinnamon roll before curiosity over her friend's words won out. "Why do you say that?"

Lacy shrugged. "Because you're both mature and intelligent—too much so to risk missing out on this opportunity. Plus, you're perfect for each other."

Hannah finished her roll and sat back in her chair with a sigh. "Your turn."

"For what?"

"Tell *me* something."

Lacy's shoulders rose and fell in a weak shrug. "I've been a total blob since we last spoke."

"Resting when you're not feeling well is hardly being a blob, Lacy," Hannah argued.

"It feels like it."

Hannah folded her arms across her chest. "That's because you're always going, going, going. I'm sure that even when you were resting, you still plowed through a couple of books and assembled another one of those crazy thousand-piece puzzles you love to do."

Lacy took another sip of water. "Actually, I didn't read a single book or do any puzzles. I didn't go into the barn even once."

Releasing her arms back down to her sides, Hannah gaped at her friend. "Seriously? I'm wondering if you should have gone to the hospital."

"I'm telling you, whatever I got from Mom was not fun—still isn't, based on how little energy I have." Lacy lifted her cup onto the table and worked a small smile to her lips. "But I did get a phone call from Connie Sanchez yesterday with some good news I can share."

At the mention of the church secretary, Hannah leaned forward. "I'm listening."

"Remember how the youth group was getting ready to start fundraising for the summer mission trip next month? It's been fully funded. For all twenty kids."

"Wait. Wasn't that going to cost something like a thousand dollars per teenager to go?"

Lacy nodded. "Yup."

Hannah studied her friend. "Are you saying that someone donated twenty thousand dollars flat out?"

"I am."

"Who would do that?"

"Theresa Adler."

The name pushed her back. "The owner of the Taylor Estate is a member of our church? I didn't know that."

Lacy rubbed her arms as if she was suddenly chilled. "You didn't know that, because she's not."

"Okay. I didn't think I'd missed that." Hannah pushed her coffee cup across the table. "But why would she donate that kind of money to a church she isn't even a member of?"

Wrapping her hands around the warm cup, Lacy fluttered her lashes closed. "Lots of reasons, I suppose. Maybe she wanted to do something nice? Maybe it's something about taxes and donations? Or maybe she knows one of the kids and didn't feel right helping that one and not the others?"

"I bet that's it, actually," Hannah said, causing Lacy to open her eyes. "Theresa Adler clearly has a soft spot for teens. So much so she wants to help provide them opportunities to learn and grow, and this was just one more way to do that."

"One *more* way?"

Hannah smiled. "She donated a big chunk of money to Liam too."

"Listen, I'm not saying your beau is old," Lacy said, her eyes twinkling, "but I don't think he exactly counts as a youth anymore."

Hannah hurried to clarify her words. "To the fire department, I should say. It's enough that Liam can start an explorer program for interested high schoolers in the fall at the beginning of the next academic year. It's to highlight rewarding careers that don't require a four-year college degree."

"Oh, I love that idea." Lacy released Hannah's cup long enough to pluck her coat off the back of her chair and drape it around her shoulders with a shiver. "Is it just me or is it getting colder in here?"

"I'm not feeling it, but I guess it could be."

Lacy met Hannah's worry with a firm set of her jaw. "Before you venture further down the path we both know you're on right now,

I'm confident I've turned the corner on whatever I had. Now I just need to get my strength back."

"Which would happen a lot faster if you'd let me get you a muffin or whatever else you want," Hannah pointed out. "You can't regain your strength without fuel."

"I'll eat something when I get home."

"Promise?" Hannah pressed.

Lacy pushed the coffee cup across the table. "I promise."

"I'm going to hold you to that. You'd better text me and tell me what you're eating."

"Yes, ma'am." Drawing the flaps of her coat tighter around herself, Lacy cut short a second shiver. "Now, I want to be brought up to speed on the case of the long-lost creamer. It didn't feel right to have Neil knowing more than I did when he got home from the store yesterday."

Hannah laughed. "Afraid he'll replace you as my sleuthing sidekick?"

"I'm going to pretend I didn't hear you say that," Lacy said with a scowl. "Instead, I'm going to keep staring at you until you tell me everything we know so far."

It was on the tip of Hannah's tongue to teasingly question Lacy's use of the word *we*, but she refrained. Instead, she took one last pull of her coffee and then pushed her empty cup and plate to the side as she began at the beginning, even though Lacy knew a lot of it already.

She told Lacy about when and why the creamer was made.

She told her about how it and the still-absent sugar bowl were the only items missing from the full set Vanessa's grandmother had made for Vanessa's mother before she moved out on her own.

She told her about Morgan Wyatt claiming it had simply shown up on a shelf in the back room of her shop the evening before she'd sold it to Pippa.

She told her about how that same room served as a classroom in which Morgan had taught her first pottery class that same evening.

And—

"I'm listening, Hannah, I really am, but my mind keeps circling back to what those pieces would be worth if they were sold," Lacy interrupted.

"But the creamer doesn't have the initials on the bottom."

"It was still made by the same person."

"But if no one knew that, it wouldn't have the same worth," Hannah mused aloud. "Right?"

Lacy's eyebrows quirked upward before she brought her hands to her cheeks. "I think so? I don't know. I'm a bit addlebrained at the moment."

"You and me both." Hannah was starting to feel as if she were chasing her tail when it came to the creamer. "Remember what I said about Morgan teaching her first pottery class in the very same room where the creamer suddenly appeared after forty-plus years?"

"Of course I do. I'm not quite that addlebrained."

"Pippa was one of her students," she said.

Lacy cut short another shiver. "Pippa Nelson, who gave you the creamer? Seriously?"

"My sentiments exactly."

"Anyone else we know in there?" Lacy asked.

"Doug Bell."

A flash of recognition briefly lit Lacy's eyes. "The high school history teacher who's dating Cassie Donnelson? Well, that explains Pippa taking the class."

"What are you talking about?"

"Cassie Donnelson's brother, Derrick, is a new accountant in town. Late twenties. Tall. Fairly handsome."

"Okay, but what does that have to do with Pippa taking a pottery class with Doug?"

Lacy's answering grin was cut short by a yawn. "My sources could be wrong, of course, but the word around town is that our local reporter has a crush on Derrick. Which, if correct, probably means she somehow heard Doug was taking the class and saw it as a way to get to know him better."

"I'm still not following this train of thought," Hannah admitted.

"If she strikes up a friendship with Doug, she strikes up a friendship with Cassie. And if she strikes up a friendship with Cassie, she might have a chance to get to know her brother, Derrick, better."

"That seems like a lot of work, doesn't it?"

"Pippa is a reporter, remember?" Lacy said, her grin returning.

"Good point. I've certainly never seen her shy away from a challenge." Hannah moved on. "Anyway, I spoke with Doug yesterday afternoon, and I have to tell you, he's on my radar."

"As a suspect?"

"I think so, yes."

"How? He can't be much more than forty-five, if that," Lacy protested. "Which would've made him little more than a toddler when the creamer and sugar bowl went missing, right?"

Hannah slumped. It was a valid point, and one she couldn't ignore.

A close yet muted ring sounded from Lacy's coat pocket. "Hold that thought for a minute, okay?"

"No problem."

Lacy glanced at the screen and then turned it so Hannah could see a photo of Neil smiling on a hike he and Lacy had taken together in the past. "It's Neil."

"I see that," she said, laughing.

"Which means he's outside in the car, waiting to drive me home."

"You didn't drive yourself?" she asked.

"Neil wanted to get something he'd left at the store yesterday." Lacy pressed the green circle on the screen but paused a moment as she dropped her voice to a volume only Hannah could hear. "Which actually means he's been worried about me and wanted to be close by."

Nodding, Hannah motioned for Lacy to hand her the phone. "She's on her way out to you now. And for what it's worth, Neil, your wife promised me she'd eat something at home." Without waiting for an answer, she handed the phone back to her friend. "I'll check in with you later, okay?"

"Yes, *Mother.*" Lacy stood, stepped around to Hannah's side of the table, and gave her a one-armed hug. "Don't think this is the end of our conversation though."

"Our conversations never end," Hannah reminded her.

Hannah couldn't shake her concern as her friend made her way to the door. Lacy might insist that she felt better, but not only did her gait lack its usual bounce, she looked downright unsteady.

One more thing to get to the bottom of.

Chapter Twenty-Three

Hannah returned to the table she'd shared with Lacy, set down her second cup of coffee, and resumed her seat, her thoughts unsettled. There was no denying the wrinkle her friend had created in her latest round of hypothesizing. Frankly, she was stunned she hadn't raised the age flag on Doug Bell herself.

She reached into her bag and pulled out her notebook and pen. After placing them beside her cup, she flipped through to the page she'd filled the previous night, scanned the list of questions she'd written down, and then moved on to the next empty page.

In bold letters at the top, she wrote, *Possible Motive*. She added the names of the three people who aroused her suspicion in one way, shape, or form. Then, with a quick glance around the room to make sure she still worked in private, she zeroed in on the first name on her list: *Doug Bell—the history teacher.*

He was too young to have had anything to do with the incidents of forty years ago, but surely his age wouldn't have prevented him from being involved in the creamer caper.

Turning back to the previous page, she added four new questions to her list.

Does Doug have any older siblings?

Is Doug's grandfather still alive? His father? If so, where are they? How is Doug's relationship with each of them?

She flipped forward to the motives page. Beside Doug's name, she began to write again.

Grandfather's replacement by Ray Williams prevented Doug's father from attending college.

Stilling her pen, she thought back on her conversation with Dad and Uncle Gordon the previous evening, specifically their mention of the many unexplained incidents Ray Williams had been forced to contend with after his hiring. The barn addition he'd built that had been burned to the ground. The trees he'd planted along the estate's drive that had been chopped down not once, but twice. The tires of every vehicle on the property getting slashed multiple times. Incidents that had led the local police to question and subsequently clear Doug's grandfather.

But if the loss of the man's job made it so Doug's *father* couldn't go to college, was it possible local law enforcement didn't look deep enough into the family for the culprit?

And if it had been one of Doug's family members who'd stolen the creamer and sugar bowl all those years ago, why would Doug put it where it could be found now? Especially when he obviously still held resentment over his grandfather's job loss and how it had impacted his father?

Hannah wrote some more.

Did a member of Doug's family steal Ray's wife's pottery for retribution?

She sat with the question and its various possibilities for a moment and then moved on to the next name she'd listed: *Morgan Wyatt—the pottery shop owner.*

The woman's knowledge of pottery and the fact that the creamer had come from her store were two details Hannah couldn't ignore. But, by the same token, wouldn't that knowledge have made her sell it for more? Hannah couldn't be sure, of course, but she didn't believe that Pippa would have paid a lot for a virtual stranger's birthday present. And Hannah had seen for herself how much Morgan charged for her own pieces.

"Selling it at her usual price point might be a nice one-time boost for the shop, but the publicity the sale stood to generate could also translate to a different kind of boost," Hannah muttered beneath her breath. "A longer-lasting, sustained boost. After all, Pippa the reporter has connections, and she could have spread word of the shop easily. Besides, Morgan didn't make the piece, so she made pure profit either way."

Bringing her pen back down to the page, she wrote a single word beside Morgan's name: *Publicity?*

And then, out of nowhere, another thought struck, and she continued to write.

Would the publicity surrounding the reappearance of the long-missing creamer increase the worth of the still-missing sugar bowl?

"Which could come into play for Doug or one of his relatives as well," she whispered.

Her excitement growing, Hannah moved on to the third and final name on her list: *Pippa Nelson—the reporter.* Who wasn't even alive when the creamer and sugar bowl went missing.

Shaking off the bothersome thought, she willed her focus back to Pippa's name on the page. Try as she might, she couldn't escape the idea that Pippa stood to gain something from the creamer showing up so mysteriously.

A creamer that had appeared in a room where she'd been.

A creamer she'd purchased as a gift the very next day.

A creamer she had wrapped in a box she could reasonably assume Hannah would open in front of a person who would likely know what it was.

"Kicking off the kind of multifaceted story that could showcase her prowess as a writer and put her in contention to win that award," Hannah said under her breath.

She touched the pen to the page once again.

Sinking back in the booth, she reached inside her bag for her phone and the picture of the very item responsible for her current troubles.

Spreading her fingers across the screen, she zoomed in on the creamer. "If only you could talk," she said. "Then I could just know."

Feeling silly, she took a sip of her cooling coffee and swiped to the next picture—the underside of the creamer, showing the delicate etching of a rose.

A second swipe brought her back inside the room where Morgan Wyatt claimed to have found the creamer. A room where all three of the people on her suspect list had been the night it had appeared. But they weren't the only ones.

Zooming in on the screen, she again looked at the class roster she'd unknowingly captured in her shot. Try as she might, she still couldn't make out the second name on the list in its entirety. She knew the last name was *Winfield*, that she could tell. But the first name? The only thing she was certain of was that it started with *S*. But the letters beyond that she couldn't decipher at all.

Frustrated, she allowed the picture to return to its normal size and, in doing so, spotted a piece of Morgan's bulletin board and the flyers it held in the background. Quickly she swiped to the next picture, zooming in on the various flyers she'd captured, including one for the Cave City Pottery Guild's next meeting. She took in the day's date, compared the start time to that on her watch—and grinned.

Chapter Twenty-Four

It was fifteen minutes past the start time listed on the flyer when Hannah quietly let herself into a meeting room at Cave City Public Library. Despite her late arrival, the monthly gathering hadn't yet begun, based on the chatter emanating from the handful of chairs lined up in three rows across the center of the room. To the right of the rows sat a refreshment table with an open doughnut box containing the same three or four kinds that were almost always left over at such affairs. Beside the box was a stack of napkins, a near-empty pitcher of orange juice, and a stack of small, clear plastic cups.

In front of the room was a long card table with a tabletop podium that held a stack of papers. Beside the podium on the table were half a dozen pottery pieces, lined up as if waiting their turn to speak.

Hannah took a seat at the end of the back row. Seconds later, Morgan Wyatt broke from a small cluster of women in the first row and made her way up to the podium as the others took their seats. Hannah scanned the faces around her as well as she could but saw no one she recognized.

"Good morning, fellow pottery guild members." Morgan tilted the podium's attached microphone closer to her mouth. "I know I probably don't really need this, but I'd rather everyone hear me than be asking one another what I said."

Heads bobbed in agreement as Morgan took everyone in with a nod of her own. When her gaze reached Hannah's otherwise empty row, her expression fleetingly changed from lighthearted to surprised to tense. Before Hannah could truly home in on it enough to be sure, it was gone, replaced—or covered—by a small wave and then a sweep of Morgan's hand in her direction.

"Ladies, I'm pleased to announce we have a guest with us today."

A dozen pairs of eyes turned in Hannah's direction. Some of the women nodded at her, some smiled, and others waved their fingers at her.

"Hannah, please stand and introduce yourself to the group," Morgan said. "Tell them where you're from and why you've chosen to join us this morning."

Transferring her bag from her lap to the empty chair beside her, Hannah stood. "I'm Hannah Prentiss. I live in Blackberry Valley. And—"

The sound of the door opening behind her interrupted her introduction. Hannah tracked the glances of the other attendees to the door through which she had entered mere minutes earlier. There, she spotted Pippa, notebook in hand, making haste toward the opposite end of Hannah's row.

"And we have another guest, ladies," Morgan said as she flashed a genuine smile at the reporter. "Pippa, please remain standing long enough to introduce yourself to the group, if you will."

Pippa unzipped her coat, shucked it off, and dropped it onto a vacant chair beside her. "Hi, I'm Pippa Nelson."

Before the young woman sat, Morgan waved for her to continue. "Tell them where you're from."

"Right." Pippa spotted Hannah at the other end of the row and drew back in surprise. "Oh. Hannah. I didn't see you."

Waving, Hannah sat, grateful her time in the spotlight was over.

"Pippa is one of the students in my new pottery class," Morgan said proudly. "She's also a reporter for *The Blackberry Valley Chronicle*, and I suggested that she might want to write an article that would include a mention of the small but mighty community of potters we have in our area. I'm simply tickled to see she's taken me up on my suggestion with a stop at our monthly meeting. So, a warm welcome to you, Pippa."

With a quick nod and an even quicker smile, Pippa took her seat and set her notebook on her thigh as Morgan began the meeting in earnest.

Slowly and with an air of importance, the pottery shop owner addressed the highlights of the prior month's meeting and mentioned a workshop led by a prominent potter that would take place in Louisville in late spring. Then she held up each of the pieces lined up on the table beside her, calling out the guild member who'd crafted it and waiting as polite applause and words of encouragement ensued in the wake of each showing.

When the last piece had been shown, Morgan gripped both sides of the tabletop podium and beamed. "Now, while I know everyone in this room is relatively new to the world of pottery, I have some news to share that I think you'll all find very exciting, because it is!"

Hannah exchanged a shrug with Pippa before they both returned their attention to Morgan.

"I know our guild members are familiar with the work of Peggy Shipman Williams, yes?" Morgan asked. Her audience murmured assent while Pippa scribbled in her notebook. "But did you know that not every piece she made contains her trademark initials?"

A few audible inhalations gave way to puzzled looks and whispered murmurs throughout the first two rows.

"Are you sure?" asked a gray-haired woman in the second row.

"I am."

"But how do you know?" the woman asked. "Peggy Shipman Williams has been dead for more than ten years."

Morgan rubbed her hands, her blue eyes dancing with excitement. "Because I had one of the pieces in my shop this past weekend, and it's been confirmed to be one of Peggy's."

A few people clapped their hands over their mouths, and others' eyes widened in shock.

"But how can you be sure they were Peggy's work if her initials weren't on it?" an elderly woman in the first row challenged. "She put her initials on all her work."

"Not on the piece I had," Morgan corrected smugly. "Which, by the way, is part of an entire dining set that Peggy made for her daughter, Rose."

More whispers rose up in clusters in front of Hannah before giving way to Morgan's voice once again.

"And that's what Peggy put in place of her initials," Morgan said. "A rose."

"Did someone bring it in to show you?" the woman in the second row asked.

Morgan's eyes slid briefly in Hannah's direction before returning to the woman who'd posed the question. "No. But I saw it, and I held it."

And sold it, Hannah thought as her own gaze traveled the line of empty chairs beside her to the lone person at the other end. The same person who had purchased the very piece Morgan spoke of.

"Can you imagine what an exclusive Peggy Shipman Williams would go for?" a woman in the second row mused aloud to the women on her left and on her right.

Hannah took note of the high guesses bandied about by the woman and her friends for a few moments until Morgan clapped her hands.

"Attention!" Morgan clapped a second time. "May I have everyone's attention, please? I'm sorry, but I just checked my watch, and we've run a little longer than I intended. I've got to get to my shop now, as I'm supposed to open in ten minutes. So the January meeting of the Cave City Area Pottery Guild is now adjourned." Morgan waved her hand at the pottery items beside the podium. "Thank you to those of you who brought pieces to share today. Please be sure to pick them up before you head home."

Rising, Hannah grabbed her coat and made her way over to Pippa, who was also preparing to leave. "Hey, Pippa."

"Hi, Hannah." Pippa slid her arms into her coat and stuck her notebook and pen into an inside pocket. "I got absolutely no indication that anyone in this room knew about Peggy Shipman Williams's mystery piece, did you?"

"I didn't."

"They're absolutely right that Vanessa's mother could sell her dining set and make a *lot* of money."

Hannah glanced around and saw that Morgan must have left. She lowered her voice so only Pippa could hear. "Can I ask what you paid Morgan for the creamer?"

Pippa's cheeks flushed pink. "Reporters don't exactly make a ton of money. Especially at a paper the size of the *Chronicle*."

Hannah held up her hands. "Pippa, I'm not asking because I want to know how much you spent on my birthday gift. I'm asking because of what the piece is."

"If you're asking for the reason I think you're asking, she clearly didn't know what she had." Pippa lowered her voice too, so the few remaining lingerers couldn't hear. "Morgan only charged me twenty-five bucks."

"And you're confident she could've gotten more if she'd known?"

"Extremely confident. You heard how they priced things today." Pippa took out her phone, tapped the screen a few times, and handed it to Hannah. "Look."

Hannah followed Pippa's finger to the screen, pulled the phone closer to confirm what she was seeing, and then began scrolling through a shopping website. "Whoa. A set of candlesticks for five hundred dollars? And a butter dish for two hundred and fifty? How on earth?"

"Because they were made by Peggy Shipman Williams, that's why."

"Are you serious?" Hannah had known that Peggy's work was valuable, but it was one thing to know that and another to see it.

"Obviously, when she first sold them all those years ago, they didn't cost that much," Pippa explained. "But as time went on and her story made its way out into the world, her work became a piece of feel-good history. People want to get their hands on it, which means its value has increased." Pippa pointed Hannah to a link beside the candlesticks. "Click there."

When she did, the link opened a page containing the story of Peggy, a live-in cook for a wealthy family in Blackberry Valley, Kentucky, who taught herself the art of pottery with an old potter's wheel found in a barn and a kiln made by her husband. "I know all of this, and still, *wow*," she murmured as she handed the reporter's phone back to her.

"I know, right?" Pippa pocketed the device. "Which means that if Morgan had known that creamer was a Peggy Shipman Williams special edition, she could have asked for a whole lot more than twenty-five bucks, and she'd have gotten it. No doubt."

Hannah considered Pippa's words. "During the meeting, she certainly made it sound like she didn't know at the time."

"I'm telling you, Hannah, this story has *almost* everything I need for it to be a true contender for the journalism award in the weekly newspaper category. It's got a touch of history while still being very much current, it has an uplifting feature component, and it's intriguing." Pippa started toward the meeting room door with Hannah on her heels.

"What do you think would clinch the win?" Hannah asked.

"Right now, I have some great base hits with this story. But I need a home run to put me over the top."

Hannah hurried behind Pippa to the library's rear door and the clear path it offered to the parking lot. "Like finding the culprit with the sugar bowl?"

Her hand on the door, Pippa's gaze snapped back to Hannah. "What sugar bowl?"

Hannah mentally kicked herself. "The sugar bowl that went missing the same time as the creamer," she said reluctantly.

Pippa shook her head, mumbled something under her breath, and then pushed her way out into the cold January day. "I have to run, Hannah. Catch you around."

With the car still in park, Hannah turned on the heater and dug in her tote bag for her notebook. The compulsion to go through her list of possible suspects was too strong to put off until after work. She set the notebook on the center console and flipped to the appropriate page, her gaze immediately landing on the last of the three names on the page.

"Oh, Pippa, are you involved in this somehow?" She rested her head against the seat's back and stared up at the ceiling of her Subaru.

"Right now, I have some great base hits with this story. But the big finish is what will put me over the top."

"'Will,'" Hannah murmured. "She didn't say 'could.' She said 'will.'"

Parting company with the headrest, she went over her notes again as the possibility that Pippa was involved warred with the multiple reasons it simply wouldn't make sense…

Pippa hadn't grown up in Blackberry Valley. She had moved there after college when she'd secured a reporting job at the *Chronicle*.

The creamer and sugar bowl had been stolen from Rose Williams Lodge more than forty years ago, a good twenty years before Pippa was even born.

The surprise Pippa had displayed when she heard about the missing sugar bowl seemed genuine.

In order for the reporter to be involved, she would have had to know about the missing items, found them, planted one, and—no, it was too far-fetched.

Hannah traveled her gaze up to the top of the page and the first name on her list. Doug Bell.

"Your age brings some questions, but you're well-versed in local history. And your family had a direct connection to the Taylor Estate at the same time the pieces disappeared," she said. "You could be the culprit. You really could. But why give up the creamer now? That's the part that's tripping me up."

She looked at the dashboard clock and then started the car. "If it's you, Doug Bell, I will find out. One way or the other."

Chapter Twenty-Five

Hannah pushed through the double doors of the kitchen and approached the man moving between the counter and the grill, plating orders like the expert chef she knew him to be. "I'm pretty sure we've had half the Blackberry Valley population in here this evening," she said, stopping beside Jacob. "You holding up okay in here?"

He slid his spatula beneath a picturesque burger patty and shifted it onto an open bun waiting on a plate beside a mound of perfectly seasoned fries. "Please. This is child's play."

Hannah laughed. "Child's play, huh?"

"That's right." Jacob topped the burger with cream cheese, fried jalapenos, and raspberry-pepper jelly and hit the bell as he placed the plated food in the pickup window. "You could multiply this by ten, and I'd be good."

"Really?" she challenged, leaning against the counter at her back. "By ten, you say?"

Lifting his right eyebrow instead of his gaze, he returned to the grill and the strip steak sizzling to perfection between two more burger patties. "Okay, fine. Maybe five."

She laughed. "So you *are* a human being with human limitations. I've been questioning it for a while."

He pointed the spatula at himself. "Moi? How dare you insult me in such a way?"

Hannah rolled her eyes. “You’re the one who started with ten and then lowered it to five.”

He flipped the steak and transferred the two burgers onto their own waiting plates. “Fine, but can you blame me? It’s been nonstop in here all evening, and we still have”—he glanced at the clock on the far wall—“three more hours to go.”

“And then we get two days off. Thankfully.” She exchanged nods with Raquel as the server hurried into the kitchen and then back out with the Five Alarm Burger.

“I can’t say I’m not thrilled at that notion. I definitely am. But with that said, you and I both know how great this kind of business is. Especially on a chilly January night, when it would be so easy for people to stay home and eat a frozen pizza while watching something on TV.”

There was no denying the truth in his words or the smile they spread across her lips. “I know.”

“Your gut told you a place like the Hot Spot would do well in this town, and you were right.” He swept the steak off the grill and onto a clean plate. He snatched a pastry bag and piped a simple design of the evening’s special butter on top, which contained chives, garlic, horseradish, and cayenne pepper. “And my gut told me my evening’s special, the Brush Fire Steak, would be a hit, and I was right. I’ve made nearly two dozen since we opened.”

He set the steak, another Five Alarm Burger, a Rookie Meltdown, and a plate of Inferno Wings in the delivery window and hit the bell again.

“You’ve got good instincts. There’s no doubt about that.” Hannah crossed to the ready plates, grabbed two, and started for the door. Raquel ducked into the kitchen, secured the remaining plates, and followed her.

"I'll never let you forget you said that," Jacob called after her. "You know that, right?"

"I would expect nothing less from you, Jacob."

His laugh followed her into the dining room and over to table four where she stood by as Raquel set her own two plates down and then took the remaining ones from Hannah. "Thanks, Hannah."

"Of course. Enjoy, everyone." She left Raquel to her diners and headed for the hostess stand but stopped as her gaze fell, first on Dylan talking animatedly with a couple at the newly turned table six, and then on the now-familiar face that made up half of that couple.

She froze, taking in her server's easy smile as he talked with his favorite high school teacher, Doug Bell. Seated across the table from Doug was a pretty brunette, her eyes sparkling as she looked between Doug and their waiter, soaking up what even Hannah could see was a welcome conversation for both men. Soon, though, Dylan glanced over his shoulder at the tables behind him and then moved to take Doug and the woman's drink order, like the seasoned server he'd become.

Hannah intercepted Dylan. "Hey, I can take the drinks to table six while you get the bill for table seven."

He gave her a grateful smile. "Thanks. It's really cool to see Mr. Bell in here."

"I'm glad." Moments later, Hannah carried full glasses to table six. "Hi, Doug. Welcome to the Hot Spot." Hannah set one water glass in front of the brunette and one in front of the history teacher, her smile at the ready as recognition flared in his dark-colored eyes.

"Hello!" Doug turned to his companion and motioned to Hannah. "Cassie, this is Hannah Prentiss. She owns this place. Hannah, this is Cassie Donnelson, my beautiful fiancée."

Cassie's cheeks flushed as Hannah shook her hand. "Welcome to the Hot Spot, and congratulations to both of you," Hannah said. "How did you meet?"

"We went on a guided tour of Mammoth Cave on the same day," Cassie said, beaming at Doug. "And the rest, as they say, is history."

Hannah smiled. "Sounds to me like God had a plan for both of you that day."

"Without a doubt." Doug reached for Cassie's hand and entwined his fingers with hers. "God knew I needed someone special, and He sent me Cassie. She makes me want to be a better man, to do the right things rather than the comfortable, easy things."

"I'm glad to hear it." Tapping the table, she nodded at the couple. "Well, a warm welcome to both of you. I saw you speaking with Dylan a moment ago, and I know he'll take good care of you this evening."

With a last glance at Doug, Hannah continued on to the hostess stand and the waiting area beyond that finally showed signs of thinning out. There, she chatted with waiting guests, took a few reservations over the phone for the following weekend, fussed over a few pictures drawn by the Hot Spot's smallest guests, and tried her best to keep her thoughts on work rather than the male occupant of table six. But it was hard.

Doug Bell's grandfather had been ousted from his job at the Taylor Estate by Vanessa's grandfather, Ray Williams.

Because of that single event, Doug's father had been unable to go to college, a loss that still rankled Doug to this day, based on the anger Hannah had picked up on his face the previous afternoon.

And while Doug was too young to have taken the pottery pieces Peggy Shipman Williams had made for her daughter, might his late father or his late grandfather have done so in an act of anger he'd chosen to cover for?

It was her leading theory for the history teacher thus far. She mulled over its merits as she straightened the stack of menus at her elbow, her gaze returning to Doug's table for what must have been the hundredth time that evening.

"God knew I needed someone special, and He sent me Cassie. She makes me want to be a better man, to do the right things rather than the comfortable, easy things."

She paused her hand on top of the stack at the memory of Doug's words. Was that it? Was that why the creamer had suddenly reappeared after forty years, and in a place where Doug had taken a class? Because he was trying to right a wrong?

"Hannah? You okay?"

Shaking the possibility from her head, she turned back to Elaine, managing a smile and a nod for the hostess as she did. "I am. Better than okay, actually. Why?"

"I thought I heard you gasp."

Had she? She didn't recall doing so, but she'd been so lost in thought that she supposed it was possible.

"I'm fine, Elaine." She dropped her hand to her side and gestured to the dining room. "I'm going to check in with the guests who are finishing up their meals or waiting for their checks. Keep up the good work. We're nearing the home stretch."

Elaine grinned. "And two days off."

"Indeed." Hannah scanned the dining room and spotted customers at two tables pushing their empty plates to the side. She spent a moment with each couple to inquire about their meals and invite them to come back. Then she made as casual a beeline as possible to Doug and Cassie's table. "Is Dylan taking good care of you this evening?"

Cassie nodded emphatically. "Very much so. Did you know he used to be Doug's student?"

"I did know that," Hannah confirmed. "He told me that Doug was his favorite teacher in high school."

Beaming, Cassie lifted her water glass toward her fiancé in a toast. "Why am I not surprised to hear that?"

"Dylan was—*is*—a good kid," Doug said. "He really liked history."

Hannah was grateful to see the guests at the tables around her were enjoying their food and didn't seem to need anything. "I bet he would've enjoyed the in-depth Blackberry Valley unit you're doing this year."

Doug smiled. "I think you're right about that. He might have even joined me for the pottery class at the Clay House to better understand the cook and the lasting name she went on to make for herself beyond the confines of the Taylor Estate kitchen."

Cassie leaned forward, her gaze intent on Doug. "Is that the woman who made those bowls you have? The ones I really like? The ones with *PWS* on the bottom?"

Doug took a sip of water from his glass and then smiled at his fiancée across its rim. "Close. *PSW*. Peggy Shipman Williams."

"You have some of her work?" Hannah asked.

Doug let go of his glass and took Cassie's hand. "I do, actually. A former student's grandmother bought it from Peggy herself at a local flea market, back when Peggy had just started with her pottery. She gave it to me before she died, saying I'd appreciate it more than her family, who preferred new, more modern things."

"How sweet," Hannah said, trying to hide the excitement building in her.

"I was thrilled, of course, both as a lover of history and as someone who believes that the more tactile experience a student can have, the more they'll retain. Those bowls make me feel more connected to the artist, as if I knew her myself and understood how and why she created the way she did. I'm also using them as visual aids during our local history unit."

"Do you have any other pieces Peggy made?" Hannah asked.

"No, unfortunately. But that's okay. The bowls give the students a good window into her self-taught skill just fine."

She breathed in, held it to a silent count of ten, and then released it. She squared her shoulders. "Did you know that *PSW* isn't on the bottom of every piece Peggy made?"

If there was a reaction to her question, she couldn't be sure. Dylan appeared beside the table at that exact moment with a plate in each hand. Stepping to the side to afford him easier access to the couple, she kept an eye on Doug as he took an extended period of time to size up his Five Alarm Burger and Cassie's Underburn Salad. She found herself wondering whether he always examined food so closely, or whether he was giving himself time to get his response under control.

She waited as Dylan asked if Doug and Cassie needed anything else, refilled their water glasses, and told them he'd check back soon, before reclaiming her spot at the side of the table.

"That burger is one of the most popular items on the menu," she said.

Doug took a bite, chewed, and swallowed. "I can see why. It's awesome."

"I'm glad you like it." Oh, how she wanted to keep talking, to see if her internal radar had begun to ping for a reason, but overstaying her time with guests was not the way she did business. "Well, I hope you enjoy your—"

"Would she have used a rose instead of her initials?" he asked across the top of his burger.

She didn't mean to gasp, but she didn't have a choice.

Before she could lasso her thoughts enough to do more than nod, the teacher continued. "Yeah, I know about that."

"Did you know that a piece from the set she etched with a rose was stolen more than forty years ago?"

His jaw tightened around the bite of burger in his mouth, but he said nothing.

"And that it showed up out of the blue this past weekend?" she asked.

He stopped chewing and swallowed. "It showed up? How? Where?"

"As a gift I was given for my birthday."

"A gift?" he echoed. "From *who*?"

"Pippa Nelson."

"The reporter from the *Chronicle*?"

Doug slowly set his burger on his plate and then looked back up at Hannah. "How did *she* get it?"

"She bought it at the Clay House."

His eyes widened. "For how much? It must be worth a fortune."

"Perhaps, but she paid twenty-five dollars."

Releasing a long, low whistle, he plucked a fry from his plate. "Clearly Morgan didn't know what she had if she sold it for so little."

Hannah dove in with another question. "How did you know about the rose? Had you heard about it? Maybe seen it for yourself?"

"Maybe."

She waited for him to elaborate. When he didn't, she searched her mind for a way to ask for the story, but he spoke again before she could come up with one.

"Would you consider letting me show the creamer to my class when we get to that part of our unit at the end of next week?" he asked, midway through a second fry.

"I would if I still had it," Hannah replied. "But I don't. I turned it over to its rightful owner the moment I was told what it was. Or, rather, I turned it over to the rightful owner's daughter. Actually, you may have had her in the classroom, depending on how long you've been teaching at the high school."

"This will be Doug's tenth year. Isn't that right, sweetheart?" Cassie interjected between bites of her salad.

"That's right."

Before Hannah could do the math, a familiar voice grabbed her attention. “Hannah?”

She turned to find Raquel behind her. “What’s up?”

“I’m sorry to interrupt, but the woman at table seven wants to speak to you about having us possibly host an event in February.”

“Of course. I’m coming.” She faced Doug and Cassie again, ready to excuse herself, but swallowed her words when she saw the history teacher sagging in apparent relief. Mustering her best smile and lightest tone, Hannah said, “Enjoy the rest of your evening together. I hope to see you back again soon.”

As she followed Raquel to table seven, Hannah wondered which part of their conversation Doug had been dreading so much that the opportunity for it to be cut off had given him such a strong reaction.

Chapter Twenty-Six

The moment the last of her staff left the Hot Spot, Hannah engaged the lock on the side door and immediately texted Lacy. STILL AWAKE?

Seconds turned to minutes as she waited for a reply, but none came. Sighing, she climbed the stairs to her apartment, mentally revisiting the troubling realization she'd had halfway through the restaurant's normal closing tasks. How she'd missed it in real time, she wasn't sure, but now that she remembered, she simply couldn't shake what it likely meant.

As she stepped through the door, her phone rang, making her jump. Glancing down at the screen and the face that smiled back at her, she swiped to accept the call and then held the device to her ear.

"Lacy?" She kicked off her shoes just inside her small entryway and made a beeline for her couch. "I know it's super late, but thank you so much for calling me."

"Neil and I were less than ten pieces away from completing my latest puzzle when your text came in. We finished it up as quickly as we could, and now I'm all yours."

"Thank you."

"So are they engaged?" Lacy asked.

Hannah's mind went blank. She hadn't the foggiest idea what Lacy meant. Could she know about Doug and Cassie? It was a small town after all. "Who?"

"Marshall and Raquel. That was what the surprise date this morning turned out to be, right?"

"No. It's too soon for that. I think they're both happy with where things are right now."

"Hey, when you know, you know. I knew I was going to marry Neil after our first date," Lacy said.

"Yes, but he didn't propose until much later," Hannah reminded her.

"Trivia," Lacy replied. "So what was Marshall's surprise date?"

"Ice skating."

"Oh, that's sweet. A classic, for sure."

"It was, and she glowed the whole night."

"Isn't that Raquel's normal state?" Lacy asked, her grin audible.

"It is, but even more so than usual."

"They're cute together," Lacy said. "And, as I said before, kind of like you and Liam."

The mention of his name reminded Hannah of the text he'd sent her as the last diner was leaving. She'd totally forgotten to answer it.

"Hannah? Are you still there?" Lacy asked.

Propping her calves on the corner of the coffee table, Hannah kneaded at the growing headache above her left eyebrow. "Lacy, I have to tell you something."

The carefree lilt in Lacy's voice vanished. "Did something happen between the two of you? Are you all right? What happened?"

"Nothing, other than me forgetting to answer a text from him tonight."

"Then answer him now, Hannah. I'll wait."

She kneaded the spot harder. "Lacy, he knew it was a creamer."

"You lost me."

"He knew it was a creamer that Pippa gave me for my birthday," she said, finally lowering her hand to her lap. "How could he know that?"

"Surely you *told* him, right?" Lacy took a sip of something. "I mean, I don't know why you wouldn't have. You are dating, you know."

"Oh, sorry. I'm not talking about Liam." Swinging her feet back to the ground, Hannah pushed off the couch and wandered into the kitchen, just to be moving. "I'm talking about Doug Bell."

Lacy whistled. "He's on your list."

"He is," Hannah said.

"Tell me what happened."

Hannah opened the cabinet where she kept her drinking glasses, stared up at them, and then closed the door without taking one. She knew she was talking more to herself than to Lacy, but she and her best friend often used each other as sounding boards. "It didn't hit me until after he and Cassie left. I don't know why I didn't pick up on it when he first said it. In retrospect, it was so obvious."

"I take it Doug and Cassie were at the Hot Spot this evening?"

She made her way back to her living room and the window that overlooked the town's main street. The sidewalk below was dotted with glowing street lamps, a sight that normally brought her a sense of peace after a long day of work. Tonight, she barely noticed. "They were. I tried to get him to say something that would either keep him on my list or give me a reason to remove him. So I threw out the fact I'd gotten an exclusive piece of Peggy Shipman Williams's pottery as a gift, and that it had been missing for decades."

"Okay," Lacy prompted.

Hannah crossed back to the couch and sat down. "I never said what the piece was."

"But he said it was a creamer?" Lacy asked. "That's interesting."

"I guess that because *I* knew what it was, it didn't dawn on me until much later that I hadn't said as much out loud to him. But he knew, Lacy. Without my telling him. He also knew that Peggy put a rose on the bottom of it instead of her initials."

Silence filled her ear for a few moments before Lacy finally spoke again. "The fact that he knew those things certainly warrants further investigation, but I don't think that makes him a slam dunk as our culprit."

"You don't?" Hannah asked, tightening her grip on the phone.

"Not having kids and therefore a connection to the schools, I'll admit I don't know Doug all that well. But his age still throws up a major obstacle, doesn't it?"

"I know where you're going with this," Hannah said, returning her fingers to her head to knead her temple. "After we talked about it this morning, that was my main hesitation. But from what I've been able to gather from my dad, my uncle, and Doug himself, there may be some bad blood between Doug's grandfather and Vanessa's grandfather, aka Peggy's husband."

"And what? You think Doug's grandfather took it and passed it on to Doug?"

"Or maybe Doug's father," Hannah mused aloud.

"Why his father?"

"Because when Doug's grandfather lost his job in favor of Vanessa's grandfather, Doug's father was prevented from going to college."

"So you're thinking either his grandfather or his father stole the creamer as an act of revenge?"

"I am."

"But his grandfather died a long time ago."

Hannah stilled her fingers against her temples. "Okay, and his father?"

"I don't know his family well, but I sort of remember something about his parents moving out of state at some point."

Hannah sat with Lacy's words, weighing and processing them for a moment before she dropped her hand back to her lap and her head against the couch. "But Doug took a class in the very room where the creamer appeared. I can't ignore that."

"And you shouldn't," Lacy said.

Hannah stared up at the ceiling. "Doug told me Cassie makes him want to be a better man. Someone who does the right thing rather than the easy thing."

"And perhaps that propelled him to give back the creamer his grandfather or father took," Lacy suggested. "Or at least put it where it might find its way back to the rightful owner."

"That would make sense, right?"

"It could." Lacy yawned. "And that would be great, because I don't like Pippa being on the list."

Hannah snapped her head upright. "Speaking of Pippa, she now knows there's one more piece still missing and that it's a sugar bowl."

"How does she know that?"

"I told her," Hannah said with a groan. Pippa's words echoed in her mind again.

"Right now, I have some great base hits with this story. But I need a home run to put me over the top."

She surged to her feet, pacing between the window and the couch. "But what if she already knew about the sugar bowl? What if she has it? What if she's just waiting for the right time to "find" it and then write her story? Pretending to be the one to track down the missing sugar bowl could be the grand finish Pippa needs to have an entry worthy of that big award she's after. The creamer reappearing gives her the history and the feel-good aspects. Finding the last missing piece would bring the story home."

"But how would she have come across either of the pottery pieces, Hannah? She's in her early twenties, and she came here from some place in Missouri specifically to take the *Chronicle* job, right? As far as I know, she couldn't have known about this story before it more or less fell into her lap."

Hannah groaned. She couldn't argue with that logic.

"And I told you why I think she took the pottery class."

"Because she has a thing for Doug Bell's fiancée's brother," Hannah murmured. "Which sounds pretty convoluted to me."

"Maybe. But next time you see her, say the name Derrick Donnelson. I suspect you won't think it's so convoluted once you do."

Hannah sat with Lacy's words in silence, her disappointment growing.

"Hey, you still there?"

"I am. I just keep feeling like I've got almost all the puzzle pieces on this, and then I'm not sure I do."

"You'll figure it out. I have faith in you."

Hannah cracked a smile. "Wait. Not *we'll* figure it out?"

"It's *we* in spirit, if not in execution," Lacy said, her voice showing signs of fatigue.

"Did you eat today like you promised me?"

"I did. A little, anyway. And I feel better, for the most part. Mostly it's just occasional wooziness now."

Hannah headed back into the kitchen, this time helping herself to a glass and some water from the tap. "That'll probably go away as you get more food in you."

"I'm sure you're right."

"Should I let you get some sleep?" Hannah asked between sips. "So you can kick whatever this is, once and for all?"

"That would be the responsible thing. But my inner Bess Marvin wants to stay up and help Nancy Drew a little more."

Hannah laughed. "Nancy isn't doing so hot with this case, I'm afraid."

"You'll figure it out." A change in the pitch of Lacy's voice let Hannah know she was on the move. "One question first?"

"Of course. Shoot."

"I know why the pottery shop owner is on your list. And I know Pippa is on your list because she's the one who gave you the creamer in the first place."

Hannah lowered her water glass to the counter. "Pippa is also on it because she was one of the three people who were in the room where Morgan says the creamer suddenly appeared. She and Doug both were."

"And the third person?" Lacy asked.

"Someone who was—or is—in the area to visit family."

"Do you remember the name?"

"I couldn't read the full name," Hannah said. "The first name started with *S*. Last name was Winfield."

"I don't know anyone by the name Winfield. Maybe ask the pottery shop owner for the first name so you can do a search?"

"She wouldn't give me the names of the people in the class when I asked her the other day."

"Yet you have them," Lacy said, mid-yawn.

"Only because of a happy accident."

"You'll find a way to get the name. If they're even still in the area." Lacy yawned again. "I'm sorry. I think you're right, Hannah. I need to get some sleep. Maybe it'll take me over the last hump of whatever I've been fighting."

"Absolutely. Thanks for letting me talk through this stuff."

"I'm not sure how much good I did."

Hannah leaned against the counter and took another sip of water. "Talking to you always helps, Bess."

Lacy laughed. "I'm glad. Good night, Nancy."

"Good night, Lacy. I hope you're back to one hundred percent in the morning."

The call over, Hannah spotted a new text message from Vanessa on her screen.

I KNOW YOU PROBABLY WON'T SEE THIS UNTIL MORNING. BUT MAMA WOULD LOVE TO HAVE YOU OVER FOR LUNCH AFTER CHURCH

TOMORROW AS HER WAY OF SAYING THANK YOU. PLEASE SAY YOU'LL COME? SHE'S MAKING HER BISCUITS.

She'd actually been thinking it might be time for her to speak with Vanessa's mother face-to-face. I'D LOVE TO. THANK YOU.

Maybe Rose would be able to provide the rest of the puzzle pieces she was missing.

Chapter Twenty-Seven

Hannah fell in line behind her fellow congregants as they filed out of the sanctuary, down the hall, and into Grace Community Church's multipurpose room, drawn to the promise of hot coffee, doughnuts, and fellowship with one another. The once-a-month post-service gathering, sponsored by the men's group, had become special to many of Grace's members, including Hannah.

Yes, she saw everyone at church every Sunday, but having a reason for people not to hurry out to their cars after service gave an opportunity to catch up with one another's lives, to celebrate blessings, and to seek prayers for any trials that were being faced. The coffee and doughnuts were an added bonus.

"I got you a doughnut." Handing it to her on a napkin, Dad gestured to Uncle Gordon, who stood in front of a window on the far side of the paneled room. "And your uncle has an extra cup of coffee with your name on it."

"You guys are the best. Always watching out for me." She took the doughnut, planted a kiss on her father's cheek, and walked with him to join Uncle Gordon.

"I'm sorry Liam couldn't stay," Dad said. "I had a brief conversation with him when he first walked into church, but not enough to really hear how he's doing."

"One of his guys is under the weather, so they're short-staffed. He has to be at the station." Hannah bit into the doughnut, relished its welcome flavor, and then chased it down with a sip of coffee. "It's been that way a lot for us this week. We got to talk at the station one morning, and we took a walk one evening after work, but mostly it's been short texts, if that."

Uncle Gordon gave his coffee cup a swirl and then took a sip. "Remember when our lives were busy like that, Gabriel?"

"My life is still busy," her father pointed out.

"Walking Zeus three times a day and doing odd jobs here at the church a few days a week doesn't come close to the kind of busy you once were."

Dad grinned. "I suppose you're right, but I'm good with that. Though I wouldn't mind adding a few specific things to my plate."

She peered at her father across the top of her coffee cup. "Such as?"

"Having you come to the house for lunch today, for starters."

She gently blew off her coffee's rising steam. "I'm sorry, Dad, but I can't today. I have lunch plans this afternoon."

"No apology needed, sweetheart." Dad leaned against the wall at his back. "How about a big meal next Sunday? With Drew and Allison and the kids. And when we're done eating, we could sit in the family room together and watch some of the old home movies like we talked about."

"That sounds great, Dad. You can count me in."

"And Liam too."

She made a face. "I know he's game, but I'm not super thrilled with the idea of him getting a bird's-eye view of my many awkward phases."

"You had no awkward phases," Dad protested.

"Spoken like a true father." She took a few more sips of her coffee, finished her doughnut, and then said, "Can I ask you both a question?"

"Of course," the men said in unison.

"Remember the other night when you told me about the mishaps that happened on the Taylor Estate after Ray Williams was hired?" At their nods, she continued, her mouth struggling to keep up with the questions rapidly assembling in her thoughts. "Was there anything else that happened around that same time that people thought was suspicious?"

"You mean besides the stable addition that caught fire within twenty-four hours of Ray finishing its construction?" Dad asked. "And the trees that line the property's entrance getting chopped down not once, but twice within a matter of a few weeks? And the tires being slashed on estate vehicles?"

Hannah nodded.

"Not that I recall." Her father looked at his older brother. "Gordon? Do you remember anything else?"

"I don't."

"You said there had been rumors about who may have been behind the fire at the stable, the slashing of the tires, and the chopping down of the trees," she said.

"There were."

"Were specific names ever given?"

"Just one." Uncle Gordon picked up his bear claw from its resting place on the window ledge and set his coffee cup where it had been.

"But the police cleared that person of suspicion?" she asked.

Uncle Gordon and Dad exchanged glances. "They said he had alibis for each incident, and that those alibis checked out. But there were no more incidents after they questioned him."

Hannah glanced around to make sure no one appeared to be listening to their conversation. The last thing she wanted was to start ugly rumors without evidence. "Did this rumored suspect have the last name Bell?"

The brothers' left eyebrows arched in exactly the same way. "Actually, yes he did," Uncle Gordon said.

"And just to confirm, he's the man Ray Williams replaced at the Taylor Estate, correct?" Hannah asked.

Her father nodded at Hannah and then looked back at his brother. "Out of the blue, right, Gordon?"

"It was," Uncle Gordon said. "That was hard enough. But then everyone in town thought he started a fire and vandalized trees and cars as some sort of retaliation. He couldn't get work anywhere in Blackberry Valley after that."

She stared at her uncle. "But why would that be if he had alibis for all of it?"

"Blackberry Valley was an even smaller town back then."

"Which means?" she prodded.

Her father's sigh stole her attention. "Sometimes, a rumor can gain so much traction that even the truth is powerless to stop it."

She knew Dad was right. She'd seen evidence of it her whole life, starting on the playground in elementary school. It was sad that even if the official account cleared someone, that didn't always hold water in the court of public opinion.

Uncle Gordon took a bite of his doughnut and chewed thoughtfully for a moment. "Proverbs 12:22. 'The Lord detests lying lips, but he delights in people who are trustworthy.'"

She considered the verse against everything she'd just learned and found it leading her to one final question. "Do you think a rumor can gain so much traction that it spills into the next generation? Or even the one after that?"

"In a city or large town that sees a lot of turnover, probably not so much," Dad said. "But in a town like Blackberry Valley, where so many of the current residents have family roots here? Yes, sadly, I think it can—and probably has in many cases."

She drained the last of her coffee then collected their trash. "I'd better get going. I love you both. I'll see you next Sunday for church and for family movie night, if not before."

"With Liam," her father reminded her.

She smiled. "*If* it works with his schedule, Dad. He is a busy guy, remember?"

"Oh, it works with his schedule."

"How do you know?"

Dad grinned at her. "I already asked him."

Chapter Twenty-Eight

Hannah plugged Rose's address into her car's navigation app and slowly pulled out of her parking spot at Grace Community Church. Once on the main road, she placed a hands-free call to someone who'd been notably absent from the church service.

On the third ring, instead of the voice she expected to hear, she heard a masculine voice say, "Good morning, Hannah."

"Oh, hi, Neil." She stopped at the traffic light. "I missed you and Lacy this morning at church. Is everything okay?"

He exhaled into the phone, the sound echoing around her as the light turned green and she accelerated. "She was more like herself last night, energy-wise. But then when she woke up this morning, she felt horrendous again. She just can't seem to shake whatever this bug is."

"And I take it, if you're answering her phone, nothing has changed?"

"She's sleeping. Has been since about nine o'clock, when her stomach finally settled enough that she got back in bed."

A sense of unease traveled down Hannah's spine, and she shivered despite the heat blowing on her from the dash vents. "It's nearly noon. Lacy doesn't get back in bed, and she never sleeps this late."

"It's bothering me as well, but I'm trying to let her rest as much as possible. Though she's not going to be happy with me when she wakes up and realizes we didn't go to church."

"I just hope when she wakes up she feels better." Hannah took a right at a stop sign as her GPS directed. "And you stayed home to look after her, as you should. Besides, she doesn't want to expose anybody else to what she's got."

Neil gave a strangled laugh. "I might need you to tell her that. I'm in for an earful when she wakes up as it is."

"Happily." Hannah slowed for a curve in the road. "I'm heading to the north side of town right now to have lunch with Vanessa and her mom, but I can come out to the farm afterward if you need me to do anything in the barn."

"I appreciate it, Hannah, but Lacy's mom has been a real godsend these past few days. She feels horrible that she got Lacy sick, and she says the least she can do is cover for her daughter until she's back on her feet."

"It's not like she did it on purpose," Hannah said.

"Exactly what I've told her at least half a dozen times over the past few days."

"And you're not showing symptoms?" she asked. "No upset stomach, no lack of appetite, chills, or dizziness?"

"Not a thing."

She braked for a stop sign then proceeded through the intersection. "That's a blessing. But do you think maybe it's time to take Lacy to a doctor to get her checked out? I don't like how long she's felt this way and that every time she starts to feel better, she takes a turn for the worse again."

"If she's still feeling bad tomorrow, I'll get her examined," Neil said. "Under protest, I'm sure. She's still insisting she's fine."

"No doubt. I'm off tomorrow, so if you need anything—an extra pair of hands with the animals, to stand in for you at the bookshop, or to help you force Lacy into the car—give me a shout, okay?"

"I think we'll be fine, Hannah, but I'll let you know if that changes. Thank you." His voice held its usual kindness, but she could also hear the concern he felt for his wife.

"Thank you for keeping me up to date."

"Have fun at your lunch. Please extend a hello to Vanessa and her mom from Lacy and me, okay?"

She took a right onto Rose's street. "I absolutely will. And when Lacy wakes up, tell her I'm praying for her. And that I said she's not allowed to scold you for skipping church this morning."

"I will, not that she listens to either of us about what she is and isn't allowed to do." Neil's chuckle sounded less strained this time, but not by much. "Thanks, Hannah."

"Of course. Bye, Neil." With a push of a button on her steering wheel, she ended the call as she slowed to a stop in front of a modest yet attractive redbrick one-story house with a pair of rockers on the front porch. She cut the engine, gathered her purse, and climbed out of the Subaru.

As she started up the walk, the front door opened, and Vanessa came out and waved. "Hi, Hannah. You found us."

Hannah smiled and hurried the rest of the way up onto the porch. "I did. And I'm so happy to be here. Thank you for the invite. I've been looking forward to trying those biscuits since you first mentioned them to me."

Vanessa held the door open for Hannah to enter the house. "Mama is beside herself with joy that you're here." She cupped a hand around her mouth and stage-whispered, “Fair warning—she’s made a lot of food. A lot. Like, I cannot emphasize how much.”

“I own a restaurant, remember?” Hannah said, laughing. “I like food.”

“True, but I have a feeling you don’t understand what I mean by a *lot*. It’s truly excessive.” Vanessa pushed the door closed and then linked arms with Hannah. “Let’s go. Mama’s in the kitchen.”

Together, they made their way to the end of the hallway and into the kitchen, where Rose was bustling between the stovetop, the oven, and the refrigerator. She looked up for just a moment, long enough to say, “Hannah! I’m thrilled you’ve come.”

Hannah took in the delicious smells coming from the pots on the stove and whatever was in the oven. “And I’m so glad to be here and finally get to meet you. Thank you for inviting me.”

“Vanessa has spoken of you often,” Rose said. “So I thought it was time we got together.” She opened the oven door and used an instant-read thermometer to check the roast. “We have a little time before this is ready, so why don’t we sit for a few minutes?” She pulled a chair out from the small kitchen table, sat down, and said, “I remember seeing you around town when you were a child, but my, how you’ve grown up.”

Hannah grinned and sat down across from her. “I have. I’ve heard it’s mostly unavoidable.”

Rose laughed and then said, “Vanessa is really enjoying the lunch group every month.”

“We have a good time,” Hannah said, glancing over at Vanessa, who leaned against the doorframe.

Rose rested her hand on Hannah’s. “I can’t begin to tell you how shocked I was—still am, actually—at seeing the creamer my mother made for me after all these years. It was like a hello from her after so long without her."

"I know what you mean," Hannah said. "I lost my mother almost nine years ago. But when I hear a song she liked or see one of her beloved flowers blooming at my father's house, it's like a little hello from her."

Vanessa straightened. "Mama, I'm going to finish setting the table while you and Hannah visit. Is there anything else you need me to do?"

"Thank you, sweetheart." Rose pointed to a bookcase that held mostly cookbooks. "Would you hand me that box, please?"

"Of course." Vanessa crossed to the bookcase and retrieved a cardboard box from its bottom shelf. She handed it to Rose then turned to Hannah. "Can I get you something to drink?"

Hannah smiled up at her friend. "No, thank you, Vanessa. I'm fine for now."

And then her friend was gone, leaving Hannah alone with Rose, who carefully sifted through a stack of black-and-white photographs.

"These are my parents," Rose said, holding a picture out for Hannah to see. "Ray and Peggy Williams."

Hannah took the photograph and studied it, noting the facial similarities her friend shared with both Rose and her grandmother. "I see Vanessa in both you and your mom."

"She has my daddy's chin." Rose took back the picture, placed it inside the box again, and handed Hannah another one. "This was the house where I grew up. It was small, but it was filled with a lot of love. It was on the Taylor Estate, and I remember the sun that used to greet me through the living room window every morning when I woke up. That, and my daddy's whistling."

"This is the cottage that came with your mother's job on the estate?" Hannah asked, looking from the photograph, to Rose, and back again.

"It is. Came with her being the cook."

Hannah looked again at the simple structure framed by flowering bushes and a smattering of pole-mounted birdhouses. "You slept in the living room?"

Rose nodded. "I did. But Mama made sure I had a chest to keep my things in, so I always felt as if I had a real place of my own. Tess and I played outside a lot, but we had fun inside too. We'd sit at the kitchen table and draw, paint, or make yarn dolls and houses for them to live in."

"Is Tess your sister?" Hannah asked, handing the picture back to Rose.

Rose swapped it with another photo from the box, this one showing two young girls around ten years old. "It felt like she was then, and for probably around eight more years after that picture was taken."

"So Tess was a friend?"

"*Was*, yes. An unlikely one, on account of her being the daughter of my mother's employer."

"Antoinette's daughter?" Hannah asked. "Theresa?"

"She was Tess to me." Rose leaned toward Hannah to get another look at the picture. "That's one of the beautiful things about children, isn't it? Left to their own devices, they don't really see the trivia of circumstances. They just see someone about their own age who likes to play the same way they do."

Hannah gave the picture back to Rose as the woman continued. "The immediate surroundings in which we grew up were like night and day. My bed was a couch, my bedroom my family's living room. Tess's bedroom was almost as big as our entire house. She had every possible *thing* she could want—money, the big fancy house, and the best clothes. I grew up without any of those things. Yet, even then, I wouldn't have traded places with her for a moment because *my* home bubbled over with the kind of love that money and status can't buy."

"Do you still talk to Tess?"

Rose closed her eyes momentarily on an inhale and slowly shook her head. "No."

"Why not?"

"I guess she finally saw the differences in our worlds. I tried to keep up our friendship. When I'd call and leave a message for her, she wouldn't call back. When I came back here to visit, if I'd see her out and about, she'd walk the other way. Eventually, I took the hint and learned to respect the fact she didn't want me in her life anymore."

Rose pulled another picture from the box and handed it to her—this one of a young woman in her late teens or early twenties, her eyes warm yet determined. A tattered suitcase and a cardboard box were at her feet. "This is you," Hannah said.

"It is. I'd just turned eighteen," Rose explained. "I'd gotten a job as a seamstress a few towns over, and I was moving out of Mama and Daddy's home. I was excited and sad all at the same time. Excited because I was earning my own way. Sad because I was leaving home, a place where I'd always felt loved and accepted."

Hannah drank in Rose's young face. "I felt like that when I left home too. Only I left to attend college on the West Coast and then opted to stay there for ten years after I graduated. I loved the experience, but it really hurt to leave my family behind."

"It's always scary, but it's always worth it." Rose pointed Hannah's attention to the box on the ground beside her eighteen-year-old self. "The dining set Mama made for me was in that box, each piece carefully wrapped in newspaper and then straw. Mama thought it was overkill, but I didn't. I treasured every one of those dishes."

"Did you know at the point this picture was taken that the creamer and sugar bowl were missing?" Hannah asked.

"No."

"So it was when you had them in your new place that they disappeared?"

Rose took the picture from Hannah, studied it, and then placed it back inside the box. "No, that was when I realized they were gone. The first thing I did when I stepped inside my own little place was unpack that dining set. I didn't even take off my coat first."

"How did you get from your parents' house to your new place?" Hannah asked, her curiosity rising.

"Since Daddy had been working for the Taylors for years at that point, Mrs. Taylor let him use one of the estate trucks. We were so grateful that she hired him," Rose said. "Before that, Daddy would walk to town every morning and wait in front of the firehouse until someone hired him to do something that day. He could do anything he put his mind to, but that's why Mama's job, and the fact it came with our cottage, was so important for us when I was growing up. And it's why her teaching herself to make pottery—and how good she was at it—also mattered the way it did."

Doug's grandfather had been ousted from his job in favor of Ray Williams years before Peggy gave the pottery set to her daughter. Any mishaps that happened in the first few months following his firing would have been long over by the time Rose was eighteen, so it seemed likely no one would have thought to suspect Doug's grandfather of the thefts.

"Are you okay, Hannah? You look troubled all of a sudden."

Shaking herself back into the moment, she mustered a smile for Vanessa's mother. "No, I'm fine. Was anyone in the truck besides the two—or three—of you that day?"

"The day I moved? No, it was just Daddy and me. Mrs. Taylor had guests for the afternoon, and Mama had to go to the main house to prepare snacks for them."

"And did you stop anywhere on the way to your new place?" Hannah had assumed the sugar bowl and creamer had disappeared from the cottage or from Rose's new residence. However, if Ray and Rose had stopped for gas or lunch, perhaps someone had taken the pieces out of the truck.

But Rose quickly shot down that idea. "No, we went straight over." She seemed to think for a moment. "If you're considering the idea that someone took the pieces between my parents' house and mine, I can tell you that couldn't have happened. I taped the box shut before we left, and it hadn't been opened when I got to my new place."

Rose rummaged through a few more pictures and held another one out to Hannah. "This was taken when Mama first gave me the set, at a little going-away celebration Mrs. Taylor let Mama have for me in the big house."

Hannah studied the image. In it, young Rose sat in a grand room, at the head of a table topped with a cream-colored cloth. Beside her left elbow was what was left of a cake that had found its way onto a total of five plates. In her hands was a twilight-blue glazed dish rimmed in brown, and tears of joy trickled down her face.

"I'll never forget seeing that first dish. I was overjoyed at the notion I'd be able to eat my supper on a plate my mama had made for me. But then there was another dish, and another dish, and another dish, followed by bowls and a pair of candlesticks, a butter dish, a teapot, the creamer, the sugar bowl—all of it." Rose cleared her throat and blinked rapidly a few times. "Between her work for the Taylors and looking after Daddy and me, Mama didn't have a lot of time for her pottery. When I saw the huge set she'd made for me, I knew it had been at the cost of making the pieces she could have sold in town. It was a huge sacrifice for her to make that set for me."

"I'm sure she didn't consider it a sacrifice at all. She loved you," Hannah said, her throat suddenly tight. There truly was nothing like a mother's love.

"They both did." Running the tip of her finger across the plate she held in the picture, Rose took a deep breath. "And when I turned that first dish over and saw the tiny rose she'd put where her initials always went, I just lost it right then and there, soaking Mrs. Taylor's fancy napkin with my tears."

Hannah studied the picture, taking in every detail she could make out before handing it back to Rose. "How long after this did you move out?"

"They had that little party for me on a Sunday afternoon. Daddy drove me and my things to my place the next Saturday."

"So about a week," Hannah mused. "When did you wrap it all and put it in that box you showed me in the picture?"

"I think I did that the day after the party. I wanted to still be able to look at the pieces, though, so I didn't seal the box until the night before we left. I spent as much time with Mama as I could that last week, helping her in her garden, or in the outbuilding where she made her pottery, or up at the main house when she was cooking or baking."

Hannah packed away the information even as her thoughts actively picked through it. "What order did you wrap the pieces in? Do you remember? Were the sugar bowl and creamer at the top of the box?"

"I don't remember. If I were to pack the same box today, I would put them on top, since I'd put the plates on the bottom." She shrugged. "But I was eighteen, so who knows how I did it? All I know is I wrapped them the best I could to keep them safe." Rose's eyes suddenly filled with tears. "So much for that idea. I didn't keep them safe at all."

"Their disappearance is not on you, Rose," Hannah said. "It's on whoever took them all those years ago."

A comfortable silence fell between them, broken only by the sounds of Vanessa moving around in the dining room.

At last, Rose lowered the box to the floor and turned her attention back to Hannah. "I'll probably never know where Mama's creamer has been all these years, or why it's suddenly reappeared now. But I'm so glad it has, and I thank you for making that happen, Hannah."

Pivoting in her chair, Hannah took hold of Rose's closest hand and gently squeezed. "I don't know when or how, but I'm going to get you those answers, Rose. One way or the other, I'm going to find out what happened to your creamer."

Chapter Twenty-Nine

Stepping off the porch and onto the walkway, Hannah cast a sidelong look at Vanessa. "Does your mother feed you like that *every* day?"

"If left to her own devices, the answer to that question would be yes." Vanessa slowed her pace, her lips twitching with a smile. "But I've told her if she wants to see me meet Mr. Right, get married, and give her some grandchildren, she can only feed me like that once or twice a week. Otherwise, I'd be too stuffed to ever leave the couch."

Hannah laughed. "No kidding. You sure she was a seamstress and not a cook like her mother?"

"You've seen the tops and dresses I wear."

Hannah gaped at her friend. "Your mom makes those?"

Vanessa slowly spun in a circle, showing off the long-sleeved top she'd paired with a flowing skirt. "She does, indeed."

"What a gifted woman. But that meal just now? She could put the Hot Spot out of business if she went the restaurant route."

"Mama grew up watching my grandmother cook," Vanessa said, her eyes shining with pride. "It's as much a part of who she is as her hair and her eyes."

Hannah looked back at the modest home, took in the inviting front porch and the smoke rising from the chimney, and smiled. "I loved every minute of being here with the two of you this afternoon. It was absolutely lovely. And the biscuits were to die for, just as you said."

"I told you." Vanessa beamed.

Hannah pulled her coat tighter as she let her gaze wander around the outside of her friend's house. "I enjoyed listening to your mother's stories and seeing her photos. It's a nice reminder of how love is so much more important than things."

"I agree. Judging from the smile Mama wore throughout the meal, I think I can safely say she enjoyed your visit too."

They took a few more steps. "I imagine that if Antoinette Taylor allowed your grandparents to have Rose's going-away party in her home, she must have thought well of them, right?"

"Oh, she did. Very much so. In fact, Mama says Mrs. Taylor had a real soft spot for her. It's why she let Tess and Mama play together as often as they did." Vanessa wandered over to Hannah's car and leaned her back against it. "When they were kids they were able to see beyond the differences in their worlds. But as they grew older, Tess apparently outgrew that ability. And then Tess's daughter and I were unable to connect at all."

"What happened?" It hadn't even occurred to Hannah that Vanessa would have known Tess's daughter.

"Don't get me wrong. I wanted to be friends. But even though I grew up in *this* house, which *wasn't* on her family's estate, and neither of my parents worked for them, Stacy seemed to see me as being on a different level. A lower level." Vanessa's jaw tightened in a scowl.

"So Stacy is Tess's—Theresa Adler's—daughter?"

Vanessa nodded. "We went to school together from kindergarten until she went off to some fancy college in some big city.

Then, interestingly enough, the girl who could've had the big glitzy wedding of everyone else's dreams ended up eloping with some guy she met in whatever city she was in." Shivering, Vanessa pushed off Hannah's car and wrapped her arms around herself. "From the one person I know who still talks to her, she and her husband live in the Northeast somewhere."

Hannah stared at her friend. "The Northeast?"

"You know, Vermont, Massachusetts, one of those places."

Hannah's mind spun. When Morgan had been talking about her pottery class, she'd said two of her students were local—and one was from the Northeast. Hannah had already identified the two locals. She had assumed the visitor couldn't possibly be involved, but could she have been wrong? "Do you happen to know what Stacy's last name is now that she's married?"

"I don't. But give me a minute, and I'll tell you."

She pulled her phone from the pocket of her coat. A few taps later, she said, "Winfield. Her married name is Stacy Winfield."

Hannah handed Liam the bowl of freshly popped popcorn and took her place beside him on the couch. "What would you like to watch?" she asked, handing him a napkin.

Turning carefully so as not to spill the contents of the bowl, he rested his right arm along the back of the couch. "Would you be opposed to shelving the movie idea and just catching up with each other instead? I feel like we've both been operating at full speed lately, and I could really use a chance to slow it all down."

"That sounds perfect." She plucked a piece of popcorn from the bowl, popped it in her mouth, and then rested her head against his arm. "Vanessa's house is on the outskirts of town, so I'm not sure I would've heard any sirens unless they went right by her house."

He too helped himself to some popcorn, his gaze intent on hers. "We actually had zero calls today."

"No cats stuck in trees?" she teased.

Liam laughed. "Thankfully, no. And what about you? How was your time out at the Lodges' place? Did you get some of those biscuits Vanessa's mother makes?"

"You know about those?" she asked.

"Everyone at the firehouse does." He let out a short, low whistle. "Rose makes a batch of them for whoever is working on a holiday. Makes it so there's less squawking from those who do, I'll tell you."

She reached across to the coffee table, took a quick sip of her soda, and then leaned back against his arm again. "They were pretty amazing."

"So you did have one. I'm jealous."

She smiled sweetly. "Actually, I had two."

His laugh echoed through the room as he popped a few more pieces of popcorn into his mouth. "I would have thought something was wrong with you if you hadn't."

"And you would have been right." She breathed in the momentary silence that fell between them and then brought up what she'd been thinking about since she'd left the Lodges' house. "I came across some interesting information while I was there. Not sure it means anything, but it might."

He paused with his hand midway to the bowl. "Do you want to talk about it?"

"Maybe," she said, shrugging. After all, it was a pretty tenuous connection. There were probably thousands of S. Walkers in the Northeast. What if he thought she was reaching, desperate for answers? "I don't know. I feel like I'm still actively trying to process it."

"Sometimes talking it out can help with that."

She leaned her head back and closed her eyes to focus better. "Last week, when you were out at the Taylor Estate checking that smoke detector, did you talk to the daughter at all?"

"Sally?"

Her eyes popped open in surprise. "There are two daughters?"

"No, I think there's only one."

"I thought her name was Stacy," Hannah said.

He shook his head. "Right. Sorry. The daughter's name *is* Stacy. Where I got Sally from, I have no—wait. Sally was the name of the nurse who was there that day."

"Nurse?"

"Yes," he said, nodding. "For Mrs. Adler. Theresa."

Hannah watched him select another piece of popcorn while she considered his words. "Does she usually have a nurse there? What's wrong with her?"

He nodded gravely. "She's in the final stages of her battle with cancer. That's why the daughter, Stacy, is here. To be with her mother for what sounds like a matter of weeks now."

"I had no idea." Feeling her mood begin to plummet, she took a shuddering breath. "I know how hard that is."

Cupping his hand around her shoulder, he shifted the popcorn bowl to the coffee table. "I'm sorry our paths hadn't fully crossed when you lost your mom. I wish I could have been there to support you."

"You're here now," she managed around the lump she quickly cleared from her throat. "And that helps."

"I know you still miss her."

She nodded. "All the time. She was everything I could've ever asked for in a mother. I was blessed to have her for the time I did—deeply, richly blessed."

Liam pressed a kiss to her temple. "I wish I could have known her better."

"I wish you could have too." She managed a smile. "I hear my father has officially invited you to watch our home movies next Sunday. I'm sorry about that."

"Are you kidding me? I told you I wanted to be part of that. I'm looking forward to it. Very much, in fact."

She made a face. "You want to see me wearing braces? Getting chased by my brother? Listen to my off-pitch family singing 'Happy Birthday' to me?"

"You bet I do."

"You're crazy," she said, her mood lifting.

He reached for the bowl and held it out to her. "Guilty as charged."

"I'll make sure you're at least fed well while you're there." She tossed a few pieces into her mouth. "In fact, maybe Dad and I should consider making a turkey. Maybe with enough tryptophan in your system, you'll sleep through the movies."

"Not a chance." He grinned. "With or without turkey. By the way, I've looked into it, and the whole turkey-tryptophan thing is a bit of a myth."

She raised an eyebrow in amusement. "Oh?"

"It's true that tryptophan plays a part in the production of melatonin, the hormone that helps regulate your sleep cycle, but you'd have to have something like twenty servings to impact your sleep."

"Don't you eat twenty servings on Thanksgiving?" she teased. "Because I'm pretty sure we do at least that at my father's house every year."

His laugh tickled her ear and warmed her from the inside out. "Now *that's* a video I want to see."

Chapter Thirty

Hannah hurried up the front steps of the Blackberry Valley Public Library, pulled the front door open, and relished the blast of warm air that greeted her cold cheeks and even colder hands.

Her teeth still chattering, she made her way over to the information desk and the woman standing behind it who stared down at a piece of paper with a stunned smile on her face. "Winter is not only alive and well out there, Evangeline, but it's decided to add an exclamation point to our Monday morning."

Head librarian Evangeline Cooke continued to stare at the creased paper in her hand, her lips moving in silence. Hannah set the book she was there to return on the counter, allowed herself another shiver, and waited for her friend to finish reading.

Seconds turned to minutes before Evangeline finally raised her head and jumped. "Hannah! I didn't hear you come in. How long have you been standing there?"

"Not very long." Placing her hand on the book once again, she slid it across the counter, smiled, and motioned to the paper. "A love letter from Ted?"

Evangeline lowered her chin enough to afford a view of Hannah across the upper edge of her eyeglasses. "In the nearly thirty-five years Ted and I have been married, he's never *ever* written me a love letter. He *tells* me every day that he loves me, but putting it in a letter like you read about in a romance novel or movie is not his style."

Hannah laughed. "You were so mesmerized by it that I was sure it must be something that intriguing." She set her elbows on the counter and watched as Evangeline, still holding the letter, scanned in the newly returned book and placed it on the cart of returns. When she was done, the letter claimed her full attention once again.

"I can't believe this. I really can't," Evangeline said. "We'll be able to do so many things to make the library more attractive for teenagers—extra-comfy reading chairs and beanbags, more public-use computers, an expanded selection of books and audiobooks for them, and maybe even the ability to bring in a young adult author or two to speak."

Hannah leaned forward. "Did some sort of grant come through?"

"No. It's not a grant." Evangeline glanced up at Hannah, eyes wide with surprise and joy. "Believe it or not, it's better than that. She's gifted our library twenty thousand dollars!"

"She?" And then Hannah had a guess. "Is that letter from Theresa Adler?"

"The letter, the kind words, and the donation." Evangeline nodded. "I can't believe she's chosen the library over all the other places she could be giving money to in town. I mean, it's not like she came in here all that often—or ever, really. And that made sense. Her family didn't have a need to check out books. They could just buy what they needed or wanted to read."

Hannah's thoughts raced. "Theresa Adler didn't choose the library *over* other places. She chose the library *in addition* to other places."

Evangeline looked up at Hannah again, her joy changing to curiosity. "Meaning?"

"She donated to the fire department for Liam to start an explorer program at the high school next fall."

"Oh, how wonderful!"

"It's something he's wanted to get off the ground for quite some time now, but he lacked the funds to do it the way he wanted to," Hannah said.

Evangeline glanced back at the letter again and then pulled it to her chest. "I don't know what to say. I'm honored to have been included in her generosity."

"Oh, there's more," Hannah said. "You know how our church's youth group was about to start raising funds for their summer mission trip? They don't need to do any of that now. Theresa donated the money needed for all twenty kids to go."

"All twenty?" Evangeline echoed.

"Yes, and she doesn't even go to our church, as you know," Hannah said. "It seems that she feels compelled to do what she can to make things nicer for the youth in our town."

Evangeline looked from the letter to Hannah and back again. "Before her time on this earth is done."

"Liam told me she's in the end stages of her cancer battle," Hannah said quietly. "And that her daughter is in town to be with her."

"I heard that as well." Evangeline blew out a long breath as she set the letter with its accompanying envelope on the counter along the wall behind her. "You'll probably think I'm crazy for saying this, but I've always felt sorry for Theresa. She grew up in the nicest house in all of Blackberry Valley. She had the kinds of clothes the rest of us girls could only dream of. And all the boys wanted to date her. But—"

"Wait. You're about the same age as she is, right?" Hannah asked.

Evangeline nodded. "Theresa was a grade below me, but Blackberry Valley High is very small, as you well know. Everybody knows everybody. And everyone in town knew Theresa Taylor. I imagine she enjoyed being popular, but I always felt like she had to walk a certain line."

"What do you mean?"

"She couldn't really hang out with the other girls. The 'regular' girls with 'regular' parents. I could go to the mall with a group of girlfriends after school. Theresa had to hurry home for lessons with her foreign language tutor or to play tennis at the country club they belonged to that was about an hour away or work with a mentor to make sure her SATs would be good enough to get into the Ivy League colleges. Frankly, I'm surprised they let her attend a public high school rather than sending her to a fancy boarding school. She wasn't allowed to simply be a teenage girl."

Suddenly, Hannah felt a little sorry for Theresa. Even though she was the same Tess who had snubbed her childhood friend, Rose, it sounded as if she'd had her own difficulties. "Do you know how her relationship was with her mother?" Though based on what Evangeline had already said, she could hazard a guess.

Evangeline wandered over to the cart of returned books and plucked two off the top shelf.

"Whether it was an awards ceremony, a play, or even graduation, her mother always seemed to be checking her watch. As if there was always someplace else she would rather be." Evangeline ran a fingertip along the spine of one book, but it was clear she wasn't actually reading the title. She wore a far-away expression that told Hannah she was enmeshed in the past. "And Theresa was her *daughter*—her only child. I just couldn't imagine that, you know?"

"I can't either." Hearing about Theresa's upbringing, Hannah was more grateful than ever for her own mother.

"I always figured that was a big part of why Theresa never seemed happy at those things. She smiled for pictures, but it never quite reached her eyes. Except, of course, when I'd see her with Rose and her mom."

"You mean Rose Lodge?"

Evangeline set both books on the counter closest to where she stood and then picked up two more books from the cart. "She was Rose Williams back then, but yes. I remember thinking that at least Theresa had them. When I'd see her with them, Theresa seemed... different."

"Different how?" Hannah prodded.

"Back then, I'd have said she just seemed happy. Like her smile was real, heartfelt. But looking at it now, with adult eyes, I'd say being with them grounded her somehow." Evangeline set one of the new books on top of the first two, started another pile with the second, and then stopped and held up her finger. "I can show you what I'm talking about. Come with me."

Hannah fell into step beside Evangeline, who took her to the library's computer bank. There, Evangeline pointed Hannah to sit while she stood beside her, keyed into the system's digital archives, and pulled up a *Blackberry Valley Chronicle* issue from May of 1983.

Evangeline scrolled until she came to a page filled with pictures from that year's graduation day at Blackberry Valley High School. Three pictures in, she pointed at the one at eye level for Hannah. "See? There's Theresa Taylor with her parents."

Hannah leaned forward in her seat, her gaze coming to rest on a pretty, young blond woman in a cap and gown standing between a slightly taller woman with perfectly coiffed hair and a man in a suit, his arm around his daughter's shoulders. "That's Theresa's father, I take it?"

"It was. He died when we were in college, though I don't remember how. That's the only time I recall him ever being around." Evangeline pointed Hannah's attention to the expression on the graduate's face. "But see what I mean about Theresa's smile? It's stiff, almost as if she practiced it for a long time."

And it was. So too were the ones worn by her parents.

"But now, watch." Evangeline continued scrolling.

A photo of familiar faces caught Hannah's eye. "Actually, could I see that one first?" She leaned forward, the smile on the young Rose Lodge as bright as the sun as she stood between her parents, their pride in their daughter's accomplishment impossible to miss. "What a great photo. They look so happy. Rose told me she grew up in a loving household, and you sure can tell it in this picture."

"You could tell it in person too. Always." Evangeline started to scroll again but paused to point at the picture of Rose and her parents again. "Oh, hey. That's me in the corner. I was there because one of my friends was graduating."

Hannah squinted at the screen but drew back in confusion. "That doesn't look anything like you."

"Because that's not me." Evangeline laughed. "Look in the other corner. See?"

She followed the librarian's pointing finger and smiled at the similarities of young Evangeline to the current Evangeline. Then she studied the blond girl with the forlorn expression in the opposite corner again.

"It's hard to believe she's in the final weeks of life," Evangeline murmured.

"Who?" she asked, distracted.

Evangeline pointed to the face Hannah was still looking at. "Theresa Taylor."

Hannah stared. She hadn't even recognized Theresa without her careful smile.

Before she could process, let alone respond, Evangeline continued scrolling. Three pictures later, the screen stopped moving once again. "Voilà! A real smile."

Sure enough, when Hannah took in the black-and-white photograph in front of her, she saw the two graduates, Rose and Theresa, standing arm in arm with Peggy. All three women wore expressions of radiant joy that seemed to come from their hearts. Once again, Theresa could have passed for a different person altogether. "Wow," Hannah murmured.

"See what I mean?" At the sound of voices at the library's front door, Evangeline straightened up and patted Hannah's shoulder. "I better run. But could you do me a favor? Could you not say anything about the donation we're getting until I let the powers that be in town know? I'd like this to go through official channels rather than the grapevine."

"Of course."

"Thanks, Hannah." Evangeline bustled away to the counter, calling a cheery greeting to the newcomers.

Hannah studied the photo of Theresa, Rose, and Peggy for another moment. Then she scrolled back up to the photo of Rose and her parents. She took in their obvious love, joy, and pride before turning her attention to the young woman in the background, inadvertently captured by the camera's lens.

Like her fellow graduates, Theresa wore a cap and gown. But unlike the other graduates captured in the background, she wasn't smiling, wasn't talking to friends, wasn't accepting or giving a hug from a peer or family member. Instead, her attention was solely on the Williams trio, her mouth pulled tight in a grimace Hannah couldn't decipher. Was it anger? Hurt? Jealousy?

Shivering against the sudden chill making its way down her spine, Hannah stood, closed out of the paper's archive, and headed outside. How could Theresa appear so happy when standing with Rose and Peggy, yet so upset just minutes before or after that?

Chapter Thirty-One

Hannah started her Subaru and listened as the engine purred to life, ready to take her wherever she wanted to go. The problem was that she hadn't decided what her destination was.

She could stop in at the firehouse and see if Liam had time to talk, but she didn't need to get in her car to do that. And whether she walked or drove, she wasn't entirely sure she could rein in her thoughts well enough to take part in any sort of conversation.

She could drive out to see her father, but if memory served her, he'd mentioned something about helping out with some sort of electrical thing at the church.

She could visit Lacy's farm and use Sprout as a sounding board for the unsettling thoughts she'd been unable to shake since leaving the library that morning.

Suddenly, that solution sounded like the best one. She called her friend on the hands-free system.

While she waited for Lacy to answer, Hannah cranked up the heat and buckled her seat belt.

On the third ring, Neil's voice filled the car. "Hey, Hannah. Lacy is in with the doctor right now. Can I have her call you back when she's done?"

She set her hand on the steering wheel, the car still in park. "I take it she's not any better?"

"She's not. We thought we were out of the woods again yesterday afternoon. She'd eaten a little dinner, beat me in a round of Uno, and even spent a little time out in the barn with the animals. But then this morning she felt terrible again." Neil sighed. "It's like every time she gains some ground, she loses it. And I don't like how that keeps happening. I told her it was time to see the doctor and figure out what's going on."

Hannah glanced in her rearview mirror at a man hurrying down the sidewalk, his head bent low against a cold that was made worse by a strong wind from the north. She recognized Archer Lestrade, Liam's best friend and fellow firefighter. "Hopefully the doctor will figure it out and Lacy will be on the mend in no time."

"I'm sure he will. In the meantime, is there anything I can help you with?"

She considered his offer. Neil was a great sounding board too. He had a wide range of knowledge that had come in handy in previous cases. But she couldn't take his attention from his wife. "No. Focus on Lacy, and please let her know I was checking up on her."

"Of course." A sudden change in pitch in Neil's voice told her he'd either shifted in his chair or stood. "I gotta go."

"What's wrong?" she asked.

"I don't know. The nurse is waving me back to the room where Lacy is." His voice trembled slightly. She could practically see him adjusting his glasses or running his free hand through his hair, his usual nervous habits. "Hannah, what if—"

Hannah cut him off. "No, don't think like that. It's going to be okay, Neil. *She's* going to be okay. I'm praying."

Neil took a deep breath, and then his tone sounded steadier. "Thank you, Hannah. I'll have her call you when she's able."

Lacy's name disappeared from her dashboard screen, letting her know Neil had ended the call. Hannah closed her eyes, asked God to watch over Lacy and keep her safe, and then slowly opened them to reveal the empty road stretched in front of her.

Drawing in a breath, she shifted into drive and headed for Cave City.

The bells above the door jingled her arrival as she stepped into the Clay House Pottery Shop for the third time in less than a week. Only this time, instead of being the only customer in the store upon her arrival, she saw a pair of women by the shelf of pie plates, an elderly man perusing the candlestick display, and Pippa Nelson talking to Morgan Wyatt at the counter, notebook in hand.

"Welcome to the Clay House. Please let me know if I can help you with any—" Morgan glanced up, recognition making its way across her face. "Oh, hello. You're back. Again." Hannah couldn't miss how she didn't sound particularly pleased about it. Not that Hannah could blame her. It wasn't as if she'd given Morgan any sales, and she'd been quite nosy.

Unfortunately, that wouldn't change with this visit.

"I am." Hannah made sure the door was shut behind her and then made her way across the floor to the counter. "Hi, Morgan. Hi, Pippa."

Pippa pulled her notebook to her chest and leaned toward Hannah. In a low voice, she said, "I wanted to tell you that I'm sorry."

"For what?" Hannah asked in genuine surprise.

"For worrying more about trying to win some award than being a friend." Pippa turned back to Morgan. "And for failing to use a gift God has given me to help someone who could really use it."

"You're using it now," Morgan said. "That's all that matters."

"I feel like I missed something," Hannah said, looking from the notebook to Morgan and then to Pippa.

"The *Chronicle* is going to run a full-page feature on the store this Wednesday," Morgan gushed. "With pictures and everything!"

"That's great," Hannah said. "How did that happen, since the Clay House isn't in Blackberry Valley?"

"The shop is here in Cave City, but the fact that Morgan actually lives in Blackberry Valley gives me an excuse to do a feature story on her and how she loves pottery," Pippa explained.

"Which I do," Morgan said, eyeing Hannah closely. "I've loved it all my life, in fact. My study at home is filled with books on pottery and framed art showcasing pieces from different periods. Because I *do* know pottery. I really do. I just didn't know Peggy Shipman Williams ever used anything other than her initials on her pieces. If I had, I wouldn't have sold it for a *million* dollars, let alone a measly *twenty-five*."

Hannah leaned forward against the counter, grateful that Morgan had brought up the exact subject she wished to discuss. "What would you have done?"

"Since I wouldn't have known it had been missing all these years, I probably would've shown everyone at the guild and then put it in a place of honor in my study."

"I see."

Morgan nibbled on her lower lip then squared her shoulders. "For what it's worth, I was ashamed of myself for selling something that didn't belong to me as soon as I put Pippa's money in the register. Once I had, though, I just wanted to pretend it all away so it wouldn't affect people's perception of me and this shop. Because that's not who I am or who I want to be. I want you to know that."

"We all make mistakes. And in your case, your mistake actually led to the creamer being returned to its rightful owner." Hannah glanced at Pippa. "I'm glad you're able to do a story on Morgan, if not the shop."

"Oh, I'll be sure to mention the shop," Pippa said. "Like I said, because Morgan lives in Blackberry Valley, I can talk about the shop, as well as the pottery classes she wants to run."

"Is already running," Hannah corrected.

"Well, yes, true." Pippa picked up her notebook and pen. "I'll certainly mention her current class, but I'll also have a sidebar that talks about upcoming classes readers can look into if they're interested. That way they can see the kinds of things they could learn, and feel connected to the teacher."

"That's a great idea," Hannah said, and she meant it. The feature would offer readers multiple ways to interact with Morgan and her shop, whether they bought her pottery or learned from her how to make their own.

Tapping her pen against her chin, Pippa looked back at Morgan. "On that subject, have you had a chance to check with the other woman to see if she'd be willing to talk to me on the phone since she wasn't at our last class?"

"Other woman?" Hannah echoed as she shifted her focus onto the shopkeeper. "Meaning Stacy Winfield? She didn't come to the second class?"

Morgan took a quick bite of a piece of coffee cake that was concealed behind the register as Pippa shook her head. "No. Stacy wasn't here." Morgan gave no sign of surprise that Hannah knew the name.

"Why not?" Hannah asked.

"I'm not sure. I've tried calling her number a few times since then, and it always goes to voicemail." Morgan returned what was left of her stowaway breakfast to its hiding spot and then quickly brushed her hands free of crumbs. "But she had told me she was coming."

Hannah leaned forward against the counter. "She said that at the previous class?"

"No. I called her Friday morning to remind her about our second class that night, and she said she would be there. I told her we'd be working on a creamer. I also mentioned that if it was okay with her, Pippa—who happens to be a reporter working on a story about me and the shop—might want to ask her a few questions."

"And then she didn't show," Hannah murmured, as much to herself as Morgan and Pippa.

The shopkeeper shrugged. "Something must've come up, I guess."

Or you got too close, Hannah thought.

Pushing away from the counter, Hannah pulled her key fob from the front pocket of her jeans. "I've got to run. We'll talk again soon."

Chapter Thirty-Two

Hannah had barely pulled onto the main route back to Blackberry Valley when Pippa's name appeared on her dashboard screen. Pressing the green button, Hannah accepted the call.

"Hey."

"That was a fast exit just now," Pippa said, the bob of her voice letting Hannah know the reporter was on the move, likely walking to her own car. "Especially when you never got to whatever reason you had for being at Morgan's shop in the first place."

"Sorry about that. We ended up talking about exactly what I'd hoped we would." Hannah didn't offer an explanation for why she'd left so abruptly.

"You know I'm still actively on the hunt for anything pertaining to these missing Peggy Shipman Williams pieces, right?"

"I assumed as much. And it's only one piece that's still missing," Hannah said.

"The sugar bowl."

"Right."

"But the real story—the one I'm trying so hard to get," Pippa said, "is the who behind where it is, and where the creamer was until a week ago this past Friday."

Hannah hummed noncommittally.

"You'd tell me if you knew something, right, Hannah?" Pippa prodded. "Because this could be my story—the one I *need*. You know that, right?"

"What happened to being a friend over an award-winning journalist?" Hannah slowed as a squirrel darted out into the road, paused, and then ran back to the side it had come from. "You've written a lot of good stories, Pippa. Maybe you could use one of them."

"I don't think any of them are as good as this one," Pippa said dubiously.

"What about that story you did on how firefighting was handed down from Liam's grandfather, to his father, to Liam? There were at least a half dozen letters to the editor about it in the following week's paper. Or that one you did about that dog at the animal shelter who alerted staff members to their coworker who'd had the seizure. That was such a cool story."

"You do know something, don't you?" Pippa asked, her voice tight. "About the creamer and the sugar bowl."

Hannah braked at a four-way stop, looked both ways, and continued straight. "I can't say that for sure, but I might."

"And you're not going to tell me, are you?"

"Pippa, I can't. Not yet. If I'm wrong, I'd feel awful spreading rumors about a situation that's already delicate enough."

"Come on, Hannah," the reporter protested.

"Sorry, Pippa. I'm not going to give you a theory I haven't confirmed. Give me an hour or two, okay? If I'm wrong, then I'll have subjected only myself to a wild-goose chase."

"And if you're right?" Pippa demanded.

"Then we'll figure it out from there—together."

She heard a click in the background of the call, followed by the slam of a door, and then an engine as Pippa started her car. "I don't like this, Hannah."

"I know. But I need you to give me this hour or two."

"Fine," Pippa said. "But after that, you'll call me either way, right?"

"I will." She took a left at the next intersection. A quick glance at the dashboard screen let her know Pippa was still on the line. "Can I ask you a question?"

"I guess."

"How do you get yourself in the door with people you haven't met before?" Hannah noted the start of a shoulder-high wrought iron fence lining an extensive piece of property on her left.

"You want me to give you tips on how to handle the very thing you're intentionally keeping me out of?" Pippa asked.

Hannah cracked a smile. "Temporarily keeping you out of. And yes, I would love tips. Wouldn't you rather have firm, fleshed-out facts rather than hearsay that you had to track down, which might turn out to be nothing?"

Pippa scoffed. "You've got some nerve, Hannah. I think you would have made a decent reporter yourself. Anyway, I find common ground with the person I want to interview, and I use that to get my foot in the door."

"Common ground," Hannah repeated as the driveway she sought finally came into view. "I'm not sure what common ground I have with the person I'm going to see now." Suddenly, she remembered that wasn't quite true. She knew several people who had been here before—Liam, Uncle Gordon, even her own father, though not as recently. "Unless…"

"Did you think of something?" Pippa asked.

"I think I did."

"You're welcome. Don't say I never did anything for you."

Hannah pulled to a stop in front of the behemoth stone mansion, squared her shoulders, and killed the engine. "Thanks, Pippa. I'll be in touch."

"I'll be waiting." Pippa hesitated for a moment then added, "And trying to remember my commitment to being a good friend over a good journalist."

"I'm glad to hear it. Talk to you later."

Hannah ended the call, climbed out of the car, and hurried around to the semicircular stone steps that led up to the palatial front door. When she reached it, she looked around for a doorbell but couldn't find one. Instead, she used the old-school copper door knocker and waited for a voice to appear from some unseen speaker. She couldn't imagine how anyone could hear the knock if they weren't right by the door, but she would have to hope for the best.

Fortunately, she didn't have to wait long. A moment later, the door slowly opened to reveal a young twentysomething woman with blond hair piled into a messy bun on her head and eyes that spoke to a kind of worry Hannah remembered all too well from personal experience.

"Stacy Winfield?" Hannah held out her hand. "My name is Hannah Prentiss. My uncle Gordon was out here recently to do some plumbing work for your mom and—"

A weak voice sounded from somewhere beyond the foyer.

Stacy stepped back and hastily waved Hannah inside. When the door was shut behind them, the young woman managed a small smile. "I really appreciate your uncle coming out to help us the other day. He took care of things we didn't even know were problems."

"He was happy to do it."

The voice came again, and Hannah realized it was from a partially open door halfway down the hall.

"It's okay, Mom," Stacy called. "Go back to sleep." Lowering her voice to a near whisper, she faced Hannah again. "If Gordon left something behind while he was here, I haven't seen it, but that doesn't mean it isn't here. I haven't exactly been on my A-game these last few weeks." Her chin trembled.

"I understand," Hannah said. And she did, better than she would have liked to admit.

"I can show you where Gordon was working if you'd like. You're welcome to poke around there and see if you can find whatever it was." Stacy tried to stifle a yawn as she started to lead the way down the hall, but didn't completely succeed.

Suddenly, Hannah wondered when Stacy had last gotten a decent night's sleep. Guilt sank into her stomach, heavy as a stone, at what she'd come to ask about. "Actually, I'm here about something else."

Stacy's brow furrowed with surprise. "Oh?"

Hannah decided to just come out and say it. "It's about a long-lost piece of pottery that showed up out of the blue ten days ago."

The young woman stumbled then gave a light cough before she mastered herself. "I—I see."

Hannah went on as if she'd noticed nothing suspicious. "It was a creamer that was part of a larger dining set Peggy Shipman Williams made for her daughter while they lived here on your family's estate."

Shifting her weight, Stacy looked over her shoulder at the partially open door from which the voice had emerged. She swallowed visibly.

"It was found in the back room of the Clay House Pottery Shop on the same night you took a class there."

Stacy squeezed her eyes shut and pressed her lips together into a tight line.

"I also know about the generous donations you've been giving out around town on behalf of your mother," Hannah said. She'd realized the donations were hand-delivered when she gave some thought to the envelope she'd seen at the library, which had no stamp or return address.

"She keeps saying she can't take it with her, and goodness knows I don't need it. We both decided it was the best use of her money. She asked me to deliver them myself because she was afraid to send such large donations through the mail."

"Wonderfully kind donations that will benefit the youth in our community for years to come."

"My mother is a wonderful person," Stacy said, pinning Hannah with a formidable stare. "A wonderful mother. But now, I must ask you to leave."

Hannah remained in place, her eyes never leaving Stacy's. "I know what you're going through, Stacy. I was around your age when I lost my mother to cancer. I remember the worry, the fatigue, the bargaining I did with God in the hopes she'd be healed, and the way I wanted to make sure everyone knew what a truly good person she'd always been."

Glancing into the living room beside them, Stacy blinked hard against the tears Hannah knew she fought constantly.

"I know you're the reason Rose Lodge's creamer suddenly appeared where it did after forty-plus years. And I know your intention was probably to do the same with the sugar bowl this past week before Morgan called your attention to your classmate's job as a reporter."

Stacy shook her head and stepped toward Hannah. "I'm afraid you and your crazy talk must leave my mother's house right this instant."

A voice emerged from behind the partially open door, tired yet clear. "No, Stacy. Send her in."

Stacy's mouth tightened with anger, her gaze fixed firmly on Hannah. "This isn't something for you to be bothered with, Mom. I'll take care of it."

"I said send her in, Stacy."

Stacy swept her hand toward her mother's room, her anger melting into worry once again. "Please, I don't want her getting worked up."

"I know. I won't do that."

Hannah made her way to the door, where she knocked softly before stepping all the way inside. There, reclined on a bed and covered in a warm blanket, was a pale figure, bearing a gauntness Hannah remembered so well she almost ran back into the hall. But she didn't. Instead, she leaned into the strength she knew her mother would want her to have in this moment and crossed to the bedside chair Theresa Adler pointed her to.

"Hello, Mrs. Adler. I'm—"

"Hannah Prentiss. Yes, I heard." The woman's breathing was slow and labored, but still she continued. "Please call me Theresa."

Hannah gestured to a glass of water that held a straw on a table between them. "Would you like a drink?"

Theresa shook her head slowly. When she continued to speak, it was with many pauses to catch her breath. "No, thank you. If I heard correctly, it seems my daughter is trying to fix my mistake. A mistake I told no one about until two weeks ago, when I finally told her..." Theresa inhaled with noticeable difficulty and exhaled with even more. "About one of my biggest regrets in life."

Hannah waited for her to continue, but the wheezing that followed Theresa's words so far made it clear she was struggling.

"You took the creamer and the sugar bowl from Rose," Hannah finally said for her.

A tear ran down Theresa's mottled cheek as she nodded.

"You didn't want Rose to move out, did you?"

"I didn't. But it was more than that."

Hannah waited quietly as Theresa closed her eyes and clearly worked to steady her breathing in a way that would enable her to continue. While she did, Hannah heard what sounded like very different breathing coming from just outside the door and knew that Stacy was listening in, ready to spring into action if needed. Hannah didn't blame her. In Stacy's place, she would have behaved the same way.

"Peggy was... She was..."

"The woman who taught you to be the mother Stacy loves so very much?" Hannah suggested.

Another tear made its way down Theresa's cheek, and Hannah heard a quiet sniffle from the hallway. "Yes. She made me feel loved. She listened to me. She included me, though it wasn't part of her job description. The dinners I ate with them were the best, even though it was the same food I got at home." Theresa coughed.

"I really think you should have some water, Theresa," Hannah pressed.

Theresa gave a barely perceptible nod, still struggling to catch her breath.

Hannah helped her sit up and braced her while Theresa took a few sips of water. Then she helped her settle back against the pillows.

"I didn't have love at home. I had things. Lots of things. But I would have given them all up to have what Rose had. For someone to see me the way Peggy saw Rose, as a treasure, a blessing to be cherished. To..." Theresa stopped and gave a shudder. "When I saw the dining set Peggy made Rose, I was so jealous. I wanted someone to do something like that, with that kind of devotion, for me. It wasn't picked out from a store. It was made with love. In the middle of the night. When Peggy was done cooking. When she was done caring for Rose and her father. She missed out on sleep, on making the pieces she sold for money—all to make something so special for someone she loved. Just a gesture of the endless love she held for her daughter."

Another tear made its way down Theresa's face, and Hannah gently wiped her cheeks with a tissue from a nearby box.

Theresa met Hannah's gaze. "I took those pieces from Rose. And I am ashamed."

"Is that why you stopped being friends?" she asked. "Why you never spoke to her again and avoided her when you saw her in town?"

Another slow nod, another cough.

"And why Stacy and Vanessa never connected?"

"I steered Stacy away from Rose's daughter. I'm ashamed of that too. I robbed her of a beautiful experience that she should have been able to enjoy. All because I wronged my oldest friend and refused to come clean with her, much less make it right."

"Why didn't you just give the pieces back to Rose at some point?" It had been four decades. Theresa would have had ample opportunity. And having met Rose, Hannah was certain Vanessa's mom would have been gracious and understanding.

"It was a long time before I found my footing in life. Even longer before I had Stacy, though I understand that Rose had her Vanessa around the same time. With her, I finally had what I didn't as a child. But then shame took the place of the jealousy, and I didn't want Stacy to pay the price for my wrongdoing. That's why I hid them and did my best to forget. Eventually, I even forgot where I'd hidden them, but I never forgot the shame. It's with me always."

Stacy burst into the room and hurried to her mother's side. "I looked and looked until I found both pieces, Mom. They were in Grandma Taylor's chest in the attic."

Theresa stared in wonder at her daughter. "Whatever for?"

Stacy took her mother's hand and held it to her cheek. "I wanted to make it right for you, Mom. So you could be free of the shame. I didn't want you to carry it with you."

Hannah swallowed hard against the lump she felt rising in her throat. "Why leave it in the shop instead of at the Lodges' house?"

"It would have been harder to drop it by a house without being noticed, and I was afraid that if I shipped the pieces, they might break," Stacy explained. "I thought an expert potter would recognize Peggy's work and return them to their rightful owner. I trusted Morgan to do the right thing."

"Unfortunately, Peggy used a different mark on the set for Rose than for any of her other pieces," Hannah told her. "Morgan didn't know who'd made the creamer. She ended up selling it to your classmate, Pippa, who gave it to me as a belated birthday gift. I happened to open it in front of Rose's daughter, who recognized it. So it is back where it belongs, though I'm sure they'd love the sugar bowl too."

"I'd planned to leave both pieces in the studio," Stacy said. "I was even alone in the classroom for a few minutes at one point. But as I set the creamer on the shelf, I heard footsteps and didn't have time to put the sugar bowl there too. So I figured I'd leave it in the restroom or somewhere different during the second class. But then I didn't go."

"Because of what Morgan told you when she called you that morning?" Hannah asked. "About Pippa being a reporter and wanting to interview you?"

Closing her eyes, Stacy nodded.

Theresa tugged her hand free and gently caressed her daughter's face. "You are the greatest thing in my life, my love. I am so proud of how you turned out. But what I did to Rose is for *me* to make right, not you. And I want to do that. I *must* do it."

"Would you like me to call Rose when I leave?" Hannah asked. "Tell her you'd like to see her?"

Her eyes still on her daughter, Theresa slowly nodded. "Yes. Please."

"But, Mom," Stacy said. "What happens if she tells people what you did? I can't bear the idea of her ruining your reputation after you're gone."

Her own eyes welling with tears she was mere seconds from shedding, Hannah grabbed hold of Theresa's free hand and looked at both mother and daughter. "I think I know someone who can keep that from happening."

Chapter Thirty-Three

The next morning, Hannah parked in the gravel parking lot outside her friend's barn and stepped out of the car, her breath forming white plumes in the cold January air. Cocking her head first toward the house and then the barn, she heard nothing to indicate where Lacy might be. All she knew for sure was that when Lacy had called to invite her over, her best friend sounded better than she had in days.

Which, Hannah realized, meant the barn was where she'd most likely find her. Picking her way past the chicken coop, she waved at the hens Hennifer and Eggatha as well as Rocky the rooster.

"Lacy?" she called as she stepped inside the cavernous building, the smells of hay, dampness, and animals instantly calming her. The harsh wind was cut off, leaving her in a peaceful quiet, broken only by the occasional rustling. "Are you in here?"

An answering bleat came from the far side of the barn. Her mouth spreading wide with a smile, Hannah made her way down the aisle between the empty stalls and headed for the pen that housed Mimi and her three kids.

"Hi, Mimi!" She reached over the top of the gate, unlatched the lock, and ducked inside, careful not to let out any of the inhabitants. She made a beeline for the cinnamon-colored goat now heading in her direction. When they reached each other, she bent over, and they gently butted heads. "Hi, Sprout! I brought you a treat, sweet girl."

She reached into her pocket, pulled out a carrot, and watched it disappear into the growing goat's mouth. Seconds later, a gentle nudging at her pocket made her look down to find Flower and Niblet demanding their own treats.

She laughed. "I didn't forget you two. Here." She produced more carrots, which disappeared just as quickly as Sprout's had.

"They really do love you, Hannah."

Lifting her gaze to the gate, Hannah smiled at Lacy. "Do they love me, or do they love the treats I bring?"

"They're all still standing there around you, aren't they?"

She looked back down at Mimi's kids. "They are, but that's probably because they're hoping there are more carrots to be had."

"If that was it, they'd be messing with your pocket again."

Nestling her head against Sprout's, Hannah modulated her voice to a more singsong pitch. "Then we match, don't we, girl? Because I really love you too."

The young goat gave another bleat.

She gave a quick head scratch to Sprout, then Flower, then Niblet, and back to Sprout again before rising to her feet and heading straight for the gate. When she was safely on the other side and the latch was set, she pulled her friend in for a hug. "It is so good to see you out here in the barn looking…" Holding Lacy out to arm's length, she gave her friend a thorough once-over. "Happy."

Lacy put her hands to her face and bounced up on the toes of her work boots with a giddy squeal. "I'd say that's an accurate description."

Hannah laughed. “So you’re feeling better, I take it?”

“No, not exactly. But I’m okay with it now, because I know it won’t last.”

Hannah felt her smile fade. “You lost me.”

“I know. Which is making this so much more fun for me right now.” Lacy wrapped her arms around herself.

Setting her hands on her hips, Hannah narrowed her eyes on her friend. “Can we please cut to the part where you tell me what’s going on? I could use a break from having to figure stuff out.”

“But you’re so good at it, Nancy Drew.”

She stuck her tongue out at her friend. “Nancy needs a break.”

“Fine. I’ll tell you. Or I can wait seven months, when I’m positive you’ll figure it out on your own. Likely before that.”

Hannah stared at Lacy. “Figure out what?”

“Then again,” Lacy said, dropping her hand to the front of her plaid barn coat, “once we’re out of coat weather, it’ll probably start to become pretty obvious.”

She gaped at Lacy.

Seven months.

Not feeling better, but it wouldn’t last.

Feeling tired and queasy in the morning but better in the evening.

Her gaze flew back to Lacy’s eyes and the face-splitting smile she wore. “You’re pregnant?” she squeaked.

“I am.”

Hannah dropped her hand from her open mouth and gave Lacy another hug. “Oh, Lacy, congratulations! I can’t believe it. You and Neil must be over the moon.”

"We were surprised when the doctor told us yesterday, but oh, Hannah, we are so excited for August!"

Hannah loosened her hold on Lacy, stepped back, and let out a squeal of her own. "What a very, very blessed baby this is going to be to have you and Neil as parents."

"And you as a godmother."

She covered her mouth in a futile effort to stifle her gasp. "Godmother?" she echoed. "Are you sure?"

"Positive. I wouldn't have anyone else, and neither would Neil. So what do you say?"

"Yes! Yes! A million times yes!"

"I'm glad to hear it," Lacy replied with a serene smile. "After seeing how great you are with goat kids, I can't wait to watch you spoil a human one."

Chapter Thirty-Four

"I know you've caught me staring at you even more than normal today, and I suppose I should be sorry about that, but I'm not." Liam claimed one of the two open spots beside Hannah on her father's couch and handed her a glass of water. "Just letting you know that."

She laughed. "May I ask why?"

"Why have I been staring?" he asked. "Or why am I letting you know?"

She took a sip of water and then held the glass on her thigh. "Both."

At the sudden swell of voices from the kitchen, he lowered his voice. "I'm letting you know because I want to. And I've been staring because you're glowing. I mean, actually glowing."

"It's been a good week," she told him. "One I don't think I'll ever forget."

"Being asked to be the godmother for Lacy and Neil's baby must have been incredible."

"It was, and I'm still in awe that they've granted me such an honor. But seeing Lacy so happy and knowing what amazing parents they're going to be is a real blessing."

Liam smiled. "It is."

"But there's more."

"To your glowing?"

She nodded. "Yesterday, after work, I sat Dylan down and reminded him that he's only twenty and it's okay if he doesn't know exactly what he wants to do just yet. That he'll figure it out when he's meant to. God makes each of us different, gives us different talents and abilities. And everyone's timetable is different. Dylan's, mine, everyone's. And that's okay."

Liam looked at her closely. "Seems to me that Lacy and Neil's kid is as lucky in the godmother department as in the parents department."

"I hope you're right."

"I am." He draped his arm across her shoulders. "I spoke to Pippa before church this morning. Told her what an amazing job she did on her story in last week's paper. If she submits that story for the award she wants, I'll be shocked if she doesn't win, and I told her that too."

Hannah smiled at the memory of the front-page article and the heartstrings it had pulled inside her even though she'd known the story before she'd begun reading. "She presented it the right way, for sure."

"A way she readily admitted you steered her toward after you spoke to Theresa Adler," Liam said. "You set all of that in motion. Turning what could have been a sensationalized story into something deeper, more poignant, and far more memorable."

"As a story of repentance and forgiveness tends to be."

"As a firefighter, I've seen, read, and even been a part of more stories than I can count over the years. But this one is special," he said. "Pippa made it so we could understand Theresa's pain and shame. Feel her gratitude at having Rose not only understand why she did what she did, but also forgive her. Feel her peace at knowing Rose will check in on Stacy with the same love and compassion Rose and Peggy had always shown Theresa. And then, on top of all that, to show us in a picture the very moment Rose was finally reunited with the sugar bowl Peggy made for her so long ago. Talk about a champion human-interest piece."

She sat with Liam's summation of everything that had transpired since Monday afternoon and let it bring yet another smile to her face.

"If only Peggy could've seen the way this played out."

"I believe she watched it all," Hannah said quietly. "Just like I believe my mom is watching me."

He sat back and met her eyes. "Do you think your mom would've liked me?"

"I have no doubt. How could she not?"

Leaning forward, he pressed his lips against her forehead. "I'm glad God put us on each other's paths again."

"I am too." Slowly, she pulled back, her thoughts flitting briefly to another pairing. "Did I tell you what happened when Doug Bell read Pippa's story?"

"No, what?"

"With the encouragement of his fiancée, Cassie, he faxed it to his father in Florida."

"Why would that have required his fiancée's encouragement?" Liam asked. "I thought you'd found that Theresa took the sugar bowl and creamer all those years ago."

"Doug needed Cassie's support because he also asked his dad to come clean about what he'd done as a teenager to try and sabotage Ray Williams's job on the estate."

"What did he do?"

"He burned a barn, chopped down some trees, and slashed a bunch of tires," she said, resting her head against the back of the couch.

Liam's eyes were wide with shock. "Why on earth?"

"Because *his* father—Doug's grandfather—lost his job at the estate to Ray, and that impacted Doug's father's ability to go to college."

Liam raked a hand through his hair. "And Doug knew this?"

"He apparently came across something while doing research for his local history unit that made it pretty clear, and it had been weighing heavily on him. Cassie tried to encourage him to confront his father even before this, but he was worried. It was his father, you know? And then, when the creamer showed up, Doug became worried his father had been behind that, as well, until I told him the pottery pieces had gone missing long after his dad's brief time as a saboteur."

She'd spoken to Doug, who'd explained that Pippa had mentioned the creamer—without confessing how she knew about it—on a double date with him, Cassie, and her brother, Derrick. That was how he'd known what it was without Hannah telling him. That clue, at least, had turned out to be nothing but smoke and mirrors, for which Hannah was grateful. She liked the history teacher and had been delighted when he hadn't actually been as guilty as he'd acted.

"So did Doug's father actually come clean after he saw Pippa's article?"

"He did. He called Colin."

"I'm glad to hear he confessed, but I'm surprised Colin never said anything about this to me," Liam mused. "Burning down a barn counts as arson, which is usually a felony in this state. There's no statute of limitations on a felony here."

"Rose and Theresa both asked Colin not to say anything to anyone, and Theresa has made it clear she doesn't wish to press charges. Said it was water under the bridge. They want everyone to find the peace they have after restoring their friendship. And she wants to forgive others as Rose forgave her."

Their conversation was cut off as chaos followed her father into the room. While Andrew and his crew crowded in, Dad crossed to the entertainment center with a stack of DVDs in one hand and a brand-new popcorn bowl from the Clay House in the other. "Who's ready for home movies?" he called.

A chorus of cheers rose up around Liam and Hannah as the rest of the family all got settled. Drew and Allison sat together on the love seat. AJ, Ava, and Axel sat on pillows in front of them, and Dad took the open spot on the other side of Hannah.

As her father pressed play on the remote, Hannah looked over at Liam, her cheeks warming. "We'll see how glad you are after you see me at some of my most awkward ages—wearing big clunky braces and partaking in all sorts of buffoonery."

"Frankly, I think it's only going to make me *gladder*, Hannah Prentiss. In fact, check your contacts list on your phone."

She eyed him for a moment before grabbing her phone from the coffee table and scrolling down to his name. For months, every time he'd managed to sneak her phone away from her, he'd changed the nickname on his own contact.

"See?" he said, pointing at his latest edit. "Liam 'Completely Smitten' Berthold. Because I am, Hannah. With you."

From the Author

Dear Reader,

After writing the kickoff book—*Where There's Smoke*—for Mysteries of Blackberry Valley, it sure was fun to jump back in again with this, the eighth book in the series, *Smoke and Mirrors*. As an author, I have a propensity for seeing the characters in whatever book I'm working on as friends, and it's always nice to spend time with them again. Like you, the reader, I want to know how they're doing and what they're up to. I want to know what makes them happy, what scares them, and how they handle it when they're struggling with something.

That's the beauty of books for me, both as a writer and a reader—creating/getting to know the characters as if they're people I'd want to share a meal with or go on an adventure with. Because, by the end of a book, they usually are.

Best wishes, and happy reading!
Laura Bradford

About the Author

While spending a rainy afternoon at a friend's house as a child, Laura Bradford fell in love with writing over a stack of blank paper, a box of crayons, and a freshly sharpened number-two pencil.

Today, Laura is the *USA Today* bestselling author of many cozy mystery series. She has also penned four Amish-based women's fiction novels set in and around Lancaster, Pennsylvania. When she's not writing, Laura loves to bake, travel, and advocate for those living with MS.

The Hot Spotlight

In *Smoke and Mirrors*, Peggy Shipman Williams was a self-taught potter whose work was proudly displayed or unknowingly hidden away in homes throughout Blackberry Valley and its surrounding towns. While Peggy Shipman Williams only made pottery in the author's and readers' imaginations, it is possible that you own—or at some point, have admired—a piece of pottery made by someone with a similar story to hers.

To this day, I can still recall a piece of pottery I saw in a shop in New Paltz, NY. It was a pie dish in an array of blue hues that took my breath away. For whatever reason, I didn't buy it, but I can tell you, I have thought about that pie dish many, many times since then, wishing I had treated myself to it.

Pie plate or not, though, I have developed an interest in pottery since that day. I've taken a few classes for fun, and when I'm in a shop with pottery pieces, I always look to see if maybe, just maybe, I can somehow spot that plate or one like it.

In the meantime, here are some fun things I've learned about pottery along the way.

- Some form of pottery can be found in nearly every region of the world throughout time. In fact, evidence of this has been discovered on six of the seven continents.

- The invention of the potter's wheel in Mesopotamia between 3000 and 3500 BC enabled potters to make their pieces more quickly and efficiently.
- Pottery is not actually "pottery" until heat is introduced. Until then, it's really just clay, which can dissolve back into mud if enough water is added to it. Once heat is introduced and it becomes pottery, though, it remains pottery.

Next time you're in a pottery shop, take a moment to really look at the pieces. And if you see a piece that speaks to you, get it if you can. Because it really is one-of-a-kind.

From the Hot Spot Kitchen

PEGGY'S HOMEMADE BISCUITS

Ingredients:

3 cups all-purpose flour

3 tablespoons sugar

½ teaspoon salt

4 teaspoons baking powder

¾ cup cold butter (be sure to use *cold*, as that is Peggy's secret)

1 egg

1 cup cold milk

Directions:

Preheat oven to 450 degrees.

Line a baking sheet with parchment paper.

Hint: To make the dough easier to work with, keep the butter in the fridge or freezer until it's time to add it.

Combine flour, sugar, salt, and baking powder in large bowl.

If you are working with frozen butter, grate it into your bowl and stir. If butter is refrigerated, cut it into pieces and add it to the bowl. Either way, you should be able to see the pieces of butter in your dough.

Add egg and milk and mix until combined. You should still be able to see pieces of butter.

Sprinkle a little flour on top of the dough and knead it on a floured surface half a dozen times. Combat stickiness with a sprinkle of more flour.

With your hands or a rolling pin, flatten the dough to roughly ¾- to 1-inch thickness.

Cut with a biscuit cutter or the top of a drinking glass.

Put biscuits on the prepared baking sheet.

Bake in preheated oven for 10 to 12 minutes or until tops are golden brown.

Serve with butter and enjoy!

Read on for a sneak peek of another exciting book in the *Mysteries of Blackberry Valley* series!

No Love Lost

BY BECKY MELBY

Pond Creek Coal Mine
Pike County, Kentucky
March 9, 1921

Talbert Haley braced both hands against the cold, damp tunnel floor as if he could stop the earth from shaking, its rumbles still echoing. The draft that usually flowed past his face no longer blew. Instead, thick ashy air filled his lungs.

Next to him, Oren Benton coughed. "You hurt, Tal?"

"Not bad." Talbert eased to a sitting position. His head throbbed. He gently touched his right temple, confirming the source of the pain. His pulse hammered over the ringing in his ears. "Explosion," he rasped, trying to make sense of the last few minutes.

He'd been on his feet, pickax in hand, chiding Oren and Linus Moss about working too slowly, and then the earth had flung him about like a rag doll.

Linus. He reached out with both hands. Hands he couldn't see in the thick darkness. A jolt of fear shot through him. Was he blind? "Linus?" He raised his voice. "Linus!"

"He's down." Oren coughed again. "He has a pulse though. Linus! Linus, wake up!"

A groan answered him. "Can't...feel...my legs."

Talbert forced away the panic closing his throat. How many times had he dreamt this, and then awakened with his heart pounding, his nightshirt clinging to his back? And then Viviene's arm would slide across his chest as she whispered, "It's only a dream, Tal. Everything's fine."

It's only a dream. He tried to believe it as he scooted toward the sound of Linus's ragged breathing.

A clang ricocheted off the walls as his foot made contact with something metal. He leaned down, running his hand across the uneven rock floor. His headlamp. "Either of you got matches?"

"Shirt pocket." Linus's voice was barely above a whisper.

"Got 'em," Talbert said after a moment's searching. "There's only four."

Oren's outstretched hand collided with Talbert's elbow. "Don't drop any."

Talbert gripped the four small sticks as if his life depended on them. Maybe it did. Maybe Linus's life hung in the balance and they could do something for him if they could get some light.

Holding the small brass lamp between his knees, he tucked three of the matches in his shirt pocket and stuck the end of the fourth between his teeth.

Securing the lamp with one hand, he turned the lever that would let water from the upper chamber drip into the calcium carbide in the base. In seconds he smelled the acetylene gas the combination produced. He took the match from between his teeth, scraped it on the floor, and was rewarded with a hiss and a flash. He wasn't blind. Thank the Almighty for that anyway. He held the lit match to the burner tip and murmured a prayer of gratitude as the flame, magnified by the reflector, filled the space with light.

The collapse had created a room no more than eight feet square. How long could three men...

He halted the thought before it could paralyze him. Lifting the lamp, he adjusted the reflector, directing it at Linus. His gut clenched. A beam, six by six, pinned his legs. One end of the beam was buried under the still-settling mound of rock and debris that blocked the entrance.

Talbert locked eyes with Oren. Tears made streaks in his friend's blackened face as he slowly shook his head.

There was nothing they could do for Linus.

Hannah Prentiss inhaled the heavenly scent of chocolate wafting from the Hot Spot kitchen and tried to concentrate on untangling a string of red heart-shaped fairy lights. Distracted by the what-ifs swarming in her brain, the sniffles coming from the corner booth, and the chocolate, she was making a mess of things. In frustration, she switched to addressing envelopes for the Valentine's Day birthday lunch she was planning for the young woman quietly crying in the corner.

When she'd sealed the last envelope, she stood and stretched. As she walked out of her office, she glanced up at the double-sided clock that had hung between the arched doorways since the old firehouse had been built in 1898. She surveyed the exposed brick walls covered with memorabilia from the early days of the fire station and felt the same sense of awe she'd experienced after signing the papers that made it hers.

Several of her friends in California had thought she was crazy for deciding to leave a successful career at a high-end restaurant to return home to Blackberry Valley, Kentucky, and turn the historic firehouse into a farm-to-table restaurant. In truth, there had been days—in the midst of remodeling, developing a firehouse-themed menu, sourcing local ingredients, interviewing, marketing, and transforming the upstairs apartment into a comfortable living space—when she had wondered if they were right. But now, she wouldn't trade this life for anything.

The old clock told her it was almost lunchtime. The 1942 wall calendar with dates that matched the current year told her it was

Tuesday, February 3. She had a week and a half to get ready for Valentine's Day.

She padded past Raquel Holden, the usually-upbeat server who'd shown up six hours before her shift started because "work gets my mind off things." Hannah had spent close to an hour listening to Raquel's relationship dilemma as they wrapped silverware in napkins. She'd listened and nodded, prayed and offered tissues.

She pushed through the swinging double doors to the kitchen—then stopped in her tracks. "Oh my goodness." It was all that came to mind as she stared at the thing of beauty in the center of the spotless stainless-steel table.

"Triple Dark Chocolate Raspberry Truffle Supreme Valentine Cheesecake." Head chef Jacob Forrest wiped his palms on his chocolate-streaked apron and beamed at her. "Chocolate cookie crust, smooth dark chocolate cheesecake with raspberries folded in, topped with a thick layer of satiny ganache, fresh raspberries, and handmade raspberry truffles." He bowed at the waist.

Hannah clapped. "We can't serve this. It belongs in an art gallery."

"Thank you, ma'am." Jacob straightened up. "Think a slice of this will help Raquel?"

"I'm sure it will go a long way toward cheering her up. But let's get some protein in her first. Blood sugar spikes have been known to bring on crying jags. Don't ask me how I know. What do we have for that?"

"I thought you'd never ask. I may have whipped up a too-large batch of the soup I'm testing for our spectacular Valentine's Day culinary extravaganza."

Hannah grinned. Part of her job as Jacob's boss was keeping his enthusiasm within manageable bounds, but she never wanted to squash it. She'd been promoting their reservations-only Valentine's Day dinner with words like *intimate*, *romantic*, and *elegant*. Left to Jacob, who favored words like *extravaganza*, it might come off sounding like a super sale at the car dealership down the street.

"What kind of soup?"

"Tomato Basil with Cheese Tortellini. Tomatoes grown and canned right here in Blackberry Valley, tortellini made with eggs from chickens we know by name and locally sourced cheese, and basil from my window herb garden." He gestured toward the greenery soaking up the pale February sun in a window.

"Sounds like a winner. I'll have Raquel pop back here to sample it."

A ding from her phone grabbed her attention. She slid it from her pocket and smiled at the name on the screen. Liam 'Completely Smitten' Berthold. It was the current nickname he'd given himself in her contacts list. The text read, I'M HERE.

"Tell your boyfriend to come join us for lunch." Jacob grinned.

"How did you know it was him?"

"Your smile. Dead giveaway. He's out front, right?" When she nodded, he shooed her out of the kitchen.

Hannah laughed as she went. She was thirty-six. Liam Berthold, Blackberry Valley's fire chief and the man she'd been officially dating for three months, was thirty-eight. And yet the giddiness she felt at the thought of seeing him rivaled that of any fifteen-year-old with her first crush.

Raquel must have let him in, because Liam met her in the center of the dining room with a warm embrace. After a quick kiss, he gave her a lopsided smile and an almost imperceptible nod toward his fellow firefighter and best friend, Archer Lestrade, who had come in with him. Usually brimming with *joie de vivre*, Archer seemed strangely subdued.

Hannah motioned to a four-top. "Do you have time for lunch?"

Liam nodded. Archer shrugged.

"Jacob's warming up some tomato soup." She tipped her head toward the corner booth. "I was about to ask Raquel if she wanted some."

Both heads swiveled to the shadowy corner where Raquel wiped menus with a vacant stare. She appeared to have stopped crying, but her uncustomary silence caused Liam's questioning expression as he greeted her. "Hey there, Raquel. Come eat with us."

Raquel ambled across the room and joined them. "Hi, Liam. Archer." She did a double take after her lackluster greeting to Archer. "You okay?"

Archer rubbed the stubble on his chin. "I'm growing a beard. Bryn's always said she wanted to see me with one. Though now… Anyway, it looks like I should ask you the same. What's going on?"

Raquel pulled out a chair and plopped onto it. "Marshall got a job offer in Chicago."

"Wow. That stinks." Archer, usually the one to give a quick joke to try to snap someone out of a bad mood, had nothing but empathy in his tone. "I feel your pain."

"I knew it wasn't just the five o'clock shadow. What's going on with you and Bryn?"

"You don't know? You guys are so close. I thought she would have told you."

Raquel shook her head. "I know she's up in Wisconsin where she can work on her dissertation without interruption. Is that it?" She gave a small laugh. "You're sad because she chose a place with no phone service or internet and you have to endure a few days without talking?"

"If only." Archer rested his elbow on the table and his chin on his hand. "We had a fight."

"Seriously? I talked to her while she loaded her car on Friday. She didn't mention anything about a fight."

"It was after that, so I'm not surprised."

Before he could explain further, Jacob emerged from the kitchen carrying a tray with four steaming crocks of soup. He gave a slight bow to Liam. "I took the liberty of bringing a portion of my humble soup for you, great fire chief, tamer of flames." Turning to Archer, he asked, "Will you also be lunching at our fine establishment, sir?"

His faux British accent earned him an eye roll from Liam. "Since when do chefs in 'fine establishments' eat with the clientele?"

"Since I make the food, so I make the rules," Jacob shot back. "I mean, *she* makes the rules." He gestured to Hannah. "But she has graciously allowed the lowly kitchen help to break bread—or in this case, tortellini—with her."

Hannah waved him off with a laugh. "Go get another bowl, please."

Liam nudged Archer's elbow. "While we're waiting, show the ladies your mysterious photos."

"Mysterious?" Hannah leaned in.

Archer reached into his jacket and pulled two manila envelopes from an inside pocket. His name was written in black ink in a medieval-style calligraphy on the front of each. He opened one and slid out a black-and-white photograph then did the same with the other envelope. One showed a tree stump. At its base, grass poked up through a thin layer of snow.

The other photo was harder to decipher at first. Hannah studied it, turned it vertical then horizontal. It appeared to be the top half of an arched window or doorway. "Looks a little like one of our doors here, but the bricks are different. Where was this taken, and why is it mysterious?"

"The envelope with the photo of the doorway was leaning against the door of my apartment on Sunday morning. The other one came to the firehouse yesterday."

"I found it behind the No Parking sign out front," Liam said.

Hannah rubbed her hands together. "They're obviously clues. You just have to find out where they were taken. I bet they'll lead you to more clues."

"A treasure hunt." The first smile Hannah had seen on Raquel all day lit her eyes with a tiny glimmer of her normal optimism.

Whatever this was, it might just be a much-needed distraction. "Maybe it's a contest of some sort. Or maybe Bryn left them for you. Something fun to keep you busy while she's gone."

Archer's mouth scrunched to one side. "I'm not so sure Bryn is interested in my having fun right now. You know all the stereotypes of clueless men who say clueless things?"

"Uh-oh." Hannah patted his hand. "What did you say?"

"She called when she stopped for groceries at some tiny town in Wisconsin on her way to Pittsville. She said it was probably the last time she would be able to talk to me. She'd been driving for almost twelve hours, and she sounded exhausted, so I said, 'Are you sure this is worth it?'" He sighed. "She hung up on me."

Liam clapped him on the back. "That's nothing, man. A simple, 'I'm sorry I'm a clueless insensitive dude' should clear that up."

"Maybe some flowers along with it," Raquel added. "And groveling."

"And chocolate." Hannah pressed her lips together. Archer's distress was real, but she was sure Liam was right. This wasn't nearly as serious as the young fireman thought it was.

Jacob set another bowl of soup on the table then pulled out a chair. "Sorry it took me a minute. Carrie from Sweet Caroline's delivered our bakery order."

If Hannah hadn't been looking at Archer, waiting for his reaction to her suggestion, she would have missed the twitch of his left eye when Jacob mentioned the bakery. Had he had a bad experience at Sweet Caroline's?

"No clue what you guys were talking about," Jacob went on, "but I second what Hannah said. Chocolate makes everything better, and I'll prove it to you after the soup."

Hannah picked up her spoon. "Bryn Reynolds is not the kind of woman to carry a grudge over a careless comment like that."

Archer stared at the contents of his bowl. "True. She's usually pretty quick to forgive. But that wasn't my first offense this week."

Hannah grimaced. "Dare I ask?"

"Her original plan was to hole up less than an hour away in a hotel in Bowling Green to finish her dissertation. She had all her research compiled, and she just needed a week in a quiet place to put it all together. I was totally supportive. But then I made the mistake of telling Colt that this would be the first time we would be apart for more than a couple of days."

Liam groaned. "Not Colt."

Colt Walker, the youngest firefighter over at the station, was known for his practical jokes. "What did he do?" Hannah asked.

"He suggested I write down a list of things I could do when Bryn was gone that I couldn't do when she was here. I thought he was trying to be helpful, because focusing on that kind of thing rather than missing the person can help. But I also know what a jokester he is, so I wrote things I would never, ever actually do." Archer slid his hand down his face. "It was all in fun, but then he went and gave the list to her."

"Uh-oh." This time the two dire syllables were proclaimed by a quartet of voices.

"Yeah. The next day she announced she was going to her grandparents' cabin in Wisconsin. For *two* weeks. She said she wanted time to decompress after she finished working. Walk in the woods and commune with nature in a place that holds memories for her." His cheeks puffed out on a ragged exhale. "But I think when she said it was the last time she would be able to talk to me, she meant *ever*."

The empathetic silence that followed was broken by Archer's phone vibrating against the wood tabletop. The lit screen said *Mom*. He lifted the phone to his ear. "Hi, Mom. Yeah, go ahead and open it. Can we switch to a video call?" He tapped the screen then set the phone in the middle of the table. "She found an envelope with my name on it under her welcome mat," he told the group.

Mindy Lestrade's face showed on the screen briefly. "It's a photograph." The picture flipped, and the next thing they saw was another black-and-white photo. It appeared to be part of a decorative wrought iron fence. The metal work was intricate, with two swags of ivy leaves pinched in the middle by a bow. One side of the fence was attached to a wooden post or board. The wood appeared charred.

"Does this mean anything to you?" Hannah asked. She glanced from the phone to Archer and saw the color drain from his face.

Archer made eye contact with Liam, whose eyes widened just slightly as he nodded.

"This is the balcony on one of the apartments above the jewelry store," Archer said quietly.

"Where the fire was last month?" Jacob asked.

Archer nodded. "It was a Sunday night. I was across the street, out for a run. I heard yelling, and at first I thought it was just a couple of people arguing. Then the front door of the jewelry store flew open. Two people came running out, and I saw flames behind them. They said no one else was in the building. I called it in and told them I was with the department."

"We had the fire out in under half an hour," Liam chimed in. "But the next day, the owner came in and blasted Archer, saying he shouldn't have waited for the team. He should have gone in and tried to save his inventory."

"So what do you think this means?" Raquel asked.

Archer was quiet for a long time. "I think someone's trying to tell me something. And I don't think it's something good."

Loved *Mysteries of Blackberry Valley?*
Check out some other Guideposts mystery series!

Whistle Stop Café Mysteries

Join best friends Debbie Albright and Janet Shaw as they step out in faith to open the Whistle Stop Café inside the historic train depot in Dennison, Ohio. During WWII, the depot's canteen workers offered doughnuts, sandwiches, and a heap of gratitude to thousands of soldiers on their way to war via troop-transport trains. Our sleuths soon find themselves on track to solve baffling mysteries—both past and present. Come along for the ride for stories of honor, duty to God and country, and of course fun, family, and friends!

Under the Apple Tree
As Time Goes By
We'll Meet Again
Till Then
I'll Be Seeing You
Fools Rush In
Let It Snow
Accentuate the Positive
For Sentimental Reasons

That's My Baby
A String of Pearls
Somewhere Over the Rainbow
Down Forget-Me-Not Lane
Set the World on Fire
When You Wish Upon a Star
Rumors Are Flying
Here We Go Again
Stairway to the Stars
Winter Weather
Wait Till the Sun Shines
Now You're in My Arms
Sooner or Later
Apple Blossom Time
My Dreams Are Getting Better

Secrets from Grandma's Attic

Life is recorded not only in decades or years, but in events and memories that form the fabric of our being. Follow Tracy Doyle, Amy Allen, and Robin Davisson, the granddaughters of the recently deceased centenarian, Pearl Allen, as they explore the treasures found in the attic of Grandma Pearl's Victorian home, nestled near the banks of the Mississippi in Canton, Missouri. Not only do Pearl's descendants uncover a long-buried mystery at every attic exploration, they also discover their grandmother's legacy of deep, abiding faith, which has shaped and guided their family through the years. These uncovered Secrets from Grandma's Attic reveal stories of faith, redemption, and second chances that capture your heart long after you turn the last page.

History Lost and Found
The Art of Deception
Testament to a Patriot
Buttoned Up
Pearl of Great Price
Hidden Riches
Movers and Shakers
The Eye of the Cat
Refined by Fire

The Prince and the Popper

Something Shady

Duel Threat

A Royal Tea

The Heart of a Hero

Fractured Beauty

A Shadowy Past

In Its Time

Nothing Gold Can Stay

The Cameo Clue

Veiled Intentions

Turn Back the Dial

A Marathon of Kindness

A Thief in the Night

Coming Home

Savannah Secrets

Welcome to Savannah, Georgia, a picture-perfect Southern city known for its manicured parks, moss-covered oaks, and antebellum architecture. Walk down one of the cobblestone streets, and you'll come upon Magnolia Investigations. It is here where two friends have joined forces to unravel some of Savannah's deepest secrets. Tag along as clues are exposed, red herrings discarded, and thrilling surprises revealed. Find inspiration in the special bond between Meredith Bellefontaine and Julia Foley. Cheer the friends on as they listen to their hearts and rely on their faith to solve each new case that comes their way.

The Hidden Gate

A Fallen Petal

Double Trouble

Whispering Bells

Where Time Stood Still

The Weight of Years

Willful Transgressions

Season's Meetings

Southern Fried Secrets

The Greatest of These

Patterns of Deception

MYSTERIES OF BLACKBERRY VALLEY

The Waving Girl

Beneath a Dragon Moon

Garden Variety Crimes

Meant for Good

A Bone to Pick

Honeybees & Legacies

True Grits

Sapphire Secret

Jingle Bell Heist

Buried Secrets

A Puzzle of Pearls

Facing the Facts

Resurrecting Trouble

Forever and a Day

Mysteries of Martha's Vineyard

Priscilla Latham Grant has inherited a lighthouse! So with not much more than a strong will and a sore heart, the recent widow says goodbye to her lifelong Kansas home and heads to the quaint and historic island of Martha's Vineyard, Massachusetts. There, she comes face-to-face with adventures, which include her trusty canine friend, Jake, three delightful cousins she didn't know she had, and Gerald O'Bannon, a handsome Coast Guard captain—plus head-scratching mysteries that crop up with surprising regularity.

A Light in the Darkness
Like a Fish Out of Water
Adrift
Maiden of the Mist
Making Waves
Don't Rock the Boat
A Port in the Storm
Thicker Than Water
Swept Away
Bridge Over Troubled Waters
Smoke on the Water
Shifting Sands
Shark Bait

Seascape in Shadows
Storm Tide
Water Flows Uphill
Catch of the Day
Beyond the Sea
Wider Than an Ocean
Sheeps Passing in the Night
Sail Away Home
Waves of Doubt
Lifeline
Flotsam & Jetsam
Just Over the Horizon

A Note from the Editors

We hope you enjoyed another exciting volume in the Mysteries of Blackberry Valley series, published by Guideposts. For over seventy-five years, Guideposts, a nonprofit organization, has been driven by a vision of a world filled with hope. We aspire to be the voice of a trusted friend, a friend who makes you feel more hopeful and connected.

By making a purchase from Guideposts, you join our community in touching millions of lives, inspiring them to believe that all things are possible through faith, hope, and prayer. Your continued support allows us to provide uplifting resources to those in need. Whether through our communities, websites, apps, or publications, we inspire our audiences, bring them together, and comfort, uplift, entertain, and guide them. Visit us at guideposts.org to learn more.

We would love to hear from you. Write us at Guideposts, P.O. Box 5815, Harlan, Iowa 51593 or call us at (800) 932-2145. Did you love *Smoke and Mirrors*? Leave a review for this product on guideposts.org/shop. Your feedback helps others in our community find relevant products.

More Great Mysteries Are Waiting For Readers Like *You*!

Whistle Stop Café Mysteries

"Memories of a lifetime...I loved reading this story. Could not put the book down...." —ROSE H.

Mystery and WWII historical fiction fans will love these intriguing novels where two close friends piece together clues to solve mysteries past and present. Set in the real town of Dennison, Ohio, at a historic train depot where many soldiers once set off for war, these stories are filled with faithful, relatable characters you'll love spending time with.

Mysteries & Wonders of the Bible

"I so enjoyed this book....What a great insight into the life of the women who wove the veil for the Temple." —SHIRLEYN J.

Have you ever wondered what it might have been like to live back in Bible times to experience miraculous Bible events firsthand? Then you'll LOVE the fascinating **Mysteries & Wonders of the Bible** novels! Each Scripture-inspired story whisks you back to the ancient Holy Land, where you'll accompany ordinary men and women in their search for the hidden truths behind some of the most pivotal moments in the Bible. Each volume includes insights from a respected biblical scholar to help you ponder the significance of each story to your own life.

Mysteries of Cobble Hill Farm

"Wonderful series. Great story. Spellbinding. Could not put it down once I started reading." —BONNIE C.

Escape to the charming English countryside with **Mysteries of Cobble Hill Farm**, a heartwarming series of faith-filled mysteries. Harriet Bailey relocates to Yorkshire, England, to take over her late grandfather's veterinary practice, hoping it's the fresh start she needs. As she builds a new life, Harriet uncovers modern mysteries and long-buried secrets in the village and among the rolling hills and castle ruins. Each book is an inspiring puzzle where God's gentlest messengers—the animals in her care—help Harriet save the day.

Learn More & Shop These Exciting Mysteries, Biblical Stories, & Other Uplifting Fiction at **guideposts.org/fiction**

Printed in the United States
by Baker & Taylor Publisher Services